G000141583

Nicole HURLEY-MOORE

Hartley's Grange

ARENA
ALLEN&UNWIN

First published in 2016

Copyright © Nicole Hurley-Moore 2016

All rights reserved. No part of this book may be reproduced or transmitted in
any form or by any means, electronic or mechanical, including photocopying,
recording or by any information storage and retrieval system, without prior
permission in writing from the publisher. The Australian *Copyright Act 1968*
(the Act) allows a maximum of one chapter or 10 per cent of this book, whichever
is the greater, to be photocopied by any educational institution for its educational
purposes provided that the educational institution (or body that administers it) has
given a remuneration notice to the Copyright Agency (Australia) under the Act.

Arena Books, an imprint of
Allen & Unwin
83 Alexander Street
Crows Nest NSW 2065
Australia
Phone: (61 2) 8425 0100
Email: info@allenandunwin.com
Web: www.allenandunwin.com

Cataloguing-in-Publication details are available
from the National Library of Australia
www.trove.nla.gov.au

ISBN 978 1 76029 203 4

Set in 12/18 pt Sabon LT by Midland Typesetters, Australia
Printed and bound in Australia by Griffin Press
10 9 8 7 6 5 4 3 2 1

The paper in this book is FSC® certified.
FSC® promotes environmentally responsible,
socially beneficial and economically viable
management of the world's forests.

Griffin FSC C009448

This is a work of fiction. Names, characters, places and incidents are products of the
author's imagination or are used fictitiously. Any resemblance to actual events, locales, or
persons, living or dead, is entirely coincidental.

For Ciandra, Conor and Alannah

Acknowledgements

A huge thank you to my wonderful editor Louise Thurtell, Siobhán Cantrill and the whole Allen & Unwin team.

Thanks to Tracy Stuart for all her knowledge about fires and I'd also like to thank the CFA for all their hard work in keeping us safe, especially through the long hot summers.

To Robyn at Beehave – a shout out for the endless supply of inspirational shoes.

I would also like to thank my awesome children Ciandra, Conor, Alannah and my mother, Jennifer, for all their humour and support. And lastly to my husband, Christopher, who always encourages me and reads every one of my stories even though romance isn't really his 'thing'.

Chapter 1

It was officially the worst day of Lily's life. This year was meant to be the one in which everything came together and she climbed the next rung in her career. But she'd barely got past the first week of January before it had started to go belly up.

It would almost have been comical if it hadn't been so tragic, she thought as she squinted through the windscreen at the wet road ahead. But she wasn't going to cry – she wouldn't give them the satisfaction.

Lily tapped her foot on the brake as she negotiated her small red hatchback through another sweeping bend. God, even the weather was out to get her. The late autumn storm seemed to have blown in from nowhere.

This morning felt like a million years ago. She'd woken up feeling great, thinking today was the day she'd be told the promotion she'd long sought was hers. But instead, everything had fallen apart. As if being betrayed professionally wasn't enough, she'd also been deceived by the one person she'd thought she could count on.

The life and career she'd spent years building up lay in tatters.

Damn it! It wasn't meant to be like this, but after the day she had just had, she wasn't surprised. After finishing her college certificate in applied fashion design, Lily had managed to nab a coveted internship with the up-and-coming fashion label Edwina Partell. It was a dream come true – or at least if would have been if it wasn't for her supervisor, Samantha Worth. The trouble had started after the year-long internship was up and Lily had been offered a job as a junior designer. As time went on, and Lily became more successful, Sam began to bully, backstab and undermine her every chance she got, all culminating in this morning's fiasco. As much as Lily loved working for Edwina, she couldn't let this slide and had to walk away.

But it wasn't just her career that had ended up in the toilet – how could Pietro do that to her? She'd trusted him with everything, and now there was nothing left. She'd been blindsided on both fronts.

She tapped the brake again to slow the car down as the rain started coming down in bucketloads. The once-familiar landscape around her looked blurry and alien, the stormy grey sky bleeding into the dull green of the wet bush.

And what was she doing? thought Lily. Was she facing her problems like an adult? Uh-uh, she was running home with her tail firmly between her legs. Running to the one person who could always make her feel at least marginally better: her big sister, Violet.

The rain was torrential now and Lily could barely see a couple of metres ahead. Perhaps she should pull over and wait for the storm to ease off, she thought, but she was so close now; in another fifteen minutes she'd be home. Surely it was better just to keep going and get out of this crazy weather.

Home: that was a word she hadn't equated with Violet Falls for quite some time. Still, at the moment it was the only home she had.

Suddenly, out of the corner of her eye, a grey blur appeared in her vision and she slammed on the brakes just as a grey kangaroo flew in front of the car. As she swerved to miss the roo, her tyres skated all over the wet road. In a millisecond the back end of the car swung out and began to spin towards the edge of the road.

Time seemed to stretch as Lily felt the accident unfold. Over the noise of the pouring rain she vaguely registered the crunch of the tyres sliding over gravel before the world outside spun 360 degrees once, and then once more. She wanted to scream but instead hung frozen on the steering wheel and prayed she didn't end up dead in a ditch. The car shuddered as the back hit something with a loud bang, but the impact slowed the car's spin.

Lily dragged in a breath as the car stopped moving and sat trembling in the driver's seat, her hands clenched on the wheel. The car was on the gravel shoulder on an odd angle to the road and was facing the wrong way.

Through the windscreen she could see the large kangaroo standing looking at her from the middle of the road for a second before hopping off into the bush.

Lily hiccupped and sniffed, and then she did the one thing she'd sworn all day that she wasn't going to do: she cried. The sobs were a mixture of terror, fright and the relief of not being dead.

Lily wasn't sure how long she sat gripping the steering wheel but she barely registered the car door being jerked open. A cold blast of air blew over her but all she could do was hang on, her forehead resting on the wheel, and just keep breathing. In, out. Somewhere in the distance a voice was talking to her, but as much as she tried, Lily couldn't make out the words.

She shook her head in an attempt to clear it.

'Miss, miss, are you hurt?'

'Um, no . . . no, I'm not hurt.' She felt surprised to hear her own voice as she lifted her head slowly.

'Are you sure? Do I need to ring for an ambulance?'

Lily wiped the tears away with the back of her hand before clutching onto the security of the wheel again. 'No, I'm fine – thanks.'

'Lily? Lily Beckett, isn't it?'

She turned her head towards the source of the question and looked into the handsome face of Flynn Hartley.

'Yes,' she said as she felt another tear slide down her face. Damn it, she just couldn't help it. 'Sorry.'

'Nothing to be sorry about. You've had a close call but everything is going to be okay, I promise,' he said, squatting down by the open door. He seemed to be oblivious to the rain bucketing down.

'I'm fine, I just need a second.'

'Take as long as you want, but how about letting go of the wheel and sitting back in the seat?'

Lily released the steering wheel and sat back. 'Ouch.'

'What's up?' Flynn said, his eyes narrowing. Lily wasn't sure if it was because of the rain drenching him or out of concern.

'I must have hit my shoulder somehow,' said Lily, reaching up to hold her right side.

Flynn gently touched her arm. 'Let's have a look, then. Can you move all your fingers and your hand?'

Lily gave her fingers a wiggle. 'Yeah.'

He ran his hands down her arm. 'Well, nothing seems to be broken, but I still reckon we should get you checked out.'

'Really, there's no need – I'm fine.'

'So you keep telling me,' he said with a slight smile. 'Come on, let's get you out of there and back to town.'

Lily frowned. 'Can't I drive?'

Flynn leant back and glanced towards the rear of the car before shaking his head. 'No way can you drive this, I'm afraid – the back end is crumpled. I'll drive you in and then call the garage to come and pick it up. They can do the mechanics and the panel beating for you.'

'Alright, thanks. I mean, that's really kind of you.'

'Don't worry about it. Is there anything you need to take with you now?' He peered past her at the jumble of bags and boxes stacked Tetris-style on her back seat.

Lily followed his look and gave a shrug. 'I'm running away.'

'Yeah, I reckon you are. Are you ready to go? Come on then,' he said as she nodded, standing up and holding out his hand to her.

Lily grabbed her handbag from the passenger seat before taking Flynn's hand and clambering out of the car. She swayed on her feet for a second but his arm snaked around her waist and steadied her.

'Mine is over here.' He guided her through the rain to his ute and got her settled. 'Is there anything else you need before I lock your car up?'

Lily shook her head.

'Okay, back in a tick.'

Lily watched as Flynn jogged over to the car. A couple of minutes later he was sliding into the driver's seat, bringing with him the smell of rain, wet wool and an underlying scent of crisp aftershave. She glanced over and saw that his dark hair was plastered to his head and he was drenched to the skin.

He looked at her as he turned on the ignition. 'Rotten day, hey?'

'I've had better. So has the roo, I'm sure. Sorry you got so wet.'

He gave her a quick grin. 'It's nothing. Now, let's get you home.'

Lily looked out the side window as the car took off down the road. Silence fell between them and the constant sound of the rain on the windscreen seemed to highlight it rather than fill it. For a moment she thought she should say something, but her mind was filled with replaying the accident over and over again. The minutes ticked by as the wet bush slid past.

'Listen, are you sure you don't want me to swing by the hospital?'

Lily jumped, startled by the sound of Flynn's voice. 'Thanks, but I think I just want to get to my sister.'

'If you're sure.'

She nodded as she turned back to the window. Yes, she was sure. The small rural township of Violet Falls may not feel like home, but her sister and niece definitely did. Violet had been there for Lily ever since she could remember – from the faded memories of a once happy childhood, through the awful time of their parents' death in a car accident and having to come to this place to live with their grandparents. Life with their grandparents had been okay while their grandmother was alive, but after her death their grandfather had become more and more cantankerous. Violet had butted heads with him more than once until finally, when he discovered she had fallen pregnant, he tossed her out. There was no way that Lily was going to stand by and let her sister go it on her own, so when Violet packed her bags and left, so did she.

It had been difficult but they had made a life for themselves in Melbourne – well, they had to, especially once little Holly arrived. But Violet had protected, supported and held them together through it all, and today Lily needed to borrow a bit more of her strength.

Lily had thought that she would never come back to this speck on the map. But last year her grandfather had died and left his granddaughters a shop in the main street and the old family home. Violet had seen it as a new start and moved here with Holly. Good thing too, as she not only started up her own business but found the love of her life,

Mac McKellan. Well, Lily should be thankful that at least Violet's life was beginning to pan out. Just as her sister's life was looking more than rosy, hers had nosedived, crashed, burned and exploded into tiny pieces.

The bush gave way to farms and paddocks as they neared the town. After a few minutes they were driving past a mixture of old miners' cottages and 1930s bungalows, punctuated by the odd triple-front brick house or a new building. The road widened as they went down the main street, which was a remnant from the days when mobs of sheep and cattle were herded along it on their way to market. On both sides of the street were a line of shops, the majority of which were old terraces with balconies and verandahs that jutted out over the footpaths. They drove on for another few minutes.

'Almost there,' Flynn said as he headed through town.

'Thank you again. You've been wonderful and I really don't know what I would have done if you hadn't come along.'

'Hey, no need to keep thanking me. Anyone would have done it.'

'Maybe – but I am grateful,' Lily said as they pulled into Violet's driveway.

'I'll stop by the garage and get them to pick up your car.' Flynn brought the ute to a stop. 'Alright?'

Lily nodded and gave him a little smile. 'That would be great. I know you said that I should stop thanking you, but thanks again,' Lily said as she pulled her handbag onto her lap and opened the door.

'No worries.'

Lily gave him a brief nod and a wave before hurrying up the wooden steps that led to the front door. The door flew open before she even had a chance to knock. Violet Beckett stood in the doorway with a frown on her pretty face.

'Lily? Is that Flynn? What's he doing here? What are *you* doing here? Is everything alright?'

Lily stepped into her sister's arms. She opened her mouth to speak but the words got stuck, her eyes blurring as the first sob escaped her lips. Violet tightened her hold and held Lily close as she cried onto her shoulder. From somewhere behind her she heard Flynn's deep voice.

'Hey, Violet. I don't exactly know what happened but Lily had a bit of a bingle on the road into town.'

'A bingle?'

'Yeah, she tangled with a roo and lost.'

'Oh my God!'

'She's not hurt, just shaken up, I think. I wanted to get her checked out by a doctor but she insisted on coming here. I'll get the boys at the garage to tow the car in,' he said.

'Thanks, Flynn, that's great of you. I'll take her to the medical centre.'

'Good,' he said as he went to turn away. 'Take care, Lily, and don't worry – today can only get better.'

Lily looked up from her sister's shoulder and gave him a watery smile. 'Thanks.'

'Not a problem.' With that, Flynn gave a nod and headed back to his car.

Chapter 2

Lily sat ensconced in Violet's overstuffed couch sipping a cup of tea. The air was warm but she still felt a little cold and shivery. Outside the storm had waned and left behind a dull day with some drizzly rain.

Violet sat opposite her with a frown on her face.

'I'm alright, Violet. I just had a shock,' Lily said as she put her cup down on the side table. 'You don't have to stare at me like that, I'm not going to shatter.'

'So what happened? Why were you coming to Violet Falls on a Wednesday afternoon and in the middle of a storm?'

Lily fiddled with the edge of the dusty pink throw that hung over the arm of the couch. A minute slipped by as she tried to find the right words. How do you explain that your whole world, everything you counted on, was a lie?

'Lily?'

'It's a complicated mess, but basically I've left my job and Pietro.'

'No!'

Lily nodded her head. 'Yes, I have. You remember I told you that Sam was going to show my designs to Edwina?

Well, she did, and then she took the credit for them. She stood there and lied through her teeth.'

'No way! But I thought she said she was going to help you?'

'Yeah, and the joke was that I actually believed her. God, I'm such an idiot! So after a pretty ugly scene at work, I needed a bit of support from the guy I share a life with. I went by Pietro's studio and found him wrapped around one of his current models.' It was a strange relief to finally tell someone what a complete and utter shit her now ex-boyfriend had turned out to be.

'No!'

'Yes. He even had the nerve to use the old *You don't understand, this isn't what it looks like.* I mean seriously, Violet – it was exactly what it looked like.'

'Oh, honey . . . I'm so sorry.'

Violet walked over and sat down. She put her arm around Lily and gave her a hug.

Lily sucked in a breath as pain spiked in her shoulder.

'Oh my God, you *have* hurt yourself. Why didn't you say something?'

'It's just my shoulder. I must have banged it in the impact.'

'What did you hit?'

'I'm not sure – maybe a telegraph pole or something after the car spun around a couple of times,' said Lily with a wave of her hand.

'Oh, for heaven's sake, I'm getting you checked out.'

'There's no need, really. I'm just a bit bruised and feeling sorry for myself.'

11

'Well, you have every right to be,' Violet declared. 'After today, I reckon you deserve it. So what do you want to do? Shall we get even?'

'No, I just need to lick my wounds for a while.' Lily gave her sister a small smile.

'How about we fill up Pietro's car with a couple of bags of manure? I know this farmer who might help us out.' Violet encouraged her with a grin. 'Come on, just imagine it when he opens the door and a pile of sheep shit lands on his expensive Italian shoes.'

Lily couldn't help but chuckle at the ludicrous suggestion. 'No, I don't think so, but thanks for my first laugh of the day. I guess I just need a bit of time to think and try to work out what I'm going to do. You don't mind if I stay here for a bit, do you?'

'Of course I don't! You know I've always got your back, no matter what.'

Lily looked over at her sister gratefully. 'Thanks.'

'It will be great being back together again. And you know that your niece will love it,' Violet said with a smile. 'Speaking of which, there's a little over an hour before I have to pick her up from school, so that's plenty of time to get you checked out at the medical centre.'

'Violet, I'm fine.'

'Yes, I'm sure you are but I'm still taking you there. The bottom line is that you were in an accident and I need to know that you're physically okay, even if you don't.'

'Violet . . .'

'Do this for me, Lily – please.'

'Oh alright, if it will make you happy.'

'It does. Come on, let's go,' Violet said as she stood up.

'You were always bossy,' Lily said with a faint smile.

'Yeah, that's what big sisters are for.'

***

Flynn perched on the old leather armchair and stared through the huge bank of windows that ran the entire length of the house. The skinny olive green leaves of the eucalypts in the gully outside were still dripping from the downpour. The storm had passed and left in its wake a soft, drizzly rain. Water flowed fast over the grey rocks jutting out of the creek bed and rivulets ran down the bank, hurrying to join it.

Hartley's Grange had been in his family for generations, but over the past twenty or so years the sheep run of almost eight hundred acres had become run-down and was barely making a living, let alone a profit. After his grandfather's death years ago, the place had fallen into a slow but steady decline. Flynn had been too young to help but even if he hadn't been, his grandmother had ruled the run with an iron fist – just like she had done in all things.

When Flynn inherited the place four and a half years ago, he had a decision to make: he could attempt to revive the farm or just walk away. He had toyed with the options for a couple of months. The thought of walking away and beginning somewhere else was certainly tempting, but in the end he just couldn't do it. But he knew then that if he was going to make it work, he had to try to find ways to save Hartley's Grange.

And when it came down to it, the best way to rescue the old place was to sell off a couple of pockets of land. A lot of people in town had been horrified, but it was the only way he could raise the capital he needed for the farm's improvements and to rebuild the house.

It had taken Flynn almost four years to restore the original two-storey stone house that dated back to the 1880s. It had fallen into disrepair until only the shell had remained. He'd put in every spare minute and a heap of money to bring the ruin back to life. The house was now a fusion of Victorian and modern architecture. The old facade still graced the front, but the back of the house was all glass and steel and offered an uninterrupted view of the deep gully below.

Finally, after years of hard work and living on the smell of an oily rag, things were beginning to turn around. Slowly, Flynn had been able to build up his mob of merinos, and last season's wool cheque had given him a reason to hope that everything was beginning to pay off. There was still a heap to do, but one day he hoped that Hartley's Grange would be as successful as his best mate Mac's place, McKellan's Run.

It had been a hell of a day and Flynn was glad to be home and in dry clothes. There were a hundred things he could do and even more he should, but for once he found it difficult to get off the chair. Perhaps, just for a few hours, the Grange could do without him.

The image of Lily Beckett wandered into his mind. She'd been pretty shaken up by the accident and he wondered if he should call to see how she was going. In the distance a magpie sang its maudlin song as Flynn remembered how Lily had trembled in his arms.

Yeah, the kid had had a fright alright, and she'd been damn lucky. He had run into her several months before when she'd been up visiting her sister and checking out the shop she'd inherited. It had been a surprise because in Flynn's mind Lily was Violet Beckett's baby sister, with pigtails, freckles and scraped knees, and, like a smartarse, he had said something to that effect. She'd given him a smile that he still could picture, her head slightly tilted to one side and the sun highlighting her rich brown hair as she answered that she wasn't a kid anymore.

Hell, he was more than aware of that. She'd been funny and flirty and countered each of his remarks. Their exchange had stayed with him – it shouldn't have, but it did.

He mentally shook the image away and rolled his wide shoulders. Thinking about a woman like that could open the door to all sorts of trouble. Lily was safe and sound with her sister and that was that. Besides, best friends or not, Mac McKellan would skin him alive if he went anywhere near Violet's little sister.

Flynn put down his coffee and walked over to the wide panels of glass as he pulled his phone from his pocket. Leaning against one of the frames, he pushed open a window. The fresh, damp air blew over him as he flicked through the directory on his phone and selected a number.

'Hello, Flynn.'

'Hi, Violet. Just thought I'd ring and check how Lily was.'

'Lily's fine, or at least she will be. I took her to the doctor and, other than a nasty bruised shoulder, she's shaken up but okay. Thanks so much for helping her, I really appreciate it.' He could hear the sincerity in her voice.

'There's nothing to thank me for. Listen, I organised for the garage to tow her car in and fix it. Sam Ogilvy is going to drop the rest of her stuff around to your place after work.' Flynn glanced at his watch and saw that it was almost 5.30 pm. 'I reckon he'll be there pretty soon.'

'That's kind – you didn't have to go to all that trouble.'

'No trouble at all,' Flynn said as he stared out into the bush. 'Tell her I hope that she's feeling better.'

'Sure, I'll let her know.'

'Thanks, Violet. See ya.'

There was a moment's hesitation before Violet responded. 'Bye, Flynn.'

Flynn flicked off his phone and rammed it back in his pocket. There, the whole thing was done and dusted.

* * *

Lily glanced up at the vintage clock on the wall. It was almost midnight and she should try to get some sleep. The problem was that every time she closed her eyes she was back in the middle of the storm, spinning out of control.

She still felt numb, and there was an iciness inside her that she just couldn't shake. For a few horrifying seconds she'd been sure that she was going to die. Lily scrunched her eyes shut to try to erase the memory of the car spinning around and around, and the sense of helplessness that came with it.

Then all of a sudden Flynn was there. She'd looked up into his eyes and knew that she was going to be alright.

Lily sighed. Maybe another cup of tea would help. The painkillers the doctor had given her were beginning to wear off and her shoulder was still sore and stiff; she'd better take another pill if she was ever going to get to sleep.

She would be eternally grateful that Flynn had showed up when he did. Lily had the biggest crush on Flynn Hartley when she'd been an awkward teenager. Back in high school he was popular. No, that was an understatement. Girls trailed after him, guys always thought he was a 'good bloke' and even the teachers were charmed by his combination of humour, cockiness and good looks.

Back then, Flynn Hartley didn't even know that she was alive, which was understandable given he was four years older than her. But that didn't stop her from looking, wishing and sighing every time he passed her in the corridors. Not that anyone noticed her. She was nothing more than Violet Beckett's pimple-faced, freckly, pudgy little sister.

It was hard growing up in Violet's shadow. She loved her sister more than anything, but still it was difficult measuring up to her. Violet was pretty much everything Lily wasn't: beautiful, self-assured, popular . . . oh, and slim. That was something Lily would never be. Violet was delicate and dainty, sort of like a ballerina. She, on the other hand, was

17

all boobs and hips. Yes, as she grew up she lost the puppy fat, but even now she still felt big when she stood next to her sister. Logically Lily knew she was just a different body type, but still. And of course, she still had what her grandfather had pointed out to her when she was a teenager: good child-bearing hips. Just the type of thing a fourteen-year-old who is lacking any self-esteem needs to hear.

Yeah, thanks, Grandad, nothing like being totally inappropriate. And had that remark haunted her for years? You betcha. She wanted to believe that it had been an uncomfortable back-handed compliment by a man who knew nothing about tact, but there are some comments you can never quite forgive, let alone forget. Grandad had always been bad-tempered, crotchety and insanely set against the McKellans, individually and as a whole, not to mention past, present and future generations. As difficult as he could be, it was always Violet who bore the brunt of his moods. He'd thrown Violet out when he found out that she was pregnant with Jason McKellan's baby, and no amount of talking or begging would change his decision – she knew that because she had spent days trying. But Silas Beckett wouldn't listen to reason and there was no way in hell that Lily was going to let her sister face an uncertain future on her own. So when Violet left, Lily went too and never once regretted her decision.

Sometimes, Lily thought that her grandfather still managed to affect them from the grave. It was because of him that Violet developed an iron will and refused to depend on anyone but herself – that is until Mac MacKellan came

18

along and turned her life around. After a rocky start, Violet and Mac had found each other, and Lily was so happy for them. If anyone deserved a bit of joy it was her sister.

As for herself, well she toyed with the idea that her taste in men, or lack thereof, had something to do with old Silas. He had been mean-spirited, cantankerous and neglectful when it came to his second granddaughter. So Lily always found herself gravitating towards men who were the polar opposite. If he was amiable, attentive and vaguely interested in her, Lily was already halfway in love. Unfortunately, they always started out charming, thoughtful and romantic but ended up being so very disappointing. There was no way of getting away from it: she was a shit magnet, and Pietro was just another example of her poor choice in men.

Chapter 3

Lily woke with a start and frowned when she realised she wasn't in her own bed. Then, in a nanosecond, yesterday's events swamped her.

Lying, cheating bastard.

She threw off the snowy white doona and pushed herself upright. Her head felt fuzzy and her stomach was a bit queasy as she reached for her dressing-gown.

Last night Violet had been the perfect sister. She hadn't bugged her for answers or a blow-by-blow account of the worst day of her life. Instead she kept her distance and allowed Lily to wallow in a big dose of self-pity. But she would have to fess up today – even Violet had her limits when it came to patience.

Lily shrugged on the blue silk dressing-gown, an embroidered dragon snarling down its back. The sleek material fell to her ankles and was soft and cool against her skin.

The thing was that somewhere deep inside, she had always known that her relationship with Pietro would end. But it was more than just sensing impending doom. Really, she'd witnessed the beginning of the end a couple of months ago but had been too stupid to see the true ramifications. The overheard conversation had played on her subconscious and reinforced every bit of self-doubt and loathing she carried around inside of her.

She had arrived back from a quick trip to Violet Falls to see Violet, Holly and her inheritance. She'd been feeling edgy and unsettled ever since she'd arrived back in the city that morning, and it was pointless trying to concentrate on any new designs when she felt like this. After pacing around the flat she decided to swing by Pietro's shoot before doing a little shopping.

She'd pulled into the car park next to Pietro's sleek silver car, picking up the cardboard tray holding three cappuccinos before heading over to the industrial-looking building in the middle of the lot. Built out of glass, steel and corrugated iron, it had once been an old factory but was now divided into half a dozen offices and three display areas. Pietro rented a small office and he'd converted one of the larger areas into his photography studio.

Lily let herself in the big glass door and hurried up the metal staircase, her footsteps echoing through the vast building. The faint sound of music came from the second floor and Lily followed it.

Passing a large black and silver sign mounted on the wall – Castell Photography – she opened the steel door at the end of the long corridor and a wave of heat and music swept over her. Inside were racks of clothes, a couple of makeup artists, a hairdresser and a handful of tall, beautiful models. Lily gave a nod and smile as she wove her way through them. Ahead, Pietro was standing with his hands on his hips while his assistant repositioned a large spotlight.

'No, Adam – I need you to point it that way, so the light will bounce off the wall.'

'Like that?'

'Yes, yes – see how it creates those fantastic shadows? Don't move, Anne, you're perfect just where you are.'

The designer, Jessamine, stood to one side. 'Oh, Pietro, that's wonderful. Look how the light plays across the silk – it's so 1930s chic.'

Pietro nodded his head. 'Exactly. This is what we want to achieve today.' He took a rapid series of photos. 'And now, just turn your head to me – perfection!'

Lily stood silently and watched. The model, Anne, did look as if she'd just stepped off the set of an old movie. The clothes were stunning; classic but with a slight modern twist.

But even more beautiful than the clothes was Pietro Castell, Lily's gorgeous boyfriend. Tall with hair so dark it was almost black, he and his parents had immigrated to Australia from Venice when he was twelve. Beneath his Australian twang there was still the hint of an accent. And the way he whispered her name made Lily hot just thinking about it.

Lily walked over to a table pushed against the far wall and put the coffees down. Pietro must have caught her movement from the corner of his eye as he whipped around with a frown on his handsome face, but when he saw Lily it disappeared.

'Ah, my Lily!' he said, striding across the room and pulling her into his arms. 'You came. I hoped you would.'

Lily smiled up at him. 'I brought you a coffee, and there's one there for Jessamine and Adam as well.'

'You're amazing – thanks. Are you staying for the whole afternoon?'

'I don't think so. I thought I would go and buy some fabric. I promised to make Holly a skirt.'

'How are Holly and your sister?'

'Good. Violet sends her love.'

'Look, I'm really sorry about not ringing yesterday to let you know about this. You could have spent another night up there with Holly and Violet.'

'It's okay, just forget it,' Lily said with a shrug. 'So you don't think you'll be finished for dinner?'

Pietro stared at her for a second. 'Yeah, you know, I think I can. Tell you what, why don't I meet you at home at 8.30? We can go to the new Thai restaurant around the corner?'

Lily wrapped her arms around his shoulders. 'That sounds perfect.'

He bent down and brushed his lips against hers. 'Good. I can't wait.'

'Neither can I,' Lily said as she stepped back. 'I'd better let you get on with it.'

'Alright, I'll see you later,' Pietro said with a wink.

'Don't forget your coffee,' Lily grinned before turning away and giving a general wave in Adam's direction. 'See ya!'

She made her way back through the models and ignored their curious glances. As Lily closed the heavy door behind her, the sound of the music was instantly muted. She started to walk down the corridor towards the stairs but changed her mind and doubled back to the bathroom.

The large room with about a dozen stalls had been updated and tiled in marble and stainless steel, but it somehow still had a factory feel about it. She nipped down to the last cubicle and was just hanging her bag on the back of the door when she heard a set of heels clicking over the tiled floor.

'So who was that?'

'Oh, you mean Lily?'

'Yes, if that's who Pietro was kissing.'

'She's Pietro's girlfriend.'

Lily stilled and tried to work out whose conversation she was eavesdropping on. She shouldn't listen, but they were talking about her.

'Well, I didn't think she was a model. What's he thinking?'

'Oh don't be a bitch, Zan,' said the second voice. 'Lily is lovely. She's a designer with Edwina Partell. From what I've seen, she's really talented.'

'I'm not being a bitch, Kate. I was just surprised that someone like Pietro would go out with such a frumpy little thing.'

'Yeah, right – so not being a bitch then.'

Lily silently cracked open the door and peered out at the two women. One was dark and the other blonde, and both were devastatingly beautiful. Whichever one Kate was, Lily decided she was her new best friend.

'Pietro could have anyone. Why would he choose that?' the brunette said as she applied bright red lipstick.

'Gee, I don't know – maybe he loves her,' Kate answered

as she ran her hands through her tousled blonde locks. 'As I said, she's a nice person.'

Seriously, Kate was Lily's best friend ever!

'Well, she should be careful, and maybe lose a bit of weight. With a catch like Pietro there would be a string of girls just waiting to steal him away.'

Kate turned and gave Zan a dirty look. 'God, you're pathetic – just leave them alone. You don't have to prove that you can win all the time.'

'As if she would have a chance against me. Did you see those freckles? She didn't even bother to try to cover them.'

'Oh my God, they're happy, so just stay away from Pietro,' Kate snapped as she walked out of the bathroom.

Zan gazed at her own perfection in the mirror and smiled before hurrying after her friend.

Lily had leant back against the wall and dragged in a breath. All of sudden she felt like she was back in school: not thin enough, not pretty enough and not quite clever enough to deserve to be loved. The tears pricked at the back of her eyes as she crept out of the cubicle. She had glanced up at her reflection in the mirror. Zan was right – why would he ever want to stay with her?

Well, Lily had finally got the answer to her question. Pietro didn't want to stay with her and that was that. He'd made his choice, and it was a tall, skinny and scheming model. He'd made his bed and now he had to lie in it . . . without Lily.

She drew in a breath as she yanked open the bedroom door. No point putting off the inevitable. Violet was already in the kitchen when she wandered into the room.

'Morning!' Violet's voice rang out and sounded way too cheery.

Lily headed over to the kettle but Violet shooed her away.

'I'll make the coffee, you go sit down.'

Lily didn't argue but followed her sister's instruction, just as she'd done as a child.

'Where's Holly?'

'She's over at Kylie's place with Amber. Today Meg's taking all three of them out for a shopping trip and a movie.'

Lily glanced up at the clock on the wall and saw that it was almost nine. 'Shouldn't they be in school? I mean, it's Thursday, isn't it?

'They have a pupil-free day, so Meg decided to give them a treat.'

'Oh, that's nice,' Lily said with a smile before she gestured towards the clock. 'Hey sorry, I didn't mean to sleep in. You should've given me a shout.'

'You needed it,' Violet said as she walked over with two bright pink mugs in her hands. 'Here, I reckon you probably need this too.'

'Thanks.' Lily accepted the coffee then blew over the top of the mug before taking a sip. It was hot and almost burnt her tongue, but the smell was already clearing her fuzzy brain a little.

'Alright, so are you ready to tell me exactly what happened?'

'I'm not sure where to begin.'

'I always find chronological order works best,' Violet said with an encouraging smile.

Lily sighed and then took a breath. 'It all started with a couple of designs. Edwina Partell is very hands-on when it comes to most of the clothing in her line. Usually she oversees everything, but things have been going really well for her lately – she's even opening another shop in Sydney. So she's not at the workshop as much as usual. Anyway, every year she leaves a space in her fashion shows for a piece created solely by one of her designers. It still comes under her label, of course, but the designer is given the kudos. It's seen as a reward, and sometimes it's a leg-up to the next rung in the ladder. Every designer, even the junior ones, will put forward something to our boss, Sam, who shows the top three or four to Edwina. So I ran with my design and made up a sample in a burnished coppery silk. I think I told you about it?'

'Yes, you did. We were in the coffee shop around the corner from your flat. It was just after I agreed to do the McKellan wedding.'

Lily gave a grin. 'And the next McKellan wedding is fast approaching.'

'Yes, it is.' Violet's eyes lit up with joy.

Lily watched as Violet stole a quick glance at the engagement ring sitting on her finger. A soft smile touched her lips and Lily wondered if she would ever be that happy. Lily mentally shook off the self-pity. She was happy for Violet and that was the truth. As far as she was concerned, she deserved all the happiness in the world and so did Mac.

'Anyway, I took the dress to Sam and she thought it was good enough to show Edwina. So naturally I was super-excited and couldn't wait for Edwina to come down onto the floor. But instead of talking to all of us, Sam hustled her away behind closed doors. They were locked away for ages and curiosity finally got the better of me so I went and hung around the front desk, and I saw them as they were walking out of the office. Edwina turned to Sam and said that the burnished coppery dress was the best thing she'd ever designed. I stood there with my mouth open and waited for Sam to deny it but she didn't. Even when she saw me standing there, she went on to say what inspired the design. I couldn't believe it – I was such an idiot to think that she would help me.'

'Did you say anything?'

'No, I was just too numb and gobsmacked. My mind wasn't functioning. I headed back to the design room and started getting my stuff together. After Edwina left, Sam called me into her office. She said that it might have looked as if she was taking the credit.'

'You think!' Violet said with a scowl. 'What a bitch.'

'Yeah, anyway, she said that her "muse" had left her.'

'So she's going to steal yours? Unbelievable.'

'Pretty much. She went on to say that I shouldn't mind as it was only one dress. And if I let this slide she'd make sure that I'd get all the credit in next year's collection.'

Violet tilted her chin. 'And what did you say?'

'That she could shove her collection in the nearest orifice and that I quit. Oh, and I threatened to take the dress with me.'

'And?'

'Sam accused me of being childish and that working for Edwina Partell was a privilege. Apparently I couldn't take the dress as I'd signed a contract and the material and design belonged to the company.'

'Did it?'

'Unfortunately, yes. I found the bolt of silk in the store-room, I told her that she could keep the dress but that was the only design she would ever have. And then I gracefully stormed out.'

'Would talking to Edwina help?'

'Maybe, but she was heading straight to the airport for a flight to London after she left the workroom, so she's probably still in the air somewhere.'

'Did you talk to anyone? What about the rest of the staff?'

'It turns out that none of them were surprised. Apparently this isn't the first time it's happened.'

'You're joking! I said it before, but what a bitch.'

Lily nodded. 'Yeah, she really is. Anyway, I was upset and decided that I needed to talk to Pietro and get a bit of sympathy. So I went by his studio and discovered him in the middle of a hot and heavy session with one of his models, the horribly perfect Zan.'

'Bastard.'

'Yep. As days go, it wasn't one of my best. Anyway, as he was trying to do up his jeans and catch his breath, he says that it wasn't what it looked like. I could have happily knocked him over the head with one of his bloody cameras. I spin around and head for the door and he runs after me, saying it was just a stupid mistake and that he loves me.'

'The shit.'

'Exactly. I pushed him off and went back to the flat, grabbed my stuff and came straight here.'

'Has he been in touch?'

Lily shrugged. 'I don't know, I turned my phone off. I suppose I should check.'

'Maybe you should talk to him. Not that anything excuses what the scumbag did, but even if it's only to hear him grovel a bit more. Hey, you deserve it.'

'Hmmm, I'll think about it.' Lily picked up the mug and took a sip. The last thing she wanted to do was talk to Pietro, but maybe Violet was right.

* * *

Most of the morning had drained away before Lily plucked up the courage to turn on her phone.

Thirteen messages. Twenty-seven missed calls – all from Pietro.

She took perverse pleasure in the amount of time he'd wasted calling her. Was that wrong? Of course not – the lying snake deserved it.

Lily tossed her phone on the bed and stared out the window. Something wasn't quite right – not the horrible situation or yesterday's turn of events, but something *in* her wasn't right. She realised that she wasn't as destroyed as she should be.

Lily wandered closer to the window and took a minute to mull over that thought. Surely if you find your significant other cheating on you, shouldn't it feel like your whole world has just ended?

– Instead, all she felt was a bit sad and headachy – which was odd, wasn't it?

Outside her window a big black crow stalked around the garden, picking up anything that might be edible. Lily frowned – not at the bird, but over her relationship with Pietro. It had started out all hot and sizzling, and neither of them could keep their hands to themselves. They'd met through Lily's work; Pietro had been hired to take some stills for a magazine spread. When their eyes met, for the first time in her life Lily was overcome with lust.

As the months went on their relationship deepened, and Lily was in a bubble of happiness. She was in love and loved in return – amazing. They spent every minute they could together, and Pietro even taught her about photography. She discovered that not only did she enjoy taking beautiful pictures but she had a talent for it.

But as one year rolled by and then almost another, an ever-widening crack appeared between them. Their jobs often separated them and they both blamed work and the long hours they were putting in, but it was so much more. The initial burst of light had faded and both of them had been willing to let whatever they had slip into habit and complacency.

Lily leant against the window and watched as the crow, with one last caw, fluttered up into the corkscrew willow. Perhaps her heart was made of sterner stuff than she'd imagined, or just maybe over the months she'd slowly fallen out of love.

Wow, how sad was that?

But that still didn't excuse his behaviour, although perhaps she should've seen it coming.

Chapter 4

Even though in a quagmire of self-pity, Lily still managed to notice that her sister was crazy busy, running from one meeting or responsibility to another. She seemed to be juggling all her balls in the air at the same time and, even though others may not have noticed it, Lily caught a flash of strain in her eyes.

Violet's events and party business was taking off and had become more successful than she could have hoped. It had started small at first, a few birthdays and a couple of small engagement parties. But ever since Violet's detailed, to-the-minute planning of the McKellan wedding, her bookings had increased. At first, she'd thought that the jobs were coming because people had seen what she'd been able to pull off for Jason McKellan's nuptials (even if, in the end, the ceremony never happened), but there seemed to be a wider swell in recommendations and word of mouth.

On top of her business, Violet was still a very busy mum to Holly and now, of course, fiancée of Mac McKellan. So with her work, the daily school run and looking after Holly, Violet was also trying to find time to be with Mac and plan their own wedding. Lily knew that her sister was more than

capable of holding it all together and getting the job done –
that's what Violet had always done. However, she also had
a sneaking suspicion that Violet may be starting to feel a little
overwhelmed, especially about the wedding.

The last week and a half had been a challenge for Lily.
She'd spent the first couple of days hiding out at Violet's and
licking her wounds. It wasn't until the third day that she'd felt
strong enough to talk to Pietro. He'd begged her forgiveness
and swore that it was a terrible mistake. Perhaps it was, but
in Lily's mind there was no way they could come back from
that betrayal.

He'd pleaded with her for a second chance and Lily
couldn't give it to him. Her self-esteem may have been at an
all-time low, but deep down she knew that she wouldn't give
in. She was sad, even weepy, but at no point did she crumble
as he pleaded with her. And that was the most telling
thing of all.

They were done and that was the end of it.

That same day, she arranged to pick up the rest of her
things while he was at work. She and Violet had driven
down to Melbourne while Holly was at school. It felt
weird letting herself into the flat and dismantling the life
they'd made together. They packed up her books and clothes
and, other than a handful of sentimental items, Lily realised
she didn't want anything else. The stuff in the flat was like
Pietro: it all belonged in the past. And it was a past she
didn't want to be reminded of.

Lily had wandered back into the lounge room of their
flat and picked up the final box. Balancing it on her hip,

she took one more look at the place she once called home. Turning to Violet she gave her a small smile.

'Come on, let's go – there's nothing for me here,' she said as they walked out of the flat. Lily shut the door firmly behind her.

She'd spent that night wiping away the odd tear and remembering the good times she and Pietro had once shared. But Lily recognised again that even though she was sad and wallowing in a good dose of self-pity, it didn't seem to hurt as much as it should. Would the split with Pietro cause her to die of heartbreak? Well, no. The realisation was a relief, but also kind of sad.

On the fourth day, Lily decided that she needed to get the tatters of her life together and work out what the hell she was going to do. Lily was unemployed, homeless and single – a triple threat in the negative. No, that wasn't entirely true: she sure as hell didn't need a man to define her. In fact, she was swearing off them altogether for the foreseeable future; they were way more trouble than they were worth. And maybe next time she wouldn't allow herself to be swept away by the first charming guy who turned up. Maybe she'd find someone she could not only fall in love with but could depend upon. No more falling in love with the idea of love. From now on, Lily would not fall for 'that' guy, the pretty, charming, exciting and sexy bad boy. Dependable and staid or nothing. But for now, all she wanted was some peace and quiet so she could work out what she was going to do next.

Violet had already made it clear that Lily could stay with her and and Holly for as long as she wanted, and her sister had even promised her some work helping out with several upcoming events. Which was wonderful, and Lily was more than grateful, but she needed to work out what she was going to do in the long term. The problem was, Lily didn't have any idea where she should go from here.

She had skills – she just had to figure out how to best use them and start hunting for a job as soon as possible. She also wanted to have a talk with Edwina Partell, first to ask if she would be willing to be a referee and second to fill her in on her unprofessional supervisor. But so far she'd been unable to get in touch with Edwina. She'd rung the office a couple of times but had been informed that Edwina was still in London and would get back to her as soon as she could. Lily had her doubts: Edwina's PA was best friends with Samantha Worth. Until she managed to speak to her in person, Lily couldn't count on Edwina's recommendation – whatever job she went for would be down to her.

Lily pored over her portfolio and made sure it was up to date. The book held all her sketches, technical drawings, colours, fabric swatches and photographs of all her designs. As much as she was still smarting over the whole affair with Pietro, she had to give him credit for introducing her to photography. She had been a quick and eager student and learnt not only how to use the equipment but also about lighting and composition. Lily had taken photos of all her creations and was more than pleased with the results. Generally she did the makeup herself and hired Tina, the struggling actress from the flat below hers, as a model. Well, hired was a loose term – basically she paid Tina in coffee, pastries and the few dollars she could scrape together.

Having a hard-copy portfolio was great, but she needed to create a digital version too. Lily spent a couple of days chained to her laptop as she put together a document showcasing her body of work, one that could be emailed along with any job application.

A week and a half after she'd run back to Violet Falls, Lily finally felt that she was ready to start putting out feelers and looking for a job. Her personal life may still be in tatters, but at least she could take a hold of her professional one. Step one was a job, step two would be a place to live. She just couldn't let herself become overwhelmed.

In between these huge life decisions she would also need to deal with the question of her inheritance, and what she was going to do with it. The old Beckett shop was just sitting there gathering dust, which was kind of crazy when Lily could certainly do with the added income renting it out would bring in. She'd checked it out with Violet months ago but had never got around to organising the work that needed to be done to bring the old place up to scratch.

The best thing to do was look at it again, just to confirm what needed to be done. She headed down the main street to her shop, one of the pretty two-storey buildings with wrought iron lacework and a verandah that stretched out over the footpath. It had been in the Beckett family for over a hundred years, but Lily was still surprised when her grandfather left it to her in his will.

Lily rattled the old key in the lock and pushed the door open. She wandered onto the old shop floor and gazed around the room. There was an air of neglected gloom, but a couple of coats of paint would make a big difference to that. Lily had already decided to hire Darren Johnson – otherwise known as Johnno – and his crew to undertake some renovations, as both Violet and Mac had recommended them. From her last visit, she knew that the kitchenette out the back and the bathroom needed attention.

Her idea back then had been to rent it out to bring in some extra money, but she'd been busy at work and put her plans on the backburner. Maybe it was a blessing in disguise. Things were different now – all she had was time.

Lily leant against the old glass counter in the centre of the room. The windows at the front were big and brought in much-needed light – well, they would once she removed all the newspaper and gave them a good clean. The room had a high ceiling, deep mouldings and an intricate ceiling rose depicting a festoon of ivy and flowers. With a bit of elbow grease and some white paint, Lily could transform this space into an elegant shop floor.

A sigh escaped her lips. It would make the perfect dress or bridal shop – or even better, a boutique to showcase her very own bespoke designs.

Lily shook her head; she shouldn't allow her imagination to run away like that. What she needed to do was to put together some more designs, finish sewing a couple of sample dresses she was in the middle of working on, and start sending out applications and inquiries. She didn't have the luxury of being indefinitely out of work, and if Lily wanted to make a name for herself, she needed to find work with a good designer. She only hoped that she could find someone as up and coming as Edwina.

But a little voice whispered again in her head: wouldn't it be better to design for herself and not be another anonymous team member behind someone else's label?

Lily frowned as she pushed herself off from the counter. Silly thoughts like that could get her in all sorts of trouble. But just imagine a shop of her very own, which specialised in unique handmade frocks that lent themselves to special occasions.

Lily twirled around and took the whole space in. She could almost visualise what it would look like. Not just a shop but a showroom, catering for brides not just in Violet Falls but right through the surrounding area, to Bendigo and maybe even in time all the way to Melbourne.

Was she crazy? Yeah, she was out of her mind. The whole thing could fail spectacularly.

But if it did, at least she would have tried to make her dreams a reality.

She paused for a second and stared at the windows. In her head she could picture the perfect dress for display, a full length evening gown in a pale green silk with a crystal embellished bodice. Lily chuckled; she was letting her imagination get the better of her.

What she needed right now was a paying job, not some airy fantasy. Besides, she'd never make it onto the great fashion catwalks of the world by having her own little shop in Violet Falls. Making it as a recognised designer overseas was what she really wanted right now, wasn't it? Or was it autonomy over her designs? The questions swirled around her head.

It took Lily another two days of mulling it all over. She'd gone back home and written three extensive lists. The first listed all the repairs and renovations that had to be done to the shop. The second one was all the reasons she should stop dreaming and go back to Melbourne and find a decent paying job. And the third was a list of why she should open her own business. The more she stared at the third list, the more points she added. Soon it was almost twice as long as the Melbourne one. When she found herself adding inane little points like 'cleaner air', Lily dropped her pen and stood up in disgust. Was she just talking herself into it, or was it truly a conflict between heart and head?

Lily took a breath and tried to look at the situation honestly. Why would she want to stay in a place she'd never thought of as home? But maybe that was it: other than wanting to be closer to her sister and Holly, maybe the one thing Lily needed right now was a home.

* * *

'You're going to what?' Violet asked as she sunk back against the couch.

'I'm going to open my own shop,' Lily said with a smile. 'That is, if you don't mind me staying here for a while.'

'Of course I don't mind! God, how could you even think that?'

'Well, we haven't lived together for ages, and I don't want you to feel that I'm encroaching on your space.'

Violet shook her head fiercely. 'As if. Now, tell me everything.'

'Okay, I know it sounds a bit crazy, but I want to open my own dress shop. I'll make up some samples for the shop floor but the majority of it will be bespoke orders. I already have design samples that I did separately from Edwina Partell's, and I've been building up my portfolio over the past couple of years. So I've been thinking: I can go back to Melbourne and try to get a job with another designer, or I can use the shop and attempt to make it on my own.'

'That's amazing,' Violet said with a smile. 'Look at you, all fired up.'

'Yeah, I think it's more panic and nervous energy. But ever since I came back here I've had this weird feeling.'

'Like what?'

'Oh, I don't know – it sounds kind of silly. I thought that after a few days of hiding I'd be ready to go back to the city and start over, but the funny thing is, I think I want to stay here with you and Holly. Maybe I need a bit more moral support than I thought.'

'That's not weird – we love you being here! And you can have as much support as you want.' Violet slid over on the couch and gave Lily a hug.

'Anyway, I'd really like to work with each client to make the perfect dress, one that suits not only their body but their personality, too. All my dresses will be unique and made especially for the customer.'

'It sounds fantastic, but it's going to take a lot of hard work and money to get it off the ground.'

'Yeah, I know. I'm not afraid of the work, and with the bit of money Grandad left me as well as my savings, I should have enough to hire Johnno and his crew to fix up the back of the shop. Hopefully there'll be some left over for some paint and material.' Lily drew in a quick breath. The idea excited and terrified her all at the same time.

'You know that I'll help in any way I can,' Violet said.

Lily let out a laugh. 'Oh, I'm counting on it, big sister.'

'Uh-oh, what have I let myself into?' Violet said, a look of mock horror on her face.

'Well, you can't take it back now. I'm holding you to it because I'll need all the help I can get.

Chapter 5

'Have fun. Say hi to the girls from me.'

Lily glanced at her sister. 'Why don't you come in and say it yourself?'

'Nah, maybe next time. Go on, this is the first time you've caught up with them in the actual physical world in years.'

Lily leant forward and stared at the café across the street where two women sat at a table in the large window. Her school friends, Hailey Waters and Jill Burnley, were waiting for her.

'I'm nervous – crazy, right? It's just that I haven't seen them for such a long time.'

'Well, you can't back out now,' Violet said as she gave her a pointed look. 'Besides, they're your friends, and it's not as if you haven't stayed in touch.'

Violet was right – even when they had run away to Melbourne all those years ago, Lily had still managed to email and text Jill and Hailey. For the first couple of years they had kept any correspondence secret, just in case her grandfather was looking for them. He'd kicked Violet out but, legally, Lily at fifteen was still officially in his care when they left town. Her friends had been loyal and neither one of them ever broke Lily's confidence, even when Mac McKellan was grilling everyone in town trying to find out Violet's whereabouts.

'Go and have some fun – you deserve it. We're not in hiding anymore.'

'I'm not hiding!'

'Of course you're not.'

Lily wrinkled her nose. God, she hated when Violet used that parent tone, the one which meant *I know you're lying but I'm giving you my support anyway.* 'I'm busy planning, designing and sewing so I can get the shop open, remember?'

'Yes, and it's been almost a month and you've barely been outside the front door.'

Lily frowned as she kept her eyes on the café. 'Maybe that's true, but I'm still not hiding.'

'Okay, okay, if you say so. I'm just getting worried about you, that's all. So if you're not trying to duck out, why are you still sitting here? Get your arse in there – your friends are waiting. They're going to be happy to see you, and after a few minutes it's going to be like you never left town.'

'Hmmm, I suppose.'

'Oh, stop being such a wuss and get out of the car!'

'Okay, okay!' Lily glanced at Violet and grinned as she picked up her handbag and opened the car door.

'What?'

'You're beginning to sound like Mac.'

'Oh shut up, I am not,' Violet laughed. 'Give me a ring if you want me to pick you up.'

Lily got out of the car. 'Thanks, but I'll probably walk. It only takes fifteen minutes, and the fresh air will do me good.'

'Okay, I'll see you later,' Violet said with a wave.

Lily watched Violet drive away before she took a breath and walked across to the café. Stepping inside, she squared her shoulders and put a smile on her lips before heading to the table.

'Oh my God, look at you!' Jill squealed as she jumped up and grabbed Lily into a fierce hug. 'You look fantastic!'

Lily clung to the petite blonde with short spiked hair and pushed down the lump that was forming at the back of her throat. Jill had always had an elfish vibe going on when they were kids, and from what Lily could see nothing had changed.

And I didn't want to come in because I thought everything would be different. Idiot, she thought to herself.

'It's great to see you, Jill.' But as Lily began to pull away, she was firmly held in place as Hailey came in for a hug as well.

'I've missed you so much!' Hailey said with a laugh, clasping her tighter. Tall and lean with an enviable athletic build, her brown hair was pulled back in a ponytail.

'I've missed you too. Sorry it's taken eight years to do this in person.'

'You're here now and that's all that counts. Besides, we've been living vicariously through your emails for years. Come and sit down and tell us everything,' Jill ordered as she scooted over into the chair by the window.

Lily laughed as she sat down. 'Well, I don't know about that – my life in Melbourne wasn't that interesting.'

'Hah, are you kidding? You in the big city and us stuck in this backwater?' Jill grinned.

45

'You do remember that we ran away without any money or a plan on how we were going to survive, don't you?'

'Yeah, as I said, excitement. I was here serving in Mum's supermarket and basically watching paint dry,' said Jill dryly. 'So, tell me everything. Why are you back and how long are you going to stay?'

'Well, I don't know exactly where to begin.' Lily glanced down at the menu to gather her thoughts.

'How about with that sexy boyfriend of yours?' Hailey asked as she picked up the menu and started reading it.

'Ah, that would be ex-boyfriend,' Lily admitted.

'No! What happened? I thought you and Pietro were solid,' Jill said, giving her arm a quick squeeze.

Lily shrugged and let out a sigh. 'So did I, but I guess I was wrong. I found him with one of his models in a more than compromising position.'

Hailey and Jill let out simultaneous cries of outrage.

'I know. I'd left work early and gone to his studio.' Lily shook her head and gave a small laugh. 'He'd told me that morning he had an important meeting and shoot on that afternoon.'

Jill grabbed her hand and gave it a squeeze. 'Not your fault – the guy's a scumbag and doesn't deserve you.'

'Thanks. Anyway, the upshot of the whole thing is that I've decided to move back to Violet Falls.'

'That's great!' Hailey exclaimed as she put down her menu. 'It'll be just like the old days. Hey, are you guys ready to order? I'm starving.'

Lily shook her head as she looked down again to scan the

menu. 'Um, no, sorry – just give me a sec. I think I'll go for the roast vegetable salad.'

'Me too. I ordered that last time and it was amazing,' Jill said. 'So, I suppose you're going to be looking for work around here?'

'What about your old job? I thought you loved it?' Hailey asked.

'I did, but I just felt it was time to move on. Anyway, I've decided to open up my own store. It'll be custom-made designs plus some accessories.'

'Fantastic! I suppose you'll be fixing up the old Beckett shop?' Hailey asked.

'That's the plan. There'll be a few on-the-rack dresses but I'll be concentrating on making bespoke event dresses.'

'So, custom-made – like wedding dresses?' Hailey asked.

'Yes, as well as any other special event.'

'Great – that means I can continue living vicariously through you and your new business,' Jill grinned.

'Anyway, that's enough about me. So, Jill, how's the supermarket going?'

'Pretty good. Do you remember how much I used to hate having to do my time on the floor when I was a teenager? Well, funnily enough, I love it now that I've taken over from Mum, although I'm more behind the scenes than on the registers.'

'That's great,' Lily said. 'And what about you, Hailey? How's life at the Town Hall?'

'I'm still on the front desk at the council. It's a pretty good job.'

'If you want to know what's going on in the town, ask Hailey. I swear, she knows everything,' Jill said with a smile

47

as she looked into her half-filled coffee cup. 'So have you run into anyone else since you've been back?'

'No, not really. I've been basically holed up at Violet's place, planning my next move.'

'Which is?'

'Have the shop fixed up, finish some more designs and take the first wobbly steps towards world domination.'

Hailey and Jill dissolved into giggles. Yeah, some things never change, Lily thought. 'Oh, I did run into the lovely Flynn Hartley on the day I arrived.'

'Oh, do tell,' Hailey said.

'Nothing much, really. He helped me out, that's all.'

'What do you mean?'

'It was the day of that big storm, do you remember? Anyway, I was just coming into town when I swerved to miss a roo. The car spun a couple of times and I ended up hitting a pole. Flynn happened along and gave me a ride to Violet's.'

Jill waggled her perfectly shaped eyebrows. 'I remember you had the biggest crush on him at school. Maybe after all these years you could finally act on it. Hmmm, there's food for thought.'

Lily chuckled. 'I don't think so. And even if I hadn't sworn off men – like forever – Flynn would be the last guy I'd go for. No, I've learnt my lesson: from now on, I'm staying away from the drop-dead sexy type.'

'Oh, but they're such fun,' Hailey said with smirk.

'Nah, they just lead to trouble, an empty wallet and a broken heart. Quiet and dependable all the way.'

'Sounds boring,' Jill said as she raised her coffee cup. 'Here's to all the drop-dead sexy types.'

Hailey picked up her cup and raised it in front of her. 'I've got a better toast: to old friends and better futures.'

'Ooh, I like it,' Lily said as she lifted up her cup. 'I'll drink to that!'

'Me too!' Jill clinked her cup against the others. 'To us!'

* * *

Flynn stared out the country rolling down before him. Eight hundred acres of rich grazing land, bush, gullies, hills and almost two and a half thousand merinos – on a day like today, it made you feel just that bit closer to heaven.

He knew every inch of it, which wasn't surprising as he'd spent his entire life at the Grange. The property had been in the Hartley family for generations and when his grand-mother, Edith Hartley, died, he'd inherited the whole thing.

Flynn walked along the ridge of the hill; it was still early morning but he could already feel the warmth of the sun. He headed to an ancient ghost gum and sat down beneath its shady boughs. To the left the dirt road snaked its way past a clump of peppercorn trees towards the crossroad in the distance. From here, Flynn could just make out the 1950s weatherboard house that stood on the track, just before the turn-off to Violet Falls. It had once been part of the Grange but as soon as Flynn had inherited he'd sold it off, along with half an acre of land.

Some memories needed forgetting.

His grandmother had been a hard woman. She'd taken him in and raised him, a fact she never let him forget, when his mother had abandoned him as a baby. Gwen Hartley had been seventeen when she ran away from Violet Falls.

Did he blame her? Yes, no . . . well, damn it, maybe.

She'd never come back and he still had no idea if she was even alive. As a kid, Flynn often wondered what his life would have been like if Gwen had taken him with her. Some nights, when the air was still and the house silent, he'd prayed she would come back and save him from his grandmother's indifference.

Things changed when he was older and strong enough to stand up to her, but as a young child Flynn's upbringing was as harsh and brittle as his unbending grandmother. Oh, she made sure he was fed, clothed and had a roof over his head – it was her duty, and he should've been grateful for everything he'd been given. But he knew in his heart that she had never loved him and he was nothing more than a nuisance and an embarrassment. When he was old enough to work around the farm he was at least finally useful to her mind, but Edith Hartley never had a kind word for her grandson, let alone any affection. He was a blight on her life: the bastard son of a runaway daughter and living proof of a deep shame.

And not a day went by that she didn't tell him so.

Thank God for the McKellans. If it hadn't been for them he would never have known what it was like to be part of a family. Mac treated him like a brother, Sarah had mothered him and John McKellan had called him 'son' and given him advice. The day he died, it felt as if Flynn had lost his own father, and the pain of it still smarted after all these years.

He leant his head against the white bark of the tree and sighed, pushing the memories back down and slamming the door shut. He had a million things to do and it was too bright a day to sit around and wallow in self-pity and the gloomy past.

'Jeez, what the hell's the matter with me?' he muttered as he stood up and brushed the dust off the backside of his jeans. He walked back along the ridge and towards his house without a backwards glance.

Let the ghosts sleep – it's safer that way. Besides, he had better things to think about, Charlotte Somerville for one. They were hooking up that night; at least that was the plan. They had a thing, an arrangement, that they'd hook up whenever neither of them had anything else on. A commitment without a commitment. It was the closest thing Flynn had ever had to a relationship – maybe that was sad but it was all he could manage, and it suited him.

* * *

Lily blew out a breath and stared down at the cream silk on the table. The pattern was pinned to the fabric, now all she had to do was cut it out. This was the part that always gave her pause, no matter whether she was cutting into hundreds of dollars' worth of silk or a cotton offcut. She stood back and walked around the table again, just to make sure that everything was perfect.

She put down the scissors and sighed.

The last thing she needed was a distraction from trying to build a business up from scratch, but today she just couldn't concentrate as her mind kept wandering to the past. Perhaps it had something to do with being back in this house again. Even though Violet had done a fantastic job renovating the old place, Lily still caught a trace of her grandparents. And while Violet probably wouldn't agree with her, for Lily there had been some good times here.

Violet and their grandfather always butted heads, even before she started going out with Jason McKellan. Lily had tried to be the voice of reason and the family peacemaker, but Silas never wanted to be placated. It was a difficult time when Lily's parents were killed in a car accident. Up until that point, visits to Violet Falls had been few and far between, though these were happy times on the whole when they occurred. But things became very different when Lily and Violet were taken in by their grandparents. Silas blamed everything and everyone for the death of his only son. He raged against the injustice of it all, which both girls understood and would've sympathised with, except for the fact that he seemed to dismiss the death of their mother. Their whole world had been destroyed and yet Silas didn't seem to see that, so caught up was he in his own pain.

The girls had gravitated to their grandmother, a kind and gentle woman. Lily knew that her father's death had affected her grandmother deeply, because whenever she said his name her grandmother's eyes would mist over and her voice would catch. But she put her pain aside and tried her best to make a home for the two girls. It was through her grandmother that Lily developed her passion for sewing and design. She taught Lily to use a sewing machine, cut out a pattern and even to embroider. It was here in this very room that Lily found some sort of peace, sitting quietly next to her grandmother sewing.

Added to his grief over the loss of his son, Silas Beckett had held a grudge against the entire McKellan clan, both living and dead. At times it went from general dislike to almost psychotic hatred. Both Lily and Violet had to suffer through endless rants about how the McKellans had ruined the Becketts' fortunes; it was a load of nonsense, but for their grandfather it was the truth. And then, of course, Violet went and committed the ultimate sin by falling in love with one of them. As it turned out it was the wrong one, but at least now she had found Mac and everything had been set to right.

Her grandfather's relationship with Lily was far less tempestuous than with her sister. In fact, half the time Lily suspected that he forgot he had a second granddaughter at all and mostly addressed her with a grumpy indifference. When their grandmother died, Lily had taken over the job of trying to smooth the waters with her grandfather but not with much luck. So Lily had retreated to the one place she could still find a little peace, her grandmother's sewing room.

Even when Lily had left with Violet after he'd thrown her out, Silas had never bothered to look for her. She pretended that it hadn't hurt, but that was a lie.

It was an awful thing not to be wanted.

Chapter 6

'Sorry I'm late. Have you been waiting long?' Lily asked as she hurried forward and clasped Darren Johnson's hand.

He shook his blond head and gave her a grin. 'Nah, I've only just got here.'

'Oh, that's a relief. Well, I suppose you'll want to see the shop.' Lily pulled an old-fashioned key out of her handbag and headed for the front door. 'Come in. Structurally the place seems to be sound but it's in dire need of sprucing up,' she said as the lock clunked open.

'Have you decided on what needs fixing?'

They walked into the shop and Lily placed her oversized bag on the old glass counter.

'I know what I'd like to do, but it really depends on how much it will cost. I'm afraid my budget is fairly tight. I would love to say fix the whole place but I know that's not going to happen.'

Johnno nodded. 'So what did you have in mind?'

'I definitely need the kitchenette and bathroom updated. And if you come through here,' Lily said as she walked towards the back of the shop, 'maybe, you could redesign this stockroom into a couple of decent-sized dressing rooms.'

'Sure. And the kitchenette?'

'Oh, it's just through here. See, the kitchen and the bathroom are on either side of the back door.'

Johnno stuck his head around the door of the rundown kitchen area. 'It's not big, is it?'

Lily gave him a smile. 'I think that's an understatement. So, is it doable?'

'Anything's doable, for a price. What are you going to do with upstairs?'

'At this point, I'm just going to paint it and turn it into my stockroom. And then the attic will be my second workroom.'

'You have another workroom?' asked Johnno.

'Yes, at Violet's place.'

'You don't mind if I just have a nosey about, do you?'

'Not at all. I'll wait for you in the front,' Lily said with a nod as she started to retrace her steps. Walking over to the window, she peeled off a bit of the old newspaper and spent the next few minutes staring out onto the main street. It was a cold day but the sun was shining, which made the temperature easier to bear. Lily glanced at her watch; it was ten minutes past nine. The street appeared to be fairly busy for that time of the morning, especially midweek. After about ten more minutes, Lily heard Johnno's footsteps over the bare wooden floor.

She turned around and smiled. 'All set?'

'Yeah, I'll go back to the office and work out some options and prices for you. Give you a ring later this afternoon.'

'Great, thanks, Johnno,' Lily said as she opened the door and waited for him to pass.

Once he stepped onto the footpath he turned back and waited for Lily to lock the door.

'I meant to ask, what sort of style did you want?'

'Well, even though the shop is old, I want the bathroom and kitchen to be sleek and modern. The rest of the place can be a nod to Victorian sentimentality, but I like my amenities contemporary. Nothing too pricey, just clean and classic.'

'Alright,' Johnno said, 'but you do know that there is probably a heritage overlay on this place?'

'What does that mean?'

'Well, nothing too serious, except a bit of bureaucratic bullshit with Council permits. It shouldn't be too much of a problem because it's inside, but you will need permission to restructure. Anyway, leave it with me, and I'll let you know.' He went to turn away but thought better of it. 'I'm glad you're back. Do you know the old saying? "There's always a Beckett in Violet Falls".'

'Well, thanks, Johnno. And it looks like the town now has three if you include my sister and niece,' Lily said with a self-conscious laugh.

'Talk to you later,' he said with a grin.

'Looking forward to it.'

* * *

A strand of hair had worked its way out of her ponytail. Lily tucked it back behind her ear as she ran up the steps of the old bandstand in the middle of the botanical gardens. Once she made it to the top, she bent over and tried to catch her breath. The air was icy and with each exhalation her breath turned into a mist. Lily tried to fit a run in each morning. She liked being alone with her thoughts, and some of her best designs had materialised at these times.

Some mornings she'd do a straight run from Violet's house, along the creek and finish with a circuit of the gardens. Other days she'd head out in the opposite direction over the old bridge towards Mac's place. And if she was feeling really pumped she'd run all the way to the falls.

But today she wasn't thinking about dresses or fabric. Today she was going over the figures Johnno had quoted her the night before. His charges were a bit higher than she had anticipated, though she probably shouldn't have been surprised; everyone in town, including Mac and her sister, insisted that Johnno and his crew were the best.

Lily leant on the balustrade and looked out over the gardens, bathed in early morning light. She could cover the costs, just. Things were certainly going to be tight and she may have to take up Violet's offer of working on some of the upcoming events she had booked. Lily felt bad about that – she hated that she'd actually take a wage from Violet when normally she'd help out for free, but if she wanted to open her own business there seemed to be little choice.

She blew out a long breath before jogging back down the steps and making her way through the gardens, feet pounding on the damp crushed pebble path. She needed to adjust her business plan and figures, be a little more savvy. Edwina Partell bought the backbone of their supplies from a small fabric warehouse in Melbourne called Stitch. Lily had got on very well with Stitch's owner, so perhaps if she went and spoke to Maria she'd be able to source the fabric she needed at a discount. The same went for any beads and embellishments; there were a couple of places she knew in Melbourne that were great value for money. And if she couldn't get everything she needed, there was always the internet.

As Lily headed back home, an ember of determination began to glow inside her. She would put every cent and every bit of herself into making her business not just reality but a success. No matter what, she was determined to make it happen.

Buoyed by her resolve, Lily grabbed a quick shower and a slice of toast before she jumped into Violet's car and headed off to Melbourne. Her day was spent in a flurry of hunting through endless bolts of material, making connections and sourcing the best deals she could find.

After a long day and a long drive, Lily pulled back into the driveway at home, feeling both elated and exhausted. Violet stepped out onto the verandah and waved. Lily grinned back as her sister came down the steps and over to meet her.

'How was it?'

Lily opened the door. 'It was good.'

'So did you manage to get everything on your list?'

'And then some,' she said as she handed Violet a fistful of canvas shopping bags with STITCH written on the front. 'Can you take these?'

'Yep, I've got them.'

'But more importantly, I stopped at our favourite

deli.' Lily reached over to the passenger seat and grabbed a cardboard box.

'Oh, you got the cheese pastries, didn't you?'

'Sure did.'

'I love those!'

'I know and that's why I bought them.'

'Ooo, gimme, gimme, gimme!'

Lily laughed as she handed the box to Violet. 'Somehow, I don't think they're going to last to dinner.'

'Are you mad? As if that was even a possibility.'

'Aunty Lily – you're back!' Holly called out as she ran along the verandah and down the steps.

'Hey sweetie,' Lily said as she wrapped her up in a hug. 'Did you have a good day?'

Holly rigorously nodded her head. 'Ah-huh – can I help?'

'Of course you can.' Lily walked around to the back of the car and opened up the hatchback. She pointed to a couple more fabric bags. 'Do you think you could manage them?'

'Sure can,' Holly said as she took the bags.

'Hey kiddo, guess what – Aunty Lily brought us back cheese pastries from our old deli.'

'Oh, they're my favourite!'

Violet chuckled. 'That's exactly what I said.'

'So anything exciting happen since this morning?' Lily picked up the last of her purchases.

Violet shook her head as all three of them headed up the stairs. 'You're forgetting where you are. Nothing ever happens in Violet Falls.'

'Nothing then?'

'Well, nothing other than that Holly has decided she wants to learn dancing. Just so I don't forget, she's been mentioning it every five minutes.'

'Kylie and Amber are doing lessons and they said it was great. Kylie thinks it would be fun if I could go too. You think it's a good idea don't you, Aunty Lily?'

Lily chuckled. 'Oh, don't drag me into your dark and devious plots, sweetie. It's up to your Mum.'

Holly let out an exaggerated sigh as they walked up to the front door. 'That's what Mac said.'

'You've already talked to Mac about it?' Violet asked in surprise.

'Yeah, he said that it was up to you. But he said maybe he'd talk to you about it – just like he did with Tiger and the other kittens.'

Lily bit back a laugh as they went inside. She reckoned that there would be dance lessons in the near future. Violet was a strong woman but let's face it, there was no way she could resist the combined efforts of both Holly and Mac.

* * *

'Thanks for coming early,' Charlotte said as she opened the door of her sleek modern townhouse.

'Not a problem, you said it was important.' Flynn stepped into the small hallway and headed towards the open-plan living area. The interior matched the outside of the building, a blend of clean lines and contemporary furniture. The only softness came from the colourful artwork on the walls and a large vase of orange gerberas on the coffee table. Flynn always found Lottie's place a bit on the sterile side, but everyone likes different things – whatever floats your boat, he supposed. 'So, what's up?'

'Have a seat,' Charlotte said as she gestured to the grey leather couch. 'Would you like a drink?'

'Shit, Lottie, what the hell's the matter? You're acting weird.' Flynn sat down on the couch. As he stared at her, he could have sworn she blushed.

'Um, I know that we're meant to be going out to dinner, but I really needed to discuss something with you.'

'So, get to it. What's up?'

'God, why does this sort of stuff have to be so hard?'

'Okay, that's ominous,' Flynn said as he leant forward. 'Just spit it out, Charlotte.'

'I think we have to re-evaluate where we stand,' she said as she sat on the arm of the opposite chair.

'Okaaay,' Flynn said, a frown deepening on his forehead. He leant back and stared hard at her.

'Look, this has been fun and I've really enjoyed the time we've had, but I'm ready for something more.'

'Listen, I don't think I can—'

Charlotte held up her hand. 'I know, I'm not asking you to.'

'But I thought that was the attraction? A relationship with no ties, no commitment.'

'It was at first, but you must know that's not a relationship by any standard,' Charlotte said as she pushed her long red hair back over her shoulder. 'I'm not trying to be cruel, but I'm at a point in my life when I need something more.

I need a real relationship, Flynn, something that has a shot at a future.'

'I thought this was what you wanted.'

'It was, but not anymore – that's why I'm walking away. It's self-preservation, really. I want to fall in love, I want to be someone's everything, and that's not you – we both know it. I need commitment, and commitment isn't your thing.'

A chill went through his body and all of a sudden Flynn felt very alone. It was his own fault; he should have seen this coming. He'd dropped his barriers a fraction and now he was paying the price. Charlotte was walking away and he didn't blame her. Resignation settled in his gut like a stone: everyone always left.

He pushed himself up from the couch and gave her a small smile. 'It's okay, Charlotte, I understand.'

Charlotte jumped to her feet. 'Listen, Flynn, I like you so much but you never let me in. If I thought there was a chance . . .' Flynn's eyes met hers and Charlotte shook her head and sighed. 'Yeah, that's what I thought.'

'I'll see you around,' he said as he started walking towards the door. 'Take care of yourself, Charlotte.'

'Flynn.'

He looked over his shoulder. 'There's nothing else to say, Lottie – let's just leave it at that.' Without another word, Flynn let himself out.

Chapter 7

The weeks slipped by quickly and for Lily there didn't seem to be enough hours in a day. Autumn had disappeared and been replaced with a cold and rainy winter – not that Lily took much notice; she was consumed with work. Even though her plan was to make bespoke dresses for her individual customers, she knew that she would also need samples that were not only examples of her style but could also be used as floor stock.

She'd been lucky with her shopping trips to Melbourne when it came to sourcing all the supplies she needed for her designs. Maria from Stitch had been excited by Lily's new venture and given her an amazing discount on the fabrics, which was fantastic, as every cent counted.

Lily had worked on five of Violet's events – three birthday parties, one retirement soiree and a wedding – which was both a blessing and a curse. On the one hand, she was extremely grateful to have the added income and thrilled that Violet's business was really beginning to take off. But on the other, each party took her away from her sewing machine – especially the wedding, as they were always so much work. As well as helping to set up the various venues and being a general dogsbody, Violet also asked Lily to take photos of the decorations and table settings at each event to add to her growing website.

Finally, in the third week of July, Johnno and his crew arrived bright and early at the old Beckett store to start work. It was a day Lily had circled on her calendar in red, as well as a handful of stars. Apparently he was in big demand and booked up for months, but was going to squeeze her into his schedule in between jobs, and the only reason he was doing that was because he was doing Mac a favour. Lily was thankful for it, even though she wasn't generally one for pulling strings, because now everything seemed like it was finally beginning to come together.

Darren Johnson was the type of guy who inspired confidence. He always met Lily's questions with a smile and was more than willing to put down his hammer and outline what exactly was happening with the reno. Johnno had told her that he had made the first applications to the heritage committee concerning the structural changes to the rooms, and that they had inspected the rooms and given him the go ahead, although he still needed the official paperwork. As far as Johnno was concerned, it was all systems go!

***

Flynn did the only thing he could and that was keep himself busy and eye-deep in work. Last week he'd hired a couple of farmhands to help bring the flock of pregnant ewes down from the top paddock. He put them in the paddock closest to the house where there was a small sheep shed on the western fence and several clusters of old gums dotted around the boundary and dam. He wanted to keep an eye on the girls as there had been several warnings from graziers over the past couple of weeks that something was going around the area killing new lambs. No one had caught a look at what was doing the killing but the general consensus was that it was a small pack of dogs.

So far Flynn had counted thirty-two live lambs, including a set of twins. He never tired of watching the little lambs standing on wobbly legs next to their mums. Every lambing season brought a few tragedies, but so far there'd only been a couple of stillbirths and one ewe lost, although her lamb was very much alive. It took time to hand rear a lamb; they needed a bottle every couple of hours for a few weeks.

Time was something Flynn didn't have that much of so he'd given Jennifer O'Reilly a call and crossed his fingers that she'd take the little guy on. Jennifer, who lived over by Moonlight, was an animal lover in her sixties, and a bit on the eccentric side. Any stray kitten, bird, dog, lamb or joey would find its way there. Jennifer would patch them up, feed them, and find them a home. Thankfully, she was more than willing to take the orphaned lamb. Flynn had wrapped him up, grabbed a bag of sheep milk replacement formula and headed over to the other side of town. He was greeted with a hug, Jennifer exclaiming that the lamb was a 'darling little thing' and that she knew the perfect family that needed a new lawnmower. By the time Flynn had left her place, full of tea and orange cake, the lamb had already been fed once, was wearing a bright red knitted jumper and had been christened Winston. It had been a weight off Flynn's mind and he smiled as he drove home: after a shaky start, Winston may have just won the jackpot.

Flynn had spent the morning pottering about the sheep shed and helping birth another lamb. He had just finished double-checking that the paddock fence was dog- and fox-proof when Mac's ute wound its way up the driveway. He stretched his back before ambling over to the car.

'Hey,' he said with a nod.

Mac pulled himself out of the ute. 'Hey yourself. You've been ducking my calls for more than a week now. I thought I'd better come out and see if you were still alive.'

'Well, as you can see, I'm fine.'

'Not very convincing, mate. So, you want to tell me what the hell's going on?'

Flynn stared at him for a second, considering if he wanted to get into this. 'Nothing, I've just been busy with work, that's all.'

Mac stared back. 'Don't bullshit me, Flynn.'

Flynn hesitated for another second. 'Listen, I could do with a coffee. Want one?'

'Sure,' Mac said, falling into step with his friend as they headed towards the house.

Flynn was silent as he moved about the kitchen, putting on the kettle and hunting out a couple of mugs.

'You're stalling,' Mac said.

Flynn leant against the kitchen bench. 'Yeah, I know. I guess I was hoping you'd just drop the whole thing and we could move onto something interesting, like which horror movie we should hire next.'

Mac chuckled and shook his head. 'Yeah, like that's going to happen. So, come on – what's up?'

'Charlotte dumped me.'

'Aha. Sorry about that, but I didn't know it was serious.'

'It wasn't. We just hung out when it was convenient.'

'So, if that's the case, why does it matter?'

Flynn shrugged. 'I don't know. I guess it blindsided me a bit, that's all.'

'Do you love her?'

Flynn glanced quickly at Mac. 'No, no, I don't. It's just . . .'

Mac sat down on the nearest stool and leant his arms on the counter. 'Oh, I get it now. It's because *she* left you?'

Flynn looked down at his hands while he considered the question. 'Yeah, I suppose that's it. It's pretty stupid, isn't it?'

'No, it's not. Your mum left, and your grandma was as mad as a snake afterwards. These things can leave scars on people, mate.'

'I looked for her you know.'

'Who, your mum?'

'Yeah. But it's pretty hard to find someone when they have a twenty-year head start,' Flynn said with a grim smile.

'What would you have done if you'd found her?' asked Mac.

'Oh you know, asked her some questions. Like, why did you go, who's my father and why the hell didn't you take me with you? I'll probably never find out the answers now.'

'Maybe one day . . .'

Flynn shook his head. 'It's too late, anyway. Maybe she thought she was doing the right thing; maybe it was the only option she had. But there's a point where you finally have to go, fuck it, I don't care anymore. I haven't gone anywhere – if she wanted to see me . . . well, she knew where I was.'

'Flynn—'

'It's alright – I have to let the past go and just get on with it,' said Flynn, turning around and busying himself with making the coffee. 'Granny always said Mum left because she couldn't handle having me, so what would be the point.'

'Yeah, which is complete rubbish. Come on, we all know what your grandmother was like – I bet your mum ran away from *her*, not you.'

'I know, I know. I guess that sometimes it still gets to me.'

'And you never commit to a relationship because you've got abandonment issues,' Mac added bluntly.

Flynn plonked the coffee mug in front of Mac. 'Been reading Violet's magazines again, have we?'

'No . . . well, maybe. All I'm saying is, next time you're interested in a girl and you think she could be the one, maybe try to do things differently. Don't assume that she's going to leave you, and don't end it before she has a chance to. If a real relationship is what you're after, then at some point you're going to have to take a gamble – on her and yourself.'

Flynn sighed. 'Yeah, but that's the hard bit.'

Chapter 8

What was left of July disappeared in a flurry of dust and old wood as Johnno and his crew tore out the old kitchen in the back of the shop. Added to that, Lily was run ragged between finalising some new dress designs for the store, trying to finish Holly's flower girl dress and helping out Violet, who had back-to-back events in the first two weekends of August. She enjoyed setting up the events with her sister and marvelled at how Violet always knew what each space needed to make it pop. Every one of her events was beautiful, fun and totally unique.

For once, Lily felt confident and in control of her life; the betrayals of a few months ago had finally begun to heal. Life was moving forward and beginning to fall into place and her days were on the whole smooth and uncomplicated – so she should have known that it wouldn't last.

Lily was upstairs hauling out a box full of musty fifty-year-old newspapers she'd found when Johnno appeared in the doorway.

'Hi. Do you need a hand with that?'

Lily looked up and gave him a quick smile. 'No, I think I've got it, but thanks.'

Johnno grinned at her; she had to admit he had a pretty devastating smile. Lily got the feeling that if he put his mind to it, most of Violet Falls' sisterhood could quite easily be in peril. There was a certain appeal when a man leaned casually in front of you with a three-day growth, sandy blond hair, overalls and a grin.

'It's after five, so the guys and I are about to head off for the day.'

'Gosh, I didn't realise it was so late, already,' Lily said as she put down the box.

'I was just wondering . . . would you like to go out to dinner sometime? I mean, that is, if you're not seeing anyone.'

Lily shook her head automatically. 'No, I'm not seeing anyone. Um, I hadn't really thought about it . . .'

'Hey, no pressure. Anyway, have a think – it's just dinner,' Johnno said with a smile.

'I will. And thanks.'

He gave her a wide smile before turning away. 'See ya tomorrow.'

'G'night.'

Lily was lost in her thoughts as she headed home. She hadn't dated anyone since coming back to Violet Falls – romance was probably the last thing on her mind. And of course, there was that promise she made to herself: to be smart about her next relationship. But then, this wasn't a relationship; Johnno had only asked her to dinner.

She walked up the wooden steps to the verandah and let herself in the front door.

'Hiya – we're in here!' Violet called out from the kitchen.

Lily hung up her coat on the old hall stand and walked down the hallway. She stepped into the kitchen and saw her sister and Holly sitting at the small table, grinning back at her. 'What's up?' she asked.

'We're celebrating!' Holly said, jumping up from the table and skipping over to give Lily a hug. 'Look, we've got cupcakes and pink lemonade.'

Lily dumped her bag on the floor and hugged her niece back. 'Really? What exactly are we celebrating?'

'A number of things,' Violet said. 'First of all, I got a call today from Holly's teacher.'

'Uh-oh, now how many times have I told you not to light a bonfire in the quadrangle, sweetie?'

Holly giggled as she grabbed Lily's hand and led her to the table where a plate of pale pink cupcakes with silver sprinkles sat. 'I didn't, silly.'

'Well, that was my first thought too,' Violet said with a wink. 'But according to Ms Potter, Holly is doing remarkably well and is a pleasure to have in the class.'

Lily bent down and tapped Holly on the nose. 'Sounds like you've got a very clever teacher.'

'Secondly, Holly has also been accepted into Moonbeams and Stardancers.'

'Hey, that's fantastic, kiddo – that's the dance school you wanted to go to, right?'

Holly nodded. 'Yep, Kylie and Amber go there too – it's the best.'

Lily looked back to Violet with a smile. 'So we do have a lot to celebrate.'

'Sure do – I just landed the Anderson wedding as well.'

'That's great,' Lily said as she reached over to give Violet a hug. 'And huge. Congratulations.'

'Thanks. Yep, this wedding is going to be big, but we've got nine months – we'll pull it off.'

'Of course we will. So, does that mean I can have a cupcake?'

'Indeed you can. To celebrate we're having backwards dinner, starting with dessert,' Violet said.

'Yay!' Lily and Holly said in unison as they both snagged a cupcake.

'So, anything interesting happen to you today?' Violet asked.

Lily licked a bit of the pink icing before she answered. 'Hmmm, Darren Johnson asked me to dinner.'

Violet's eyebrows shot up in surprise. 'Ooh, and you said?'

'That I'd think about it,' Lily said with a smile. 'I don't know. Johnno's really nice, but I guess I hadn't looked at him in that light before.'

'Well, from what I gather, he's a straight-up kind of guy and everyone in town likes him.'

'Yeah, I guess.'

'He's got his own business, and let's not forget he isn't exactly hard on the eyes,' Violet added with a wink.

'I know, I know, you're right. It's just that it came out of the blue – I suppose I wasn't expecting it.'

'You don't like him?'

'No, it's not that. He's just different to the type I would usually go out with.'

'Hey, I don't want to sound mean but maybe that's a good thing? You need someone you can depend on and who actually looks out for you for a change.'

'I guess. Anyway, I'll think about it. I like Johnno, I just hadn't ever thought about him in that way before.'

* * *

Lily walked into the bakery the next afternoon and lined up with a sea of hungry people. She bit back a sigh. This was going to take longer than she thought. Maybe she should just skip lunch? As if in answer, her stomach growled in protest. Yeah, who was she kidding – she was starving, and she'd already skipped breakfast.

Lily checked her watch and saw that she'd landed right in the middle of the lunchtime rush. There was nothing for it but to be patient. The air was filled with the scent of freshly baked bread and coffee, which made her hunger pangs even worse. She glanced around the crowded shop and gave a smile to the woman next to her. Her gaze kept wandering until it latched onto the wide shoulders of Flynn Hartley standing a little in front and to the side of her. It was wrong to ogle but, heaven help her, she just couldn't avoid it – the man was well put together.

As if sensing her stare, Flynn turned his head.

'Hi, Lily,' he said. His dark eyes warmed as he smiled.

Damn. Her stomach had that feeling she used to get when she was a teenager and he'd walk past her in the school corridors.

'Hi, Flynn. Whatcha up to?'

Flynn's smile widened. 'Well, I'm getting lunch.'

Lily wanted the ground to open up and swallow her whole. Of course he was getting lunch: it was lunchtime and they were in the bakery. She felt heat in her cheeks.

'Ah, I meant in general.' Nice save – not.

'I'm just teasing,' he said as he angled his body around to face her. 'I'm actually in town picking up a new chainsaw – I managed to kill the last one. So I thought I'd treat myself to one of Helen's chocolate éclairs while I was here. They're the best.'

'Don't tempt me,' Lily said.

'Go on, you know you want one.'

'You're the devil,' Lily said with a shake of her head.

'How's your day going?' Flynn asked with a smile.

'Hectic. Johnno and his team have started renovating the back of the shop and I have to help Violet measure up the community hall for the sixteenth birthday party she has coming up. Then drop back to the shop in case Johnno needs anything before zipping up to Bendigo to buy some fabric. I'm kicking myself – I went to Melbourne last week for a fabric shopping adventure and forgot to buy the lining for Holly's flower girl dress.'

'So you're staying in Violet Falls?' Flynn tilted his head to one side and studied her.

'Yes, I'm going to open up a store that specialises in event dresses.' Lily glanced away. She was having trouble meeting his dark brown eyes and just prayed she could rein in her inner giggling fourteen-year-old schoolgirl.

'Sorry, event what?'

'Dresses that you wear for events and big occasions – you know, special dresses, like the ones for weddings, engagements and formals.'

'Right – got it.' He leant a little closer. 'I'm glad you're staying.'

Lily's stomach tied in a couple of knots as her eyes locked onto his.

'So, what else have you been up to?' Flynn asked.

'Um, a lot of sewing, and I've been helping Violet out with some of her events. Oh, and I've been trying to get about fifty layers of old paint off the woodwork so I can repaint it.'

'That doesn't sound like much fun.'

'I have to admit, it's not one of my favourites.'

A voice suddenly broke Lily's awkward focus. 'Next! Who's next? Flynn, is it you?'

He turned around and gave the slightly harassed woman behind the counter a grin. 'Hey, Helen. No, Lily can go next – she's a busy woman.'

'Flynn, you don't have to do that,' Lily said.

He reached back and grabbed her by the hand and pulled her to the front of the queue.

'Go on,' he urged. 'Before Helen serves someone else.'

'Thank you.'

'What will you have?' Helen asked.

'Um, a couple of salad sandwiches on rye, an apple juice and two cappuccinos, please.'

The woman gave her a quick smile as she hurried away.

'You forgot a chocolate éclair,' Flynn whispered close to her ear.

Lily tried not to focus on the sensation of his warm breath against her neck. 'No, I didn't.'

Trapped in the lunchtime crowd with Flynn standing behind her, Lily would have liked to say that she couldn't wait to get out of the bakery, but the truth was she was enjoying having him that close. This was not the plan – the plan was to stay well away from addictively charming men. She should focus on her work and the errands she had to run, and that sweet, dependable Darren Johnson who had asked her out on a harmless dinner date. Anything else was just asking for trouble.

Get a grip, Lily.

She took a deep breath and tried to ignore the heat emanating from Flynn's body as he was pushed against her in the crowd.

Within a couple of minutes, Lily's sandwiches and coffees arrived and she paid for her purchases. As she turned to leave she glanced up at Flynn. 'Thanks for letting me go first. Bye.'

'No worries,' he said before he gave her a nod. 'I'll see you around, Lily Beckett.'

Lily scurried out of the bakery as fast as she could and made her way to the community hall. She glanced at her watch – she'd arranged to meet Violet there five minutes ago. Quickening her pace, she tried to forget how her skin had tingled when Flynn had whispered in her ear.

Lily ran up the steps of the hall and opened the door with an accidental bang. The noise made her sister jump and swing around.

'Sorry, sorry, sorry!' Lily called out as she hurried forward.

'You scared me half to death,' Violet said with a shake of her head.

'Sorry, I didn't mean to burst through quite so enthusiastically,' Lily said with an apologetic smile and a shrug.

'Forgiven – that is, once I get my heart back in my chest,' Violet chuckled.

'Well, you have to forgive me because I brought coffee and food – and besides that, I'm your only sister.'

Violet frowned for a second as if debating the whole thing. 'Well, I guess you did bring me coffee . . .'

Lily pulled a face. 'So, what exactly are we doing in this empty hall?'

'The layout for the party, of course. We're turning this empty hall into something that a gaggle of sixteen-year-olds will love. I'm thinking moody lights – it's a big open space and I want to try to give it a more enclosed sort of feel. There's nothing more disheartening than a bare hall and fluorescent lights for a party.'

'So, not country chic then?'

Violet grinned. 'Not this time. So you can just put that in the box with the timeless elegance.'

Lily let out a laugh as she headed over to shut the door which had blown open. It was chilly outside but at least there was a hint of sun. 'Does this place have heating?'

'Yep, but as we are lowly party planners we don't get it turned on.'

'Well, that just sucks.'

'Tell me about it.'

It was almost another hour before Lily made it back to the shop. She gave Johnno a wave as she slipped in the back door.

'You had a delivery while you were out,' he called as he stopped what he was doing and walked towards her.

'Really? That's funny – I wasn't expecting anything.'

'Anyway, I got him to leave it on the old counter,' he said, a frown creasing his forehead. Without another word he turned away and disappeared into what would be her new kitchenette.

'Thanks,' Lily said as she walked through into the front room. Sure enough, a small white cardboard box was sitting on the glass counter. A bright yellow sticky note was stuck on the top of the box. *Let me tempt you* was written in black ink and a bold hand.

Lily grinned as she opened the box and saw a chocolate éclair nestled inside.

Yep, definitely the devil.

* * *

Lily was beading the lace appliqués for Violet's wedding dress when there was a knock on the front door. With lace in hand she headed down to answer it, hoping that whoever it was wouldn't hold her up. She needed to finish what she was doing and then get ready to go out.

'You've forgotten, haven't you?' Jill said as Lily swung the door open.

'Of course not – we're going to the movies and have to leave at half six.'

'Uh-huh, exactly,' Jill said with a grin as she walked into the house. She was followed by Hailey and another woman who Lily didn't recognise. 'And what's the time now?'

'Oh no, it's not six thirty already, is it?'

Hailey chuckled. 'I see some things never change – you were always running late, even when we were kids.'

'Five minutes – I promise I'll only be five minutes!'

'Sure. Oh, but before you fly off, this is a friend of ours, Mandy,' said Jill, pulling the other woman forward. ''Bout time the two of you met.'

Mandy smiled and nodded in Lily's direction. She was about the same height as Lily, with shoulder-length blonde hair and pretty hazel eyes.

Lily held out her hand and smiled. 'It's lovely to meet you, and I'm so sorry that I'm holding everyone up.'

'Not a problem. I've heard a lot about you,' Mandy said with a friendly smile.

'I'll be back in a tick, I promise,' Lily said as she handed Jill the lace she'd been working on. 'Could you put this back on my work table?'

'Sure. Hey, this is beautiful.'

'Thanks. It's one of the straps for Violet's wedding gown,' Lily said before hurrying back down the hallway, letting her hair down from its messy knot as she went. In her bedroom she pulled off her hoodie, grabbed a pair of jeans that had managed to escape her painting efforts and hunted for her favourite green top. After a spritz of perfume, eyeliner and a bit of lipstick, Lily walked back down the hall, shrugging into her brown leather jacket on the way.

She found her friends in her workroom.

'See, I told you I'd be ready in five.'

Hailey turned her head and smiled. 'A good thing too, because I don't want to miss a minute of the yummy Amos Valter.'

'Don't you mean you don't want to miss a minute of the movie?' Jill teased.

Hailey shook her head. 'Nope, I meant what I said.'

'We'll make it, won't we? I mean, Bendigo is only forty minutes away,' Lily said.

'Don't worry, we'll make it. I factored in you being late – the movie doesn't start for another hour and fifteen minutes,' Jill said with a wink.

'I resent that!' Lily said with mock indignation.

'And that's your right, honey, but at least we'll be on time.'

'Hey, you made this, didn't you?' Mandy asked as she pointed to Violet's wedding gown on the dressmaker's dummy.

'Yes,' Lily answered. 'I mean, I'm still making it.'

'It's exquisite. Really, it's beautiful.'

'Thanks. I hope I get the same reaction from my sister. She didn't want too much structure, just something that was flowing and dreamy.'

'How could she not love it? It's ethereal, and romantic. Do you think I could take some photos of it? And do you have anything else?'

'Sorry?' Lily said, turning slightly to cast Jill a confused look. 'I don't quite understand . . .'

'Oh, sorry, I should have said,' Jill said as she put up her hand. 'Mandy here is a journalist for the *Violet Falls Gazette* – although she's meant to be off-duty when we're going out.'

'Well, I can't let a movie – even an Amos Valter one – get in the way of a story,' Mandy said with a laugh. 'But seriously, this dress is beautiful, and I would love to do a story on you and the shop. Are you taking orders yet?'

Lily opened her mouth and then closed it again as Hailey broke into the conversation.

'Sorry, that was me – I told Mandy you were opening a dress shop. It wasn't a secret, was it?'

'No, of course not,' Lily said with a smile. 'It's just that I'm nowhere near opening it yet. I mean, the shop is still being renovated.'

'Tell you what, how about sometime I do a little article on you and some of your designs? We could do a small series of them leading up to the opening. I think it would really create a buzz,' Mandy said.

'That would be fantastic, thanks! I'd have to see if Violet would be okay about having the dress photographed or if she wants to keep it as a surprise until the wedding. But in any case, I already have some other pieces.'

'Great! I'll get onto it.'

'Come on, you two,' Hailey said as she glanced at her watch. 'If we miss the beginning of the movie you have to shout us all popcorn.'

Chapter 9

'I thought I might find you here.'

Lily looked up to see Flynn standing in the doorway of her shop. Damn it, why did he always have to look so good? She swallowed hard and tried to subdue her hormones. She'd sworn off men – well, she'd sworn off everything that Flynn Hartley seemed to embody.

'Oh hi, Flynn. What are you doing here?' She tried to sound offhand and nonchalant but was pretty positive that she hadn't pulled it off. She put down her paintbrush and gave him a small smile.

'I was thinking about all those layers of old paint that you mentioned and wondered if a sander might help,' he said, putting the power tool on the floor.

Lily eyed it cautiously. 'Um, thanks. You didn't have to do that.'

'No problem, I'm not using it at the moment,' he said with a shrug.

All this week she'd kept running into him. On Monday it had been outside the supermarket – no coincidence there, you always ran into someone. On Tuesday they literally bumped into each other as she rounded the corner near the health food shop. Flynn had grabbed her in his arms to stop her from landing flat on her arse on the footpath so that she could feel the muscles beneath his thin cotton shirt. Not good, really not good.

Then on Thursday she saw him as she left the café with Hailey and Jill. He'd given her one of his most devastating smiles, leaving her momentarily speechless. That was until Jill jabbed her in the ribs.

Although she wouldn't admit it to anyone else, today when she walked down the street she'd looked for him. That just wasn't right, was it?

And now here he was, standing by her door and looking more than tempting.

'I appreciate it, Flynn. Hopefully I won't do any damage.'

He laughed as he stepped over the threshold and made the room seem smaller.

'So, how's the renovating going?'

'Pretty good. I'm mainly painting upstairs, hiding from the dust and noise, since Johnno and his team started demolishing the bathroom. I'm hiding from the dust and the noise. But today I needed to get the shop door painted – I don't know, some sort of symbolic gesture to give the old place a new lease on life.'

'Sounds like a plan.'

Lily found the tin of paint she was looking for and prised open the lid with an old screwdriver. 'Everything is going to be white in the shop and I thought a pretty mid blue would look great on the door. However, it seems that it's got to be heritage colours, so I'm stuck with this browny red stuff.'

'I like it. So is there a lot to do?' He took a step closer and sunk back onto one hip. Lily watched him with a prick of jealousy. Flynn appeared to be at ease with both her and himself. She, on the other hand, had a series of knots twisting tighter in her tummy. In an attempt to ignore the effect, Lily put the lid back on the paint and busied herself finding the drop sheet and brushes she'd need.

'Most of it is just cosmetic, but I'm having a new kitchenette and bathroom put in. Johnno is squeezing me in between other jobs, and I'm doing whatever bits and pieces I can – like this.'

'Maybe you should get someone else in to do the painting,' Flynn suggested. 'It would free up your time for opening the shop.'

'That's true, but my budget probably wouldn't stretch it that far,' Lily said, thinking of the stack of notes she'd handed over to the mechanic yesterday afternoon when she picked up her car. If only she had got comprehensive insurance instead of third party. It was too expensive at the time, but it had ended up costing a lot more. It had hurt – really, really hurt – but she was happy to get her little red car back.

'Oh, sorry, I didn't mean to pry.'

'Not a problem,' Lily said with a quick smile.

'So, do you need a hand with anything?'

The knots tightened. His gaze locked onto hers; it was time to go into defensive mode. Or was she just imagining a change in his meaning?

'No, I think I'm alright, but thanks again for the loan of the sander.'

Flynn dug into his pocket and pulled out a scrap of paper, then grabbed a pen that was sitting on the counter nearby.

'Well, here's my number, just in case.'

Lily reached out and took it, her fingertips grazing his. A tingling sensation sparked and travelled across her hand.

Lord, Flynn Hartley was dangerous.

She hid her reaction and gave him a nod. 'Thanks, that's really lovely of you.'

'I'd better get back to it, but you've got my number if you change your mind,' Flynn said as he stepped back. He gave her a grin that made her feel warm all over.

'Okay, I'll keep that in mind.'

'Do that,' he said with a wink as he stepped through the doorway.

* * *

A week passed and Lily had made quite a bit of progress. She had swept, scrubbed, de-cobwebbed and almost finished painting the two rooms on the first floor. On top of that, she'd helped Violet set up little Angie Buchanan's sixth birthday party on Saturday morning and finished the beaded bodice for the pale blue chiffon.

The two upstairs rooms she had earmarked already: the front one that opened up onto the balcony would become her office, and the other would be her stockroom. The only major job she had left was tackling the attic. It was still cluttered with generations of junk that Lily wanted to clear out to turn it into her ultimate sewing workroom.

Lily had spent the morning clearing and sorting the attic. From what she could make out, the family had stopped storing things up there decades ago. Along with the dust and cobwebs she'd found a few treasures, but, with the exception of some of the furniture, the dressmaker's dummy and the ubercool old cash register, everything else was junk.

Lily opened a desk drawer and picked up the first few pieces of paper. She frowned as she went through them. Three delivery receipts, a page torn from a ledger and a shopping list that included cotton wool, Mercurochrome and hair oil.

Why would anyone keep book work and receipts from 1953? And what the hell was Mercurochrome?

Lily stuffed the papers into a garbage bag and carried on. Twenty minutes later, the desk was cleared and Lily stood back to view the small pile of treasures she'd decided to keep. There were four glass marbles, including a huge one with a swirl of pink and blue spiralling in its centre, an old box of matches with a cool black cat on the front and an old-fashioned key ring with a dozen keys on it. Lily picked up the key ring and turned it over in her hand – there was something intriguing about it. Some of the keys were small and very plain but there was one that caught her attention. It was about eight centimetres long and had a Florentine knot–like head.

'Hey, Lily – you up there?'

Lily jumped at the sound of Johnno's voice; she'd been lost in her own little world.

'Yes, I'm here,' she said as she walked over to the top of the stairs and looked down.

'The boys and I are off for lunch. We'll be back in about an hour.'

'Oh, okay.'

'I've locked the front door but the back one is still open. Do you want me to bring you anything?'

Lily smiled. 'Aw, thanks, but I brought a salad from home.'

Johnno gave her a nod. 'Alright then, see you later.'

'Okay, bye.'

Lily felt a stab of guilt as she watched him walk away. He'd asked her out and she had never got around to giving him an answer. It was hanging between them – it was a space, a gap that was almost uncomfortable. Generally, they both carried on as if Johnno had never asked but every now and then, Lily would catch something in his eyes and half expect him to mention it. She was avoiding the decision, she knew it, but there was something that held her back. Perhaps she was still feeling burned by her last relationship and she was unwilling to start something new. Well, maybe unwilling wasn't exactly the right word; maybe it was more akin to scared to death of being made a fool of again. So until she faced that particular demon, avoidance appeared the best course.

Lily turned away and wondered what she should tackle next. The sound of voices and footsteps died away as Johnno and his boys went out the back door. There were a couple of chests and some boxes stacked on top of each other by the far wall. She was hoping the chests might hold some more trimmings and braid, like the ones Lily had discovered on her first trip up to the attic. She moved the boxes aside and opened the first metal chest.

'Well, that's disappointing,' Lily said as she stared into the empty chest. There was not even a scrap of paper or a snippet of lace. She closed the lid and put it to one side to get to the one underneath. This one looked like an old steamer trunk and was far more substantial. It was made of wood and metal with leather trim and straps. It wasn't very big but it was certainly intriguing.

Lily sat down in front of it and unbuckled the straps. She tried to open the lid but it wouldn't budge – it must be locked. Lily tapped her fingers together as she stared at the etched brass lock. Her gaze travelled back to the bunch of keys on the desk.

It wouldn't be that easy, would it?

She jumped up and grabbed the keys before settling back on the dusty floor.

'Right, then – here we go.'

One by one, Lily placed each key in the lock and gave it a twiddle. Some were too big, others too small and some fitted in the slot but wouldn't turn.

'Great, I'm the Goldilocks of the keys,' she muttered under her breath. 'Only two left.'

She picked up the key with the Florentine knot and slipped it into the lock. Lily sent up a silent prayer and held her breath as she turned it. Much to her surprise she heard a soft click.

Please don't be empty . . . or have mummified remains, she thought to herself.

Gingerly she raised the lid and saw that inside was a metal tin. Lily frowned: why would anyone bother putting such a small box in such a big chest? She picked it up and prised open the lid. A brooch fashioned into a little bunch of purple violets lay nestled on a piece of blue velvet. It appeared to be made out of silver and painted enamel, and in the centre of each flower was a tiny citrine. Lily smiled as she took it out of the tin. Maybe she really had found a family treasure after all – the brooch certainly put the old bunch of keys and marbles to shame. She picked up the brooch and walked over to the window, the stones glittering in the light as she turned it from side to side. It was pretty and delicate and she already had the perfect dress to pin it on. In fact, if she believed in fate, one could say that the violet crystal pin and the dress were a match made in heaven.

Lily wondered if it could have belonged to her ancestor, the first Violet Beckett. The setting could be late Victorian, which would put it at the right time period. It would be wonderful to prove that it had once belonged to the family legend, but unless the brooch came with a little note saying *I belong to Violet* or there was an old photograph of the woman wearing it, there wasn't much hope of knowing.

Once, long ago, the Becketts had been the founding family in this area when one of Lily's ancestors discovered gold. The family's fortunes rose, and as the town developed, they owned a big slice of it. That is until at its peak, tragedy struck when the Becketts' eldest daughter – the first Violet Beckett – was swept away into churning winter floodwaters. In deference to the family and the lost girl, the town renamed itself Violet Falls in her honour.

The original Violet had always been a ghostly figure haunting Lily's childhood. Their grandfather, Silas Beckett, had been a hard man. He'd spent their formative years lecturing them on their illustrious family history and the weight the Beckett name once carried in Violet Falls. He'd also ground into them that all McKellans were a crafty lot of beggars who could never be trusted, and the Hartleys weren't much better purely by association – according to Grandad, they always backed the McKellans and were thick as thieves. Lily had learnt to tune out her grandfather's drawn-out family rants; none of it really mattered to her.

But Lily had to admit there was something about standing in the silent attic of the family shop and holding onto a trinket that could have been the first Violet's. All of a sudden, it made the woman more tangible. Instead of the vague ghostly image of a faceless girl who perished in the falls of Landoc Creek, all of a sudden she appeared to have substance.

* * *

Flynn frowned as he knocked on the door for the second time. Where the hell was she? Johnno had mentioned when he'd run into him at the café that she was still at the shop, so why wasn't she answering the door?

He swapped the cardboard container that held two of the Hummingbird Café's large coffees to his left hand so he could turn the doorknob.

'Lily? Lily, are you there? It's Flynn,' he called out as he walked into the building.

He waited by the back door but all was silent. Flynn wandered through the rooms looking for any sign of her. It wasn't until he stood by the stairs that he thought he heard a scrape of a noise from upstairs.

Flynn took the stairs two at a time until he reached the first floor. After poking around the empty rooms for a minute, he spied the open door and the steps that led to the attic.

He walked up the staircase and was about halfway when he saw Lily. She was sitting on the floor beneath the window staring at something in her hand. A shaft of light illuminated her dark hair and there was almost a glow around her.

'Lily?'

Her head jerked up and for an instant she looked startled.

Flynn walked up a couple more steps. 'Sorry, I didn't mean to scare you. I did knock and call out but I guess you didn't hear me.'

Lily gave him what looked like an embarrassed smile as she shook her head.

'I brought you this,' he said as he walked over and handed her the cup. 'I saw Johnno in the café and figured you could use a coffee around now.'

Lily stood up and took the drink. 'Oh, thanks.'

Flynn gave a shrug with his wide shoulder. 'It's nothing. It's a cold day and I was in the café . . . you know.' Why the hell did he feel so uncomfortable all of a sudden? He stared down at her. Stop looking at the freckles . . . stop looking at the freckles. He glanced at her eyes and for a moment was lost in their golden chocolate orbs – damn, that was even worse.

'Well, thanks anyway – it's really nice of you. So what are you doing in town?' She gave him a smile and perched on the corner of an old desk.

He stood opposite her, drew in a breath and tried to centre himself. 'I was just picking up a few things then wondered if you might need a hand sorting this place out.'

Lily looked at him for a second and blinked. 'Really? You want to help me?'

'Sure. It looks as if you have a big job here. That is if you want me to?'

'Um . . .'

'Hey, it's no big deal. I just thought I could help you lug some of this junk out of here.'

She kept looking at him. Had he grown an extra head or something?

'Actually, that would be great. Thanks, Flynn, I'd appreciate a hand.'

He let go the breath he'd been holding. Bloody hell, what was the matter with him? 'Alright, just tell me what you want me to do.'

Half an hour later, Flynn was taking another overstuffed garbage bag of rubbish downstairs to the courtyard when he heard a female voice and the distinctive click of heels across the old wooden floor. He paused at the bottom of the stairs as the familiar voice of Charlotte Somerville carried through the shop.

What was she doing here?

His first instinct was to turn around and head back up to Lily. But then he'd be just a bloody coward. He'd purposely avoided Charlotte since she had ended it. Oh well, they were bound to bump into each other eventually.

He hoisted the bag up on his shoulder and made his way to the back door. In the kitchenette, Charlotte had cornered Johnno.

'So do you think you could come around and check it out?'

Johnno nodded. 'Sure, I'll drop by after I finish up here – about quarter to six, I reckon.'

'That'll be great, I appreciate it.' Charlotte turned her head and saw Flynn by the door. 'Oh hi. I didn't expect to see you here.'

'Hi, Charlotte. What are you up to?'

'Oh, I've got a leak by the back door – the rain has made the wood swell or something. Anyway, I'm having trouble opening and closing it, so I dropped around to beg Johnno to come and have a look.' She glanced back at Johnno and flashed him a smile.

'Right. Hope you get it sorted,' Flynn said and went to walk away, but her voice called him back.

'So, why are you here?'

Flynn gave a shrug. 'Just helping out.'

'Since when do you do that?'

'Since now. See you around,' Flynn said with a parting nod as he headed for the skip bin out the back.

Chapter 10

Flynn stretched his back and let out a loud sigh. He'd just finished digging the last damn post hole, which was a good thing too as it would have to be one of his all time least favourite jobs to do. A large branch had fallen off the nearby gumtree and pretty much destroyed the old gate on the boundary fence of the bottom paddock. All he had to do now was sink the post and throw in some concrete. Young Ben, Mac's farmhand, was going to swing by in the afternoon to help him hang the gate.

This wasn't how he'd planned to spend his Saturday morning but what could he do? It had started just after dawn when he'd got a phone call from one of his neighbours saying they had just seen a handful of Flynn's sheep hightailing down the road. It had taken him a couple of hours but he had finally wrangled the runaways back onto his property.

It had taken him almost as long to clear away the branch. He'd cut it up in a few sections and then wrapped a chain around the pieces and dragged them out of the way with his ute. The gate had been totalled, and Flynn wasn't really surprised as it had been there for the past thirty-odd years.

When he'd rung the local farm suppliers, he'd been lucky that they had a braced gate in stock that would fit. It all depended how you defined 'lucky' he guessed. So far the branch had cost him the morning, around three hundred dollars for the gate and hours of mucking about with runaway sheep and the bloody post hole digger.

He'd planned to have a quiet day, just doing a few chores, watching the game over at Mac's and maybe swinging by and seeing Lily. But none of that was going to happen now. Maybe he'd have better luck next week. He could never say that farming was boring – you never knew what it was going to throw at you next.

Flynn dropped the posthole digger on the ground and let out a slow breath.

Damn it, maybe he'd just make some time. Young Ben probably wouldn't show his face until after the game anyway. Perhaps Flynn could carve out an hour or so and just drop by Lily's place to see what she was up to.

Besides, it wasn't as if his endless list of jobs wouldn't still be here waiting for him when he got back. Everyone needed to stop every now and then to smell the roses – even him. What harm would it do if he just took off for a little while? Anyway he reckoned after the morning he'd had, he deserved it.

Without another thought, he walked towards the house. He needed to get cleaned up before he headed back into town.

* * *

'Lily! You up there?' Flynn called out as he strode up the attic stairs. 'I knocked, but the back door was wide open.'

'Yes. I think Johnno and his crew have just gone to grab a couple more sheets of plasterboard,' Lily called back. 'Anyway, I'm in here, Flynn. I've discovered a forgotten hidey hole.'

He walked across the bare wooden floor and towards her voice. Behind a stack of boxes, bags and the odd bit of furniture, a small door stood ajar.

'Are you okay?'

'Of course I am. Look what I've found!' Lily's voice floated out from the dark recess. 'Someone had painted over the door, which makes no sense at all. I've spent an hour scraping off fifty million layers of paint and prising the damn thing open.'

Flynn stood in the doorway and peered into the gloomy cupboard. It was long and narrow and ran all the way to the exterior wall. It was decorated – or maybe the better word would have been festooned – with enough cobwebs to make even Miss Havisham proud. He frowned into the tight dark space and coughed as the dust tickled the back of his throat.

Lily gave him a bright smile. 'I was hoping for treasure but there doesn't seem to be anything here. But check this out,' Lily said as she took another step towards the back wall of the cupboard. 'Look, it's a tiny little window that someone had painted over as well. It's as if they were trying to hide that this even exists.'

'Yeah, well maybe they had a reason. Best come out of

there before you go through the floor,' he said as he held out his hand.

'Oh, I think the floorboards seem firm enough.' Lily started walking towards him when her foot caught on a broken board. With a surprised gasp, she started to tumble.

Flynn dashed forward, trying to catch her before she hit the floor, but as he moved he bumped the door and it banged shut behind him. As his arms tightened around Lily the dark crowded in on him. He sucked in a breath and held onto her tightly.

'Thanks,' she said in a muffled voice, her face against his chest.

But Flynn barely heard her. For a second he scrunched his eyes shut and repeated the safe words over and over again in his head.

There's nothing there. There's nothing there.

He tried to ignore the wave of panic that threatened to break over him. He blew out a breath and then inhaled. *There's nothing in the dark . . . except Lily.*

'Hey, Flynn – are you alright?'

He shook off the clammy cold feeling as best he could. 'Yeah, I just get a bit claustrophobic sometimes, ever since I was a kid.'

Lily rubbed her hand over his back in a gesture of comfort. 'Why don't I get the door and then we can get out of here.'

She moved out of his arms and Flynn felt the loss of her warmth. In the darkness he could hear her fiddling with the old doorknob. He focused on his breathing and tried as hard as he could not to remember childhood fears. A shiver ran down his spine as he imagined a faint scratching from some-where behind him.

'Um, sorry, but it seems to be stuck,' Lily said.

Of course it was.

Flynn reached out in the darkness and ran his hands over her shoulders. 'Here, let me have a go.'

She brushed against him as they changed positions. Lily was soft and warm; her spiced floral scent wound around him and kept the terrors at bay.

Flynn waggled the doorknob but it wouldn't turn. There was only one thing he could do, unless they wanted to stay trapped until someone found them. He put his shoulder to the door and gave it a hard shove. After a moment of resist-ance the door flew open. He went to stand back to let Lily go first but felt her hand on the small of his back.

'You go ahead,' she said as she gently pushed him forward.

He didn't need to be asked twice. He stepped out of the darkness and into the attic, into the light. Flynn reached behind and pulled her with him.

She squeezed his hand. 'Are you okay? I think you look a bit pale.'

'Nah, I'm alright. I just get claustrophobic every now and then, sorry.'

'There's nothing to be sorry about. We all fear something, Flynn. You should see me around clowns.'

'Clowns?'

'Hell, yes, damn creepy things. I guess I was about four or five when my parents hired a clown for Violet's birthday party. I was terrified and spent the whole party crying under a table. I refused to come out until he was gone.'

'Clowns, huh? Aren't they meant to be fun?'

'Oh yeah, it's all fun until they pull out a knife and try to cut out your heart,' Lily said with a delicate shudder. 'They hide their faces, so you never really know what they're thinking.'

'Right, so clowns are out.'

'Absolutely. So what about the claustrophobia?'

'I just got stuck in a cupboard when I was a little tacker,' Flynn said as he shrugged his shoulders.

Lily looked down and was surprised to notice she was still holding his hand. Quickly she let go. 'It's funny how things that happened to us when we were little can still have an effect.'

'Yeah, I suppose. Listen, I could do with another coffee – want to go and get one with me?'

Lily looked up and gave him a bright smile. 'Sure, it sounds like a plan.'

* * *

'So how is everything with you? Haven't caught up in a while,' Mac said as he pushed the pizza box over to Flynn.

'Yeah, it's all good. Thought I'd get an early start. I've been busy clearing some of the scrub away from the top fence and making sure I've got decent firebreaks. You?' Flynn said as he reached down and snagged a piece of pizza.

'Pretty much the same. They reckon this summer is going to be a bastard as far as bushfires go.'

'Let's just hope they're wrong. I've got a lot of sheep up in the top paddock, and I don't know if the top dam will be enough for a hot summer.'

'How many have you got up there now?' Mac asked.

'About a couple of hundred. I think I'll move them down near the house – there's more shade there and that dam has never once dried up.'

'Good idea. Do you need a hand?'

'Maybe,' Flynn conceded.

'I'll swing by with young Ben first thing in the morning, if you like.'

Ben Jamison was Mac's farmhand. What had started as a part-time job had turned into something more and the kid was now a near-permanent fixture at McKellan's Run. After escaping his abusive father, Ben idolised Mac as a cross between a father and a big brother and now lived above the stables. As far as Flynn knew, Ben hadn't been near his father in months.

'Hey, that would be great – appreciate it.'

'No worries.'

'So how's the family?' Flynn said with a grin. 'And why are you hanging out with me instead of your girls?'

'Hey, sometimes a man just needs beer, pizza and a movie.'

'Uh-huh.' Flynn took a sip of his beer.

'And it may have something to do with the fact that Violet, Holly and Mum are over with Lily talking about wedding dresses. I love her, but I just can't do the girly dress talk,' Mac said as he shrugged. 'I try to pay attention but my eyes glaze over.'

'So I'm the backup plan – that hurts, Mac, it really does,' Flynn said with a sigh and a sad shake of his head.

'You're an idiot,' Mac said with a laugh. 'So what are we watching tonight?'

'Well, we can go with zombies, action with explosions and car chases, or a drag your soul to hell horror – your call.'

'My vote is for the drag your soul to hell horror.'

'Okay, but I would just like to point out you'll be the one driving home down dark and lonely bush tracks, not me.' Flynn got up from the couch and grabbed the movie. 'Speaking of creepy things, I managed to get myself trapped in an old cupboard the other day.'

Mac straightened in his seat and put down his beer. 'How?'

'At Lily's shop. She'd found this old storage space in the attic. It had been painted shut but she opened it. Anyway, I was talking to her in the doorway and she stumbled on something. So when I went to catch her, I knocked the door and the damn thing swung shut on us.'

'Hell. Did you freak out? Because you're allowed to, you know.'

'Nah, I was alright. Everything closed in for a second but it was okay. The door was just a bit jammed and we were out of there pretty quick,' Flynn said as he put the DVD in the player. He walked back to the couch and scooped up the remote before he sat back down.

'I'm glad to hear it. So you were okay with it?'

'I suppose. Don't get me wrong, I'd rather not get stuck in another bloody closet again – even if it is with Lily Beckett,' Flynn said with a grin.

'So, you want to run by me why you were with Lily in the first place?' Mac asked as he turned and looked at his friend.

Flynn stared straight ahead. 'Oh, shut up and watch the damn movie.'

Chapter 11

It was a glorious spring morning. The sun was shining and there was something hinting of summer in the air as Lily pounded along the botanical garden footpath. September had been busy but she'd made great progress on the dresses for Violet's wedding. Since the wedding was scheduled for the end of summer, she felt that she had plenty of time to finish them. Her normal daily routine of splitting her time between the shop and sewing had been slightly interrupted with Holly's school holidays. She tried to help Violet out and take on a little more events planning to give her sister some much-needed one-on-one time with Holly. She'd also taken her niece to the movies a couple of times, which had been great.

But now it was the first week of October and school had officially gone back, so Lily was able to concentrate on business. Well, that and the money pit that was her shop renovation. No, that wasn't really fair: up until this point everything with the new kitchen and bathroom had gone well and pretty much to the time line Johnno had first laid out for her. Oh, there had been a few hiccups, but nothing major – that was until last Sunday night when a huge storm ripped through the town. The wild weather had torn a section of the old corrugated iron off the roof. Consequently, the rain had poured through the attic and down one of Lily's newly painted walls on the first floor. It was a setback and a costly one, but Lily just had to take a breath and wear it.

So she should have been mulling over her budget, the new repairs that had to be done, and which one of her designs she should tackle next. Instead her mind kept wandering back to Flynn. Since being locked in the cupboard she'd only seen him a few times, and they had been accidental meetings at that – at the service station, outside the bakery and once when she dropped off Violet at McKellan's Run. Their exchanges had been friendly but brief. It was better this way, but if she was being truthful, there was a part of her that regretted him not popping in to see her.

Lily fell into step with the beat of the music as it pumped through her earphones. She should just let it go and not dwell on it, she thought as she ran back towards home. Problem was that was easier said than done.

She hit the shower and grabbed a quick breakfast with Violet and Holly before heading over to the shop to see how the roof repairs were going.

Walking upstairs to the attic, Lily was confronted by a large metal ladder disappearing into the manhole in the slatted wooden ceiling, a pair of workbooted feet sticking out at the top.

'Is that you up there, Johnno?'

'Oh hey, Lily – yeah, it's me. I was just checking out the roof trusses. So do you want the good news or the bad news?' Johnno said as he climbed halfway down the ladder.

Lily dropped her head back and scrunched her eyes for a second. 'Ooh, really? Okay, damn it, hit me with the bad news.'

'I have to replace a couple of the beams.'

'And the good news?'

'I don't have to replace the whole thing,' he said with a smile as he climbed all the way down. 'Here, why don't you go up there and have a look? I'll point out the bit that has to be fixed.'

'Okay,' she said as she started to climb up. 'What exactly am I looking for?'

'I've left a light up there. When you reach the top of the ladder, look to the beam on your right,' Johnno said as he followed her up, standing just a couple of rungs below her. 'Just reach over and touch it.'

Lily did just that, a little piece of it broke off in her hand. 'It's rotten.'

'Yep, it sure is,' Johnno said, making no attempt to move. 'These things happen. The shop is old and just needs a bit of TLC.'

Lily was conscious of Johnno standing too close, his body brushing against hers. She looked back at him. 'Um, can we go down now?'

'Oh yeah, sure.'

Lily felt his hand on her back as she took the last couple of rungs. 'Thanks.'

Johnno gave her a smile. 'Anyway, it will add a bit of

time and expense to the job of fixing the roof. I'll do some costings and give you the figures later.'

'Alright,' Lily said as she went to go back downstairs, but Johnno called her back.

'So Lily, have you had time to think about us going out?'

Lily hesitated for a second. Johnno was a good, decent, stable guy, and it was only dinner, not a commitment for the rest of her life. Why shouldn't she say yes? It wasn't as if Flynn . . . damn it, why was she even thinking of him at a time like this?

'Sure, why not, Johnno – thanks.'

'Great,' he said with a beaming smile. 'How about next Saturday?'

'Sounds good,' Lily said before she walked back down the stairs. 'It'll be nice.'

And it was just that – nice. The next Saturday, they went to a trendy little bar in Bendigo that had a cool and intimate vibe, followed by dinner at Lemongrass and Orchid, one of the best Thai restaurants in the area. The food was fantastic, the conversation was pleasant and Lily did have a nice time, but there was something missing. When Johnno kissed her goodnight it had been gentle and sweet and didn't raise her heartbeat, not even for a second. As Lily walked back up the steps to the verandah, she couldn't help but wish there was a spark between them. The truth was that no matter what her head said, her heart wanted fireworks.

* * *

Flynn had tried to put Lily out of his mind. He'd caught the look of concern in Mac's eyes when he'd let slip that he had been with Lily and guessed he couldn't blame him. Mac was his best friend and, like anyone else in Violet Falls, knew about Flynn's long and meandering trail of failed love affairs. However, Mac understood the reason why Flynn had trouble committing and why things always seemed to go belly up. Normally Mac wouldn't say a word, and Flynn knew that he could always count on him, but this time things were different. This time, Mac wasn't only Flynn's mate but almost Lily's brother-in-law.

When Mac and Violet had got together, he knew he was getting an instant family. He'd been in love with Violet Beckett for years and nothing made him happier than knowing that soon she'd be his wife and Holly his daughter. But he also knew that Violet and her sister, Lily, had a strong bond. Violet had been responsible for Lily since she was a kid and she worried over her like a mother hen.

So Flynn understood Mac's look of concern the other night, and for that reason Flynn took a step back. He stayed at the Grange and rarely went into town, but even on the handful of times he did, he still managed to run into her – perhaps it was fate, or maybe just bad timing. Each meeting left him feeling rattled and aware that no matter how hard he tried to ignore it, Lily Beckett had an effect on him.

Monday afternoon found him standing in line at the post office. The line was long and to kill the time he stared out the window. The bakery was just across the road and the more he looked, the more he thought that maybe he should grab one of their éclairs and a coffee before heading home. As he stood there he overheard a couple of women who were ahead of him in the line. One was Mandy from the newspaper and the other one was Jill; she glanced over her shoulder and caught his eye and he nodded a greeting in return.

'So on Saturday we went to dinner before catching a late screening at the movies,' Mandy was saying to Jill.

'Nice. Where did you eat?' Jill asked.

'Um . . . what's it called? You know, the Thai place – Lemongrass and Orchid.'

'Oh great – the food is fantastic there.'

'It was. Hey, I ran into your friend there, Lily.'

'Really?'

'Yeah, she was there with Johnno.'

Something in Flynn's gut contracted when he heard the words. He stopped himself from barrelling into their conversation and demanding all the details. He shouldn't be jealous but he was. Rationally he knew that he had absolutely no right to feel this way. It wasn't as if he and Lily were going out or anything. It was just the idea of her in some dimly lit restaurant with another guy that didn't sit well with him at all. Flynn picked up his parcel and then hightailed out of there as quickly as he could and headed to his car. No point heading to the bakery now, all of a sudden he seemed to have lost his appetite.

***

108

The Violet Falls agricultural show had been held on the last weekend of October for the past hundred and two years. There was a woodchopping contest, a horse show, a petting zoo for the kiddies, the sideshow carnival and horse rides, and the old pavilion showcasing entries in the various competitions, including the best jam or preserve, patchwork quilt, knitted item or rose grown in the local area. Several members of the community took the agricultural show very seriously and made an effort to enter as many categories as they could. It was common knowledge that old Mrs Patterson, for instance, was the undisputed champion when it came to strawberry jam and quince jelly and had walked away with the blue ribbon for the past forty-five years.

The show always opened with a parade on the Friday evening. Starting up one end of the main street, it made its way to the local oval on the other side of the railway track. The parade was heralded by the Violet Falls highland band and included floats from the primary school, sporting clubs and other community groups as well as fire engines and a collection of antique cars.

Lily stood alongside Violet and Mac outside her shop and waited for the parade to begin. The Violet Falls primary school was entering a float this year as usual, but Holly had decided that she wanted to be with her new dance school, Moonbeams and Stardancers. The main street was lined with people, all waiting to cheer the participants on.

'Is Holly nervous?' Lily asked.

Violet nodded as she glanced her way. 'Yes, but she's got Kylie and Amber with her, so I hope she'll be okay.'

Mac put his arm around Violet and gave her a squeeze. 'You worry too much – Holly will be brilliant. Once the parade gets going she'll have a ball. Look,' he said as he gestured towards the post office, 'it's starting.'

Lily turned her head and looked up the street as the first drumbeats sounded in the air. The drums were quickly joined by the drone of a dozen bagpipes as the band began to march down the street to the strains of 'Scotland the Brave'.

After the band came the Violet Falls kindergarten, with a dozen or so preschoolers sitting on a float dressed as acorns.

'That's adorable!' Lily said with a chuckle.

'Yeah,' Mac said with grin as he nudged Violet. 'Hey, you want to start working on our own little forest later?'

Violet blushed. 'Shhh Mac – someone will hear.'

After the kindergarten came the school, all the kids dressed up as their favourite book characters. The boys and girls from Holly's dance group followed.

'Oh, there she is!' Violet said, waving to her daughter as Mac pulled out his phone and started snapping a few photos.

With the help of her two best friends, Holly walked down the middle of the road carrying the Moonbeam and Stardancers banner. All the girls from the dance school were dressed in pale pink tutus and had their hair pulled back in the classic ballerina bun.

Holly gave her Mum a little wave and smile as she walked past.

'See, I told you she'd be alright,' Mac said as he nudged Violet. 'Didn't I, Lily?'

Lily grinned back. 'Yes, you did, Mac.'

'Come on, let's head down to the oval,' he said, slipping his phone back into his jeans and putting his arm around Violet again.

The three of them wove their way through the various groups of people and headed towards the sportsground. The music was fading into the distance and being drowned out by the clapping and voices of the crowd. They stopped several times as they were greeted by friends. Seriously, Lily began to think that Mac must know every single person in town.

Once inside the sportsground, they waited by the fence for the whole parade to circle once. Then, after a final blast of the fire engine siren, the parade broke up and all the children were gathered up by their parents.

'Did you see me, Aunty Lily?' Holly said as she ran forward into Mac's arms.

'I certainly did! You were great out there.'

'You were beautiful, fairy,' Mac said as he swung her around before putting her down in front of Violet.

'Thanks, Mac!' Holly scooted over and gave her mum a hug. 'What did you think, Mummy?'

'That you were my very favourite ballerina out there. Good job, kiddo – I'm really proud of you for walking in the parade, even though you were nervous. Now I know you like the tutu but I brought your jeans and boots to change into. It's going to get cold soon,' Violet said as she handed Holly a bag.

Holly took the bag but her eyes travelled past her mother to the sideshow with all its rides. 'Mummy, can I go on some of those?'

'Hmmm, I guess. Which ones?'

'That one,' Holly said with a grin, pointing to a great metal monster. The ride had eight arms with a passenger car attached at each end. Not only did the cars go around and around but they also went up and down with a loud whooshing sound.

Lily looked at Violet and could have sworn that her sister's face had paled.

'Um, I'm not sure . . .'

'Oh, please, Mummy – it looks fun. Mac will take me, won't you?'

He glanced at Violet, who still didn't look convinced. 'Well, that's up to your mum.'

'Oh please! Aunty Lily, get Mummy to say yes.'

'Hey, leave me out of this,' Lily said with a laugh.

'Why don't we get you changed and have something to eat, and then I'll think about it,' Violet said.

Holly took her mum's hand in hers and then Mac's. They looked like the perfect family and all of a sudden Lily felt like a fifth wheel. They should have this night as a family unit and not have poor old Aunty Lily tagging along.

'You guys go ahead. I think I'll just wander around and check out the pavilion.'

'Don't you want to get something to eat?' Violet asked with a frown.

'No, not yet – go and have fun. I'll see you later.'

'But . . .'

Lily shooed Violet away with her hand. 'I'm fine – go.' She added a hard look just to get her message across. She watched as they turned away and wandered off into the growing crowd. Not a lot happened in Violet Falls, so the show was an excuse for most of the town and district to turn out. Lily headed down to the far end of the oval where the old pavilions were. For Lily the word pavilion always stirred up romantic visions of some bygone Victorian era, but the pavilions at the Violet Falls sportsground were really just big sheds.

By the time she stepped through the door, the place was already filling up with people. She took her time looking at all the entries in the different sections. This year there was a small photography division and she wondered if maybe next year she should enter.

She bumped into Mac's mother, Sarah McKellan, down in the floral area.

'It looks as if congratulations are in order,' Lily said as she pointed to the large blue first prize ribbon next to Sarah's vase of three blood-red roses.

Sarah turned around and smiled. 'Oh hello, darling, and thanks – I wasn't sure if I'd pull it off this year but it appears I did, which is lovely.'

'Well, your roses were always so beautiful.'

'Ah, that's so sweet. Have you just got here?'

'Um, yes.'

'Well, you've just missed a great drama. One that will be talked about for at least a good week,' Sarah said with a wink.

'What do you mean?'

'It seems that Sally Ford – do you know her? She's one of Violet's friends, I think?'

'Yes, her daughter is best friends with Holly.'

'Well, it seems that young Sally has managed to pull off a coup. She's just beaten Mrs Patterson to first place with her strawberry jam, and Mrs Patterson was far from happy.'

'Whatever happened to being gracious in defeat?'

'Grace is something Elvira Patterson has always been lacking in. Anyway, she's just said – very loudly, may I add – that the whole thing was rigged and that she has never been so insulted in all her life. She stormed out of here with a red face swearing to get to the bottom of it.'

'Gosh.'

'Ah yes, it's high drama in Violet Falls. So, are you here by yourself? I thought you'd be with Violet, Holly and my son.'

'I was – we watched the parade from outside the shop. But I thought that they should be by themselves, as a family.'

Sarah reached over and gave Lily's hand a squeeze. 'That was lovely, dear. You are more than welcome to stay here with me, if you like.'

'Thanks, but I'm kind of enjoying just wandering around by myself.'

'I'm on duty here until the fireworks. Apparently, I'm the muscle who is meant to stop anyone from fiddling with the displays. Ah well, that's what happens when you're volunteered onto the agricultural show committee,' Sarah said with a sigh.

Lily laughed at the thought of the dainty Sarah McKellan being seen as a deterrent. Then again, she did seem more than capable of reining in her sons. Perhaps the show committee knew exactly what it was doing after all.

'Anyway, you know where to find me if you need anything.'

'Thanks. Have a great night, and congrats on your win,' Lily said before heading back out to the oval.

Lily did a circuit of the sideshows, remembering how thrilling it had all been as a kid. Even as a young teenager, the show always had a touch of magic to it, especially once the sun went down. She supposed it was a combination of the lights, rides, stallholders hawking for your business and games, like fishing for floating plastic ducks and throwing darts at balloons. Funny, as she walked through the crowd she caught a trace of that old feeling of excitement.

Lily looked up as she neared the Tornado, the ride that Holly had wanted to go on earlier. She smiled when she spotted her niece, Violet and Mac already on board. The passenger cars spun around and then the heavy metal arms lifted them high off the ground in a seesawing motion. Lily noted that her sister looked far from comfortable, but Holly and Mac were grinning from ear to ear and laughing.

She grabbed a coffee from a food van and sat down on one of the wooden benches that ran around the circumference of the oval. It was dark but the floodlights illuminated the grounds, as did the bright lights from the sideshow. She was glad that she'd brought a jacket because as soon as the sun had gone down there was a definite bite in the air.

She had just settled in to watch the first round of the woodchopping competition when Flynn Hartley appeared by her side and shoved a polystyrene box into her hands.

'What's this?'

'A hamburger with the lot. I saw you over here while

115

I was in the queue and thought you looked cold. Do you mind if I sit?'

Lily shuffled along the bench to give Flynn enough room. 'Thanks for the hamburger.'

'Not a problem. The kindergarten has put on a hamburger and sausage sizzle. They're trying to raise money for new playground equipment.'

Lily opened the lid and took a bite. 'It's good.'

'Yeah, it is,' Flynn said after he'd taken a bite of his own. 'So, why are you sitting here all by yourself?'

'I could ask you the same question.'

Flynn shrugged. 'I came in to see how my fleece went in the wool competition.'

'I haven't made it down to the wool shed yet. Were there a lot of entries this year?'

'Yeah, heaps, which is great. About five or six years ago we'd have been lucky to get a handful. Mr Alison, who's been running it for donkey's years, thought that interest around here was dying out and he'd have to shut the whole thing down. But this year we got about twenty farms entering into the different sections.'

'And how did you go? No, wait – don't tell me. I'll go and have a look after I finish this.'

Flynn gave her a smile. 'So, you still haven't answered my question.'

'I'm giving my sister and your best friend a little space to enjoy the night and each other.'

'Hey, I'm sure they don't think you're in the way.'

'No, they probably don't, but sometimes *I* feel like I am.

116

Anyway, I think I'll head off home – that is, after I check out the wool pavilion.'

'The woodchop isn't your thing?'

Lily wrinkled her nose. 'Honestly, I only sat down here so I could drink my coffee,' she said in a half whisper.

Flynn let out a laugh. 'Well, your secret is safe with me.'

They both fell into silence as they tucked into their burgers. The next lot of competitors lined up in front of the massive logs, but Lily was too distracted by the proximity of Flynn to take much notice. There was a space between them but every now and then his shoulder would innocently brush against hers, which made her acutely aware of how inadequately small the wooden bench was.

The countdown sounded and the noise of axes hitting wood and cries of encouragement filled the air.

'You know that you're setting a precedent, don't you,' Lily said as she glanced up at Flynn.

'I don't know what you mean.'

'Every time we run into each other lately, you give me food.'

'Twice, Lily, it's happened twice,' he grinned. 'Besides, it's always been my ultimate weapon. Some men bring flowers, me, I bring hamburgers.'

'For which I'm grateful,' Lily said as she stood up.

'Where are you going?'

'To the wool pavilion.'

'In that case, I reckon I'll tag along,' he said, standing up as well. Without another glance at the woodchopping, they walked to the treed end of the sportsground.

She could smell the lanolin when she walked through the

door. The long trestle tables lining the room were filled with big fluffy fleeces. She wandered along them until she spotted Flynn's name printed on a card.

'You got third!' Lily said as she pointed to the green rosette.

'Yeah,' he said as he looked at his boots. If she didn't know better, Lily would think that he was embarrassed.

'Congratulations – that's amazing.'

'Thanks. Maybe next year I'll be able to beat that one.' Flynn pointed to the fleece with a large blue ribbon across it.

Lily walked over and read the card. 'It's Mac!' she said with surprise.

'Of course it is,' Flynn said with a smile. 'Mac's sheep are legendary around here. It's not often that he doesn't get a prize or a place for his product. The big plan is that one day the Grange's sheep will rival those at McKellan's Run.'

'That wouldn't hurt your friendship?'

Flynn looked at her strangely. 'I don't know where you'd get a crazy idea like that from. Of course he wouldn't mind – he's my mate.'

'Sorry, it's just some people would feel threatened.'

'Not Mac – he's got nothing to be threatened about. If it weren't for him and his dad, my place would have gone under long ago. Mr McKellan taught me everything I needed to know to manage a sheep run, and Mac has always been there to lend me a hand when I needed it.'

Lily looked back at the wool. She felt as if she'd said the wrong thing. All of a sudden she was that awkward, tongue-tied teenager again.

'Well, I think I might call it a night – thanks for dinner,' she said quickly.

Flynn looked at his watch. 'You're going before the fire-works? I always thought they were the best bit of the show.'

'Um . . .'

'Come on, they're going to start in an hour. I'm sure we can find something to do until then.'

'Why?'

'Another crazy question – because I like hanging out with you, that's why. Stay, and I'll take you on a ride and buy you some fairy floss. And then after that, you can win me one of those big stuffed toys.'

Lily chuckled. 'I've never won anything in my life.'

'Well, tonight's as good a time as any to start.' He held out his hand and, after a moment's hesitation, Lily took it.

True to his word, Flynn plied her with fairy floss and took her on the dodgem cars and then on the old carousel. She sat on a painted dapple-grey and he on the black horse next to her. Lily held onto the gilt-painted pole as the horse went up and down, trying to ignore the curious looks from some of the nearby parents. She glanced over to Flynn and he winked back at her, which made her smile and her insides go a little tingly. The earlier awkwardness was forgotten and Lily realised just how much she liked being around Flynn. He made her smile and laugh, and Lily was pretty sure she could do with more of that in her life. There was an easiness between them, and that was something that she hadn't felt with a guy for a while, and certainly not on her date with the nice, safe Johnno.

They wandered through the sideshow together, stopping every now and again to try their luck on one of the games. It turned out that Lily sucked at throwing darts at balloons and didn't fare any better with the lucky numbers. Much to her surprise, she won a small orange beanbag toy on some evil-looking clowns and handed it to Flynn. 'It's not one of the big toys but it's the best I can do.'

'See, you did win something after all. What, I'm not sure,' he said, turning the toy over in his hand.

'Maybe it's an octopus?'

'I think it's one leg short. But nevertheless, I will treasure this poor deformed octopus and call it Monty.'

'Monty?'

'It's a great name,' he said as he took her hand again and tugged her along. 'Come on, let's go on the Ferris wheel.'

They climbed into a seat and Flynn put his arm along the back of the seat; Lily didn't pull away but didn't lean into it either. She suddenly felt awkward and fourteen again. The ride began and she turned sideways to look down at the crowd of people below. She'd forgotten how much she loved riding on a Ferris wheel. In another minute they were transported from the noise and congestion of the busy carnival and into their own little world, the whole town just specks below them. Flynn's arm seemed to brush closer to the back of her neck and she shivered involuntarily.

'It's pretty up here,' she said, trying to sound casual. 'I can't remember the last time I was on one of these.'

'Then it's obviously been far too long.'

'Yeah, I guess it has. Oh look, the lights around the oval have gone out. I wonder why . . . ah, of course,' Lily said as the first boom went off. A firework whistled up into the night sky and exploded into a shower of blue sparks.

The Ferris wheel kept rotating slowly around and around as more fireworks were let off. Lily and Flynn were almost at the top when a series of red, gold and blue lights exploded in the sky.

'Oh, it's beautiful,' Lily said, turning back to Flynn with a wide smile.

'Yeah, beautiful,' Flynn said as he lowered his head and kissed her.

Chapter 12

Lily sat on her bed and hugged the ridiculously large teddy bear that Flynn had won for her at the show. It was crazy: after she'd been kissed by Johnno she remembered wanting fireworks, and then tonight – well, tonight she'd got them literally, physically and, hell, even emotionally. There was no way that Lily could sit there and not admit that Flynn had an impact on her – he'd rocked her world with just a kiss and they both knew it.

She'd dodged Johnno's question the other night about seeing each other again with a not so graceful change of subject. But after tonight, she'd have to sit him down on Monday and explain that she wouldn't be able to see him again – at least, not in a romantic way – because if she did she wouldn't be being true to herself or to him. Her grandmother always said that you can't flog a dead horse, and Lily had thought it was an awful sort of saying, visualising some poor dead pony. But tonight she finally got what it meant, without the visual aid. There was no point trying to make anything between Johnno and herself because there wasn't anything there.

The next day, Lily found herself back at the oval again, sitting on the hard wooden benches that circled the showground along with Violet, Holly, Sarah, Mac's brother Dan and, of course, Flynn. They were waiting for Mac and his little blue heeler, Razor, to take their turn in the sheep dog trials. In bigger towns, some of these competitions went from dawn to dusk for days on end, but here in Violet Falls each year showed a decline. There were generally only a handful of entries in the trials, so they had been added to the agricultural show instead of having their own separate event. Mac was worried that the whole thing would die out so he'd decided to enter for the first time and show his support.

The sun had come out and Lily felt a sense of family as she sat on the sidelines with the people she cared about, clapping as the dogs rounded up three sheep at a time. Flynn sat close beside her and subtly pressed his hand against hers.

'Look, there's Mac!' Holly said, standing up and pointing.

Lily raised her head just in time to see Mac walk onto the oval and stand at the appointed starting point, called the casting peg. Razor sat a few metres behind Mac and waited for the sheep to be released further up the field.

'Go on, Razor – get around,' Mac called out as the sheep were freed. Razor ran in a wide arc and started moving them towards Mac in a straight line. Mac whistled as Razor ran backwards and forwards, drawing them in closer and manoeuvring them around the casting peg in a counter-clockwise direction.

Mac started walking towards the first obstacle and Razor held and balanced the sheep, stopping them from breaking formation and running in different directions. Mac whistled again and Razor herded the sheep through the first obstacle, then the second and third until finally he'd ushered them into the pen. When Mac shut the last gate, the whole clan jumped to their feet and clapped. Mac gave them all a wave before he and Razor left the field.

'Oh, they did so well,' Sarah said with a grin.

'Do you think they've taken off many marks?' Violet asked. 'Because I didn't see any mistakes, did you?'

Dan shook his head. 'Nope, only for a split second at the bridge when the lead sheep tried to run.'

'Yeah, but Razor was on it,' Flynn said.

'Sorry, what do you mean about taking marks off?' Lily asked as she glanced up at Flynn.

'That's how they judge it. Each section of the trial has marks attached to it. The cast, when the dog runs in an arc towards the sheep, the lift, when he moves them in a controlled manner, and the draw, when he brings them to Mac. The next bit is how well he gets them through the obstacles and overall general work. There's a hundred points to begin with and then marks are deducted with every little mistake.' Flynn finished the explanation with a shrug. 'Mac's been talking about it a lot over the past couple of weeks.'

Mac wandered out with Razor and sat down next to Violet.

'You were brilliant,' she said as she gave him a kiss.

Holly hugged Razor. 'You're the cleverest dog ever.'

They sat there for another hour while the last few competitors took their turns. When the contestants were called back to the arena, there was much clapping and yelling when Mac managed to take the second prize rosette.

After that, Lily and Flynn surreptitiously broke away from the others – they weren't exactly hiding their hesitant new feelings for each other, but they weren't flaunting them either. It was all still so new. They drove to the falls on the other side of town and walked along the green banks, which were sprinkled with moisture from the water mist in the air. It was good to be alone again, away from the noise and laughter of the showgrounds. They walked hand in hand, enjoying the sound of the running water and the cool air. It really was a beautiful place, and for the first time Lily didn't associate it with the untimely demise of her ancestor. On this visit she was too filled up with Flynn and the effect he had on her to think about anything else. Lily was keenly aware of how his hand felt warm and strong in hers, and how she wished above all things that he'd kiss her again.

Flynn tugged her along the path until they came to a small lookout opposite the waterfall. She lifted her head up and smiled as he brushed a strand of hair back from her face.

'It's good to get away from everyone,' Flynn said. 'Don't get me wrong, I love them but I just wanted to have you to myself for a while.'

'Me too.' Lily turned her head and glanced over at the water which gushed along. She drew in a deep breath before turning back to Flynn. 'It's always so peaceful here, I think it's one of my favourite places.'

'Yeah, it's pretty special but I always forget that until I'm standing here.'

'I try and run here once a week.'

'Really? I didn't know that,' Flynn said. 'That's quite a way from your place.'

'Which is why I only make it once a week,' Lily answered with a grin.

Flynn took a step forward, he was close now and Lily could feel the heat of his body. She reached up and pulled him down, until their lips touched. An instant fire sparked inside of her as her mouth moved under his. His hands spiked through her hair and anchored her to him. The sound of the waterfall receded and all she was aware of was Flynn, the warmth of his body and the slightly spicy scent of his aftershave. As the kiss deepened, Lily's hands travelled slowly from his shoulders and up the smooth skin to the nape of his neck. He moved and wrapped his arms around her, pulling her so close that there was not even a breath of space between them. And yet, Lily knew she wanted more.

She always knew that kissing Flynn Hartley would be dangerous, she just never realised how devastating it would be.

* * *

On Monday morning, Lily went to the shop earlier than usual. She wanted to talk to Johnno – she needed to address the whole second date thing.

Lily braced herself against the open doorway of the kitchenette.

'Um, Johnno, could I have a word?'

Two other guys on his team gave him a smirk as he walked over to her.

'Don't you clowns have something to do?'

Taking the hint, they hightailed it out as quickly as possible.

'So, what's up, Lily?'

'Um, it's about the other night,' Lily said nervously, as she ran a hand through her hair.

'I had a great time,' Johnno said with a widening smile.

Lord, this wasn't going to be easy.

'I had a lovely time as well but, well, I can't go out with you again.'

'Why not?'

'I like you, Johnno, I do . . . But I have to be honest with you: I kind of went out with Flynn as well. I didn't plan it but it happened, and now . . .'

Johnno sighed. 'And now you'd rather be with him, right?'

'I'm really sorry. I hope you're not mad with me.'

Johnno shook his head and shrugged. 'Nah, these things happen. It was one date, Lily, not a lifetime commitment.'

'Thanks for being so understanding.'

'No worries. Now, if you'll excuse me, I have a shop to finish,' Johnno said with a small smile as he turned away.

***

Later that day, Lily sat at her sewing machine as Flynn filled the doorway. She had spent the last five minutes trying to explain why they shouldn't rush into a relationship.

'So what are you saying, you don't want us to be together?' Flynn asked as he leant against the doorframe and locked eyes with her.

'No, that's not what I mean,' Lily said with sigh. 'I guess I'm not explaining myself very well.'

'I guess not.'

Lily got up and stood in front of Flynn. 'I like being with you. I like how it feels and I like how it's generally – okay, granted, maybe not right at this moment – but generally how easy it is between us. All I'm saying is, let's take it slowly. We're not in a hurry, are we?'

Flynn shrugged. 'Nope.'

'Okay then.'

'So we'll take it one step at a time and see where that leads us.'

Lily smiled. 'That's what I was thinking – no pressure for either of us.'

'Alright, I'm willing to give it a shot. But I'd really like you to answer a question first, that is, if you don't mind?'

'Of course,' Lily said lightly.

'You said that you *liked* being with me.'

'I do.'

Flynn stepped forward, his arms circling her waist. 'So are you telling me you only *like* my kisses?'

A slow smile spread over Lily's face. 'Hmmm, I suppose, though maybe it could be just a little bit more than like.'

'Maybe we should give one another try, just so you can be sure.'

Lily put her arms around Flynn. 'Maybe.'

Lily grabbed a biscuit and nibbled on its corner as she took a seat in Jill's front room. 'You know that I'm seeing him, don't you?'

'Who?' asked Hailey.

'Flynn Hartley, of course,' Jill said with a roll of her eyes. 'God, Hailey, who else would she be locking lips with?'

'Yes,' Lily said, wriggling around in the big lounge chair until she was comfortable.

'So you kissed him again?'

'Yes, I did, Hailey.'

Jill sighed. 'Ah, young love. Hey, hang on a minute. What about Johnno?'

'How did you even know about that?'

Jill wrinkled her nose. 'Small town, remember?'

Lily let out a sigh. 'Johnno asked me to go out, so I did. We went to dinner and it was nice.'

Jill blew out a breath. 'Nice, eh? Well that's a death knell if ever I heard one.'

'Kind of,' Lily admitted. 'He's a great guy, but there isn't a spark between us.'

'And what about with you and Flynn?' Hailey asked.

'There's more than a spark, there's a bloody incendiary device,' Lily said. 'So, I told Johnno that we should just be friends.'

'And what about Flynn?' Hailey reached over to pick up her coffee from the table.

'We're taking it slowly and just seeing what happens.'

'Now what the hell possessed you to do something dumb like that?' Jill asked.

'What do you mean?' Lily said in surprise. 'We're both busy, him with the Grange and me with setting up a business.'

'Oh for heaven's sake, will you just stop?' Jill said as she slumped back on the couch. 'Jeez, Lily, I swear you're doing my head in.'

'Explain?'

'Stop trying to be sensible and analyse everything! Just go with the flow for once and don't put the brakes on. Be spontaneous for a change.'

'But if Lily doesn't want to go out with him then you shouldn't bully her into it,' Hailey said as she grabbed a biscuit.

'I'm not bullying her!' Jill said with a frown. 'I'm trying to push her back into life.'

'But that should be up to her.'

'Well, of course it's up to her, Hailey. All I'm saying is there's an opportunity, so why not take it?'

'Can we all stop talking like I'm not here?' Lily said with a shake of her head. 'Helllooo, I can hear you.'

'Then take the advice,' Jill quipped as she picked up the cushion and threw it at Lily.

'I'm just trying not to make another mistake. Pietro—'

'Was a shit, but just because it didn't work out with him doesn't mean it won't work out with Flynn. All I'm saying is if you like Flynn, and it's pretty obvious that you do, then go for it. You're both adults and, as far as I can see, not hurting anyone.'

'That's true, but we all know that Flynn doesn't have a great track record when it comes to relationships,' Hailey cautioned.

'Who said anything about that? Are you going to ask him to marry you?'

Lily shook her head and grinned. 'God, no – we've only kissed a few times.'

'That's what I'm trying to get through to you. You don't have to take it so seriously Lily. Why not just have a bit of fun?'

'I don't—'

'Do fun,' Hailey cut in. 'Yes, we know.'

'Ooh, that's not fair.'

Jill sat forward and took Lily's hand. 'Look, ever since you left Violet Falls all those years ago you've been level-headed and dependable. You supported your sister and looked after Holly once she was born. You've worked hard and traded away your teenage years to make sure your family was secure. I get it, you're amazing, but we all need to let down our hair every once and a while. When was the last time you did something just for the hell of it?'

'I . . . I—'

'Exactly. You like Flynn, and it's pretty obvious that he likes you, so go for it. Not because it might lead to something else but because it'll be fun.'

'I suppose you're right.'

'Of course I am. Besides, haven't you always wondered what Flynn would be like in bed?'

'Jill!'

'Come on, you used to have the biggest crush on him when we were at school.'

'Everyone had a crush on him back then, Jill,' Hailey added, taking another sip of coffee. 'And nearly everyone hooked up with him as well.'

'Good point, even though it's exaggerated,' Jill said before her head snapped around and she stared at Hailey. 'Hang on a minute, you said everyone went out with Flynn – did that include you?'

Hailey chuckled into her mug. 'Maybe. Well, yes, a million years ago and for about a nanosecond.'

Jill stared at her open-mouthed. 'I had no idea!'

Lily jumped in. 'Oh, Hailey, I'm so sorry, I would never have talked about all this if I'd known that you and Flynn—'

'It was over before it began,' Hailey said as she reached over and squeezed Lily's hand. 'Believe me, it's ancient history. I know that you've had a thing for him for years. Go on, Jill's right – have a little fun. No one will hold that against you.'

'Are you sure?'

'Oh for heaven's sake, just go for it Lily,' Jill said again. 'Hailey doesn't give a damn – as she said, it's ancient history.'

Hailey smiled and nodded. 'Of course. Go on, Lily – if you like him then where's the harm? It's just a bit of fun after all, nothing serious.'

Chapter 13

Spring gave way to summer, and in a flash it was the end of Holly's school year. Somehow Lily had got roped into making three costumes for Holly's end of school concert: a snowflake, a candy cane and an ice princess. It was worth all the effort, however, because Holly was the cutest snow-flake ever.

Violet was also busy as she arranged Christmas party after Christmas party. Lily helped where she could. She'd been toying with an opening date of St Valentine's Day for the shop but that got blown out of the water when Johnno informed her that even though the Heritage guy had given him the go ahead, the Council had now put a stop to works until the official paperwork was received, and all they could do was wait for this to happen. On top of that, Johnno and his team had a two-week break over the Christmas and New Year period. It had been annoying but Lily took it in her stride.

Christmas itself turned out to be one of the best Lily could ever remember. It seemed to be three days filled with non-stop fun, laughter and a continuous supply of food.

Holly had been in heaven, not only did she get to help decorate a Christmas tree at her place, but also at

MacKellan's Run. Mac had decided as it was going to be the first Christmas he was sharing with Violet and Holly, they needed to have a celebration. So once again the great room at the old house was rearranged under Violet's direction to accommodate the McKellen-Beckett-Hartley clan for Christmas lunch.

On the Saturday before Christmas, Mac, Flynn and Holly went Christmas tree hunting. They went over to old Bob Newton's place on the other side of Violet Falls. Bob had set aside a couple of acres of his farm for pine trees and each year he'd open the gates and let anyone who wanted a tree to come and get one – so long as you found, felled it, carted it off the premises and left a decent donation. He planted a row of new saplings every year to replace the ones that had been taken and any money he made was donated to the local hospital's Christmas fund. It had taken a couple of hours but finally the three of them arrived back at Mac's place carrying what Holly described as the best tree in the whole town.

Lily had glanced at Violet in surprise at the size of the tree as Mac and Flynn carried it into the house.

'That's massive!'

Flynn grinned at her. 'Well, this was the one Holly wanted.'

'Are you sure this isn't just a boy thing?'

Flynn chuckled as he helped Mac manoeuvre the tree onto its stand. 'Yeah well, there may have been a bit of that involved.'

'Great tree,' Violet said as she stood by Mac and placed her hand on his shoulder. 'Thanks for doing this.'

'Nothing to thank me for – besides, we needed a big tree as we have a big room. And I thought Holly would get a kick out of it.'

'Isn't it great, Mummy? Mac let me pick it out all by myself.'

'Good job, kiddo,' Violet said with a smile. 'It's fantastic – We've never had a real tree before.'

'I like the one we've got at home but this one makes it look this big,' Holly said as she held her thumb and fore-finger up.

Lily couldn't argue with that. The pink tinsel tree they had at home was only half the size of this one and it was leaning on a jaunty angle. It hadn't started out that way, when she, Violet and Holly had put it together last week it had stood perfectly straight. That was until Tiger, Holly's tortoiseshell kitten, had decided his humans had given him his own personal jungle gym. Tinsel was strewn across the floor and Tiger hit the plastic baubles up and down the hallway as if they were soccer balls. They kept shutting the door of the front room but somehow the kitten still managed to get inside. Lily had thought that perhaps Holly should have called him Houdini instead of Tiger . . . or maybe Lucifer.

Christmas morning had started early as Holly and Tiger had 'accidentally' managed to rouse the household around dawn. With bleary eyes Lily had stumbled out of her room and bumped into her sister in the kitchen as they both headed for the kettle. However, her sleep deprivation quickly dis-appeared as she watched Holly's glee as she handed out presents from under the lopsided pink tinsel tree.

Mid-morning, when they arrived at McKellan's Run, Mac greeted them at the door. He planted a kiss on Violet before he swung Holly in the air until she giggled.

'Hey, I was wondering when you would get here,' he said as he put Holly down.

'We're running a bit late,' Violet admitted as she stepped inside.

'Not to worry – Mum and Dan have only just arrived as well.'

'Merry Christmas, Mac,' Lily said as she gave him a peck on the cheek.

'Thanks Lily – you too,' he said. 'So how's your morning been?'

'Well, let's just say it started earlier than I thought it was going to,' Lily said with a smile as she gestured towards Holly.

'Ah, holiday exuberance?' Mac chuckled.

'Yeah, something like that,' Lily said as she walked into the house.

Lily helped Violet dress and set the long table in the great room. Lily stepped back and admired their handiwork. There was a white silk damask runner down the centre of the table and dotted along it were tall white candles amongst bunches of ivy and pine twigs.

'Well, it might be getting hot outside but at least we can pretend we're in some sort of cool forest,' Lily said. 'It looks really pretty.'

'Thanks,' Violet said as she started setting the plates down. 'I think they said that it was going to hit at least 35 degrees today.'

'Thank goodness for air conditioning,' Lily said with a smile. 'Um, why are you setting so many places? I thought it was just going to be us.'

'One place is for young Ben – he considers this his home now.'

Lily frowned. 'So nothing's changed?'

'Nope, there's still a problem with his father. Ben is safer here.'

'And so who else is coming?'

Violet glanced up. 'Jason – at least I think he's coming.'

Lily exhaled. 'Isn't that going to be a bit awkward?'

'Maybe, but there isn't much we can do about it, is there? Jason is Mac's brother and of course he'd want to be here with his family during the holidays. Besides, we're all adults and I'm sure we can get through a meal without anything happening.'

'What does Holly think about it – I mean about him coming today, she knows doesn't she?'

Violet pulled out a chair and sat down. 'Yeah, she's aware that he might come. You know when I told her that Jason was her father she seemed to take it in her stride. I overheard her telling her friends that she had two fathers but other than that she hasn't said much about it. I've tried to broach the issue with her a few times and she just changes the subject and talks about Mac.'

'Maybe that's telling in itself. Has Jason been in touch or seen Holly since the wedding-that-wasn't fiasco?' Lily asked as she walked over to the sideboard and picked up the cake stand with Sarah's decorated Christmas cake. She placed it in the centre of the table and promised herself a piece later.

'A couple of times here or at Sarah's place. Both visits were pretty short and Jason didn't say much – I guess trying to build a relationship with a child you didn't know you had can take some time.'

'Uncomfortable then?'

'Kind of, but in saying that Holly seemed pretty at ease. She chattered non-stop about school, her friends, Tiger, dance class and Mac.'

'So, do you think he'll come?'

'I don't know – I guess time will tell.'

Even with Lily's misgivings about Jason, lunch had turned out to be a happy affair filled with great food and laughter. As the day warmed up, everyone was slightly relieved that a cold lunch of salads, seafood and turkey rather than the traditionally hot Christmas dinner had been decided on. Not that she had had much to do with the food prep – Dan had taken it on himself to provide all of the lunch.

Flynn sat next to her, his leg brushing against hers – it was nice to have him close. She reached over and squeezed his hand. Jason had sat between Sarah and Dan, he appeared at ease and even laughed at a couple of Holly's antics. Perhaps she should finally forgive him for the way he'd treated Violet in the past. For the sake of peace and harmony maybe she should give Jason the benefit of the doubt. But if he so much as looked at her sister the wrong way he'd have to answer to her. As Lily glanced around the table she began to realise just what it meant to have moved back to Violet Falls. Somehow she'd been enfolded into a bigger family and she hadn't even noticed it until now.

* * *

Lily shut the front door behind her and jogged down the wooden steps just as the sun was beginning to appear over the distant hills. She'd already worked out this morning's running route in her head: along the creek, a circuit of the botanical gardens and then cut through the main street on the way home. Some days she'd head in the opposite direction and run over the old bridge and out of town. Or if she was feeling uberhealthy and energetic she'd make her way to the falls, but today wasn't that sort of day and she was keeping to her 'go to' route.

Lily paused at the gate as she tightened the bright red armband she always wore; she couldn't imagine running without music. Flicking on her phone, she selected her tunes before popping in the earphones. With the fast beat pounding through her, Lily ran down the road until she reached the little dirt track that led to the creek.

She loved this time of the morning. There was a crispness that was almost cold, but you knew it wouldn't last for long, not with it being halfway through summer. There was a definite change in the air: the heat was coming and soon Lily would miss the freshness of these mornings. Lily's feet hit the dirt track and caused little puffs of dust to kick up with every step. The land was beginning to dry out, and patches of grass were already dying off. The green still clung to the banks of the creek but for how long, Lily had no idea. The talk in town was that it was going to be a stinker of a summer; the Bureau of Meteorology had predicted it and so had old Mr Boccaccio, and he was never wrong. Even the creek itself was already showing signs of the drought. The water still ran quickly but the level had shrunk down the sides of the banks. If they didn't get a decent downpour soon the whole of Violet Falls would be turned into a dustbowl. One of the town's legends was that Landoc Creek had never once dried up, that the community could always count on it even in the fiercest of summers. But if decent rain didn't come soon, it sounded like this year could be the exception.

Lily followed the track as it veered away from the creek and headed towards the town. The track turned into a paved footpath as Lily ran past the first few homes on the outskirts.

She glanced down at her watch and smiled as she ran through the tall stone gates of the botanical gardens. She'd managed to shave a couple of minutes off her normal time. To celebrate she stopped at the old Victorian-era drinking fountain for a few sips of cold, clear water.

As she ran around the large ornamental lake, Lily saw that most of the grass was still green and the big clumps of purple agapanthus were flowering. A council announcement last month had let it be known that even though they wouldn't be able to save all the lawn in the gardens, they were going to try to maintain a section, along with the old established trees, by watering them from Lady Amelia Lake. Lily wondered how long that would last, because the water level there looked as if it was dipping dangerously low as well.

Lily ran a circuit and a half before leaving through the front gates. After a couple of blocks, she found herself at the top end of the main street. It was still empty, except for the delivery truck heading towards the supermarket.

She adjusted an earphone as a new song started. This one was slower, and Lily fell in time to the beat as she jogged down the footpath.

But something ahead snared her attention. Lily's heart was in her mouth as she looked across the street at her shop. She stopped stock-still and couldn't catch her breath, which had nothing to do with her morning run.

Her newly and beautifully painted shopfront had been defaced by litres of black paint. It had been thrown over the walls, the front door and even the windows.

For a moment, Lily stood there stunned.

Who would do that? Why would anyone do that?

Lily sucked in a breath as she grabbed her phone and pulled up the number of Violet Falls police station.

* * *

'So the police don't know who did this?' Violet asked as she stood with her hands on her hips, surveying the black paint splashes all over the shop window.

'No. Their best guess is that it was a couple of local kids having a lark.'

'Some lark.'

'Yeah. Anyway, Johnno said not to worry, he'd deal with it.'

'Very nice to have your own pack of builders and handymen on call.'

'Some girls are just blessed,' Lily said with a smile. 'I'm telling myself it's just a hiccup on the path to opening the shop. Apparently my pristine newly painted shop was too much of a temptation to the youth of Violet Falls.'

'I suppose – although according to what I've heard, this is the first time something like this has happened.'

'Oh, I don't know – what about all the graffiti on the old railway fence?'

'Hmmm, maybe, but that's more pictures and tags. This, on the other hand, looks as if someone has just splashed paint out of a can.'

'Don't worry about it. Johnno assures me he'll have it as good as new in a flash.' Lily reached over and gave Violet a hug. 'Come on, forget about this – just wait until you see inside.'

Lily spent the next half an hour showing Violet around the newly renovated shop floor. She put the ugly paint sloshes out of her mind and carried on with her day. It wasn't that she wouldn't like the opportunity to give the little shits a serious talking to and get them to front up the money for the clean-up and Johnno's time. But until they were caught, there was nothing she could do, so why dwell on it.

* * *

Later that afternoon, Lily was walking down the main street when she heard Flynn call out to her from behind.

'Hey, Lily – wait up.'

She stopped, turning around to wait for him to catch up.

'Hi! I didn't think you were coming into town today.'

'I've only just heard about the graffiti on the shop. Are you all right?'

Lily gave a half-hearted shrug. 'Yeah, I guess. I reported it to the police and they think it was probably just kids.'

'Really? That kind of stuff generally doesn't happen around here. I mean, there's a bit of graffiti down around the railway, especially the underpass, but nothing like this.'

'Oh well, maybe they were just bored. Anyway, Johnno said that he'd clean it up, so it's all good.'

'Right, Johnno's going to fix it.' Flynn's statement hung in the air longer than it should.

Lily took his hand. 'Well, don't you think it makes sense that the contractor I've hired to renovate my shop is the same guy I pay to clean up the paint?'

'Yeah, I guess. I suppose for just a second there I was being a bit of an idiot,' Flynn answered with a sheepish smile.

'Yep,' she said with a grin, as she gave his hand a squeeze. 'I made my choice, you know that.'

'And a wise choice it was.'

'Well, since I'm on a roll, I think I'd better fess up.'

'About what?'

'I may have made a mistake.' Lily placed her hands on his hard chest. She could feel the heat of his taut body beneath her fingers as it seared through his cotton shirt. 'You know when I suggested that we take things slowly?'

'Yes.'

'I kind of think that I was wrong.' She laid her palm over his heart. 'Maybe I was a little hasty in that decision. It seems silly to put the brakes on something that doesn't need them. What do you think?' She looked up at him nervously.

'That you're a very wise woman.'

'I don't know about that, Flynn,' Lily said as a hint of a smile touched her lips, 'but perhaps I shouldn't stand this close to you. Otherwise I think the whole town will be gossiping about us.'

'Like I care. Besides, it's what this town does best.' Flynn glanced around and grinned. 'Maybe we should give them something to gossip about. We'd be providing a social service, really. Look, Mrs Cookson is coming down the street with Mrs Claire. I wonder what they'd say if I kissed you.'

'Flynn, don't play around like that,' Lily warned as she gave him a pointed look.

'So you're willing to take a chance and see where it takes us?'

Lily looked up and saw something behind the grin. There was a trace of longing and vulnerability in his dark eyes that made her stop in her tracks.

'Yes, Flynn, let's see what happens. Just don't do anything silly in front of Mrs—'

Flynn gathered her tightly in his arms and kissed her, right there in the middle of the main street.

* * *

The next morning, a knock sounded on the front door of the shop. Lily frowned – most of the tradies used the back door. She hurried down the stairs and into the front room of the shop then opened the door. Outside, Jill stood with two coffees in her hand.

'Hi! What are you doing here?' Lily said as she opened the door.

'Bringing my old friend a coffee and an apple danish,' Jill said as she swept past. 'Shall we eat here? And then I can fantasise about old Mrs Halsford having kittens because we're leaning on her precious counter.'

'Yeah, she was pretty tyrannical about that,' Lily said with a smile and a shake of her head.

Jill put down the drinks before screwing up her face and waving her hand. '"Get away from the glass, girl – you're fogging it up. And keep your grubby little fingers off it".'

Lily chuckled. It was true the former tenant of the shop had been a dragon of a woman. She'd run the shop as a women's clothing boutique for many years, which was obvious from her stock – it never seemed to change, just more and more variations of beige. Mrs Halsford was always polite when there was an adult in earshot; not so much if she found you by yourself with sticky hands on the display case.

Lily took a coffee from Jill and leant on the counter. It gave her a shot of perverse pleasure too.

'So what brings you here?'

'Well, I could lie and say that as we're friends I don't need a reason to visit.'

Lily nodded. 'That's true.'

'Or I could tell the truth and say that I came over to find out why you were kissing Flynn Hartley in the middle of the street yesterday.'

145

Lily's mouth dropped open for a second. 'How did you even—'

'Bush telegraph, or rather the Violet Falls gossip relay. You know you can't do anything, especially kiss a sexy man on the main street, without the gossip machine firing up.'

'I knew this would happen.' Lily cradled her head in her hands.

'Oh come on, buck up. You should be proud. I mean, we don't have much in town – a fair football team, and the cricket and netball teams are okay – but it's our gossip network that is truly spectacular. Dare I say, almost Olympic level.'

'Oh, shut up.'

'Out with it – tell me everything.'

'What's to tell? Apparently the whole town already knows that Flynn kissed me in public.'

'According to the sources, it was far more than an innocent kiss. I do believe the words "carnal" and "sordid" were used,' Jill said before she erupted into hysterical laughter.

'Oh my God! There was nothing sordid or bloody carnal about it. Mrs Cookson should mind her own damn business!'

Jill wiped her eyes with the back of her hand and tried to pull herself together.

'Don't worry, it's just that poor Mrs Cookson probably hasn't ever been kissed carnally before.'

'Ew, stop it! I'm getting a picture,' Lily said with a shudder.

'Oh come on, it's funny. Besides, as soon as something more interesting turns up, everyone will stop talking about you and Flynn and your *carnal* kisses,' Jill said as she almost broke out into giggles again.

'I suppose . . . How long do you think that will take?'

'Oh, I don't know. I guess everything will die down in a couple of months,' Jill managed to get out before she collapsed into fits of laughter again.

'I hate you so very much,' Lily said with a grin as she grabbed a danish and bit into its flaky goodness.

Chapter 14

Holly ran into the kitchen holding a large book. 'Mummy, will you read me this story?'

'Okay. Which one?' asked Violet.

Holly grinned. 'All of them!'

'Ooh, nice try, kid,' Lily said with a laugh.

'How about one?' Violet said. 'Which one do you want?'

Holly flicked open the book and pointed to the story. 'This one, because the princess looks like you. And look,' she continued as she flipped over another couple of pages. 'See, the woodsman looks like Mac.'

Violet bit back a laugh. 'I guess it does. Wow, who knew I was a princess?'

'Me and Mac – and Aunty Lily, too.'

'Well, she's got you there,' Lily said.

'Tell you what, I'll read you the story but first I've already promised Aunty Lily to try on the wedding dress, so she can finish it up. So if you give me half an hour, I'll read you the story before dinner. Do we have a deal?'

Holly nodded her head. 'Deal. Does that mean I can watch cartoons while you and Aunty Lily fix the dress?'

'I guess it does.'

'Yay!' Holly said, doing a little dance before running off to the television.

'Okay then, Princess Violet – let's do this.'

Violet shook her head and chuckled. 'Since when do fairytales happen?'

Lily grinned. 'Aw, come on, sis – always so cynical. Hmmm, how about when you marry Mac? I reckon that's pretty much a fairytale come true.'

'Point taken – you win.'

'Thank you. And now, speaking of fairytales, I would really like you to try the dress on now.'

'There's nothing I'd like more,' Violet said with a smile.

Lily stood up before pulling her sister to her feet. 'Ah, there's hope for you yet. Come on, and I promise I won't stick you with any more pins.'

* * *

Lily sipped her tall glass of iced tea and looked out the front window of the Hummingbird Café.

'You know, everyone has been talking about you,' Hailey said with a grin as she looked over the rim of her coffee cup.

'So I've heard,' Lily said as she threw a pointed look to Jill. 'All I can say is that they obviously don't have much going on in their lives,' Lily murmured. To tell the truth, she was just a bit sick of the whole thing. It had been four days since Flynn had kissed her in the street and since then she'd done her best to ignore the curious looks, secret smiles and, in some cases, hostile glares.

'Just ignore it,' Jill said, driving a fork into her salad. 'It's nobody's business but yours . . . oh, and ours, since we're your friends.'

'Mr Hodges says it's the very first bunch of flowers that Flynn has ever sent a girl. Not counting the ones he sends to Mac's mum every year on her birthday,' Hailey added as she studied Lily.

'I'd say that Mr Hodges should mind his own business and not gossip about his customers,' Lily said, looking away. 'Honestly, you'd think people would have better things to do than talk about me.'

'Wait.' Jill held up her hand. 'He sent you flowers?'

'Um, yes – a big bunch of roses and lilies,' Lily admitted as a flush of heat bloomed in her cheeks.

'Kathy from the Eureka pub said that last Saturday night was the first time she'd ever seen Flynn Hartley leave on his own,' Hailey continued.

'Oh, I'm sure that's not true, Hailey,' Jill said. 'Flynn has always been a bit of a player, but you make him sound like an alley cat.'

'It is true, and not only that, Mrs Greenly told Sue Preston that both Flynn and the mayor's daughter were at the Millstone the other night. Apparently they were sitting at separate tables and barely acknowledged one another.'

Lily frowned. 'I really don't need to hear this.'

'Ah,' Jill said as she looked up. 'Rumour has it that Flynn and Charlotte have had a thing going on. It's not serious because they both date other people, but when they're not . . .'

'They date each other,' Lily said flatly as she reached for her iced tea. 'Yes, I heard.'

'Oh, they weren't dating. It's just sex,' Hailey said with a smile. 'Or at least that's what I overheard Charlotte telling Lucy Girvens at the council offices. Really hot sex.'

'Hailey!' Jill sat back and hit Hailey's shoulder. 'What the hell is the matter with you? Why are you telling Lily something like that for?'

'I thought she should know. Lily has the right to go into this with her eyes open. What's the old saying? Forewarned is forearmed, or something like that. Anyway, I'm not trying to upset her – she's my friend and she has a right to know what's going on.' Hailey leant over the table to take Lily's hand and give it a little squeeze. 'He went home alone and that's all that matters.'

'Yes, I suppose you're right.' Lily felt torn in two. On one hand, the idea of Flynn having sex with someone else made her feel . . . what? Lily sat back in her chair. It made her feel uncomfortable, angry and jealous, and for an instant a tiny part of her wanted to pull Charlotte Somerville's glorious red hair out by the roots. On the other hand, a part of her was very relieved that Flynn had gone home alone. She shouldn't let it get to her – she and Flynn were barely at the start of something. Whatever was in Flynn's past was his business, and Lily wished that Hailey hadn't brought Charlotte Somerville up at all. Sometimes it's better to be blissfully ignorant. Flynn had a history and so did she, and the last thing either of them needed right now was to be haunted by the ghosts of exes past.

'I think we should leave Charlotte out of this. I'm looking towards the future, not the past,' Lily said.

'I agree. Even if things don't work out between you two you will at least have given it a try. Besides, Charlotte's all right,' Jill said before popping an olive into her mouth. 'Sorry, you're right – changing the subject now.'

'No, she isn't – Charlotte Somerville is a bitch!' Hailey exclaimed. 'She's far too full of herself and her family's position in the town.'

'That's a bit harsh, don't you think?' Jill asked.

'Just telling it how it is.'

'Way to change the subject. You two are like a dog with a bone,' Lily chuckled as she shook her head. 'As far as I'm concerned, people can say whatever they want. I just don't care anymore. The only people that matter to me are my family, my two crazy friends and Flynn. Everyone else can go and take a long walk off a short pier.'

Jill picked up her glass. 'Very well put, Lily.'

'Absolutely,' Hailey smiled as she clinked her coffee cup on Jill's glass.

Lily grinned and clinked her tall glass against the others. 'To the people who matter.'

* * *

'Can I speak to you for a second?' Violet asked, knocking on Lily's workroom door.

Lily sat back in her chair and shot her sister a smile. 'Uh-oh . . . what have I done?'

Violet walked in and moved a pile of fabric from the only other chair in the room before sitting down. 'You haven't done anything. I just wanted to make sure that you're okay – you know, that the shop and dresses are all panning out how you hoped.'

'Yep, it's all fine,' Lily replied, looking closely at her sister. 'But there's something else on your mind, isn't there?'

Violet ran a hand through her dark hair. 'Yeah, I guess I'm just a bit concerned about you and Flynn. Don't get me wrong, I really like him. He's Mac's best friend and he's a great guy.'

'But?'

'Well, he has a bit of a reputation. I don't think he's ever had a long-lasting, serious relationship.'

'And why is that a problem?'

Violet frowned. 'Sweetheart, it's not that I want you to rush into a relationship. I guess I just wanted to talk about the fact that I've sometimes wondered if he's capable of having one at all.'

'I know that you're just looking out for me but really, Violet, I'm a big girl.'

'Yes, of course. I just don't want to see you hurt, particularly after the last episode.'

'Believe me, Flynn is nothing like Pietro,' Lily said as she fiddled with the bit of ruby-coloured silk. 'We're just beginning, Violet – nobody's making any promises at this stage. Who knows, the whole thing could come crashing down around our ears in a couple of months, but then maybe we'll stick at it for another forty-odd years. I don't own a crystal ball and we both know there are no guarantees.'

'You're right, I should mind my own business.'

'No, I like having you worry,' Lily said with a wink. 'That's what big sisters are meant to do, right?'

'Yeah, something like that,' Violet said as she stood up. 'I'll let you get back to your sewing. I'm here if you ever need to talk.'

'I know – I'm counting on it,' Lily said before turning back to her sewing machine and putting her foot on the pedal.

Mulling over their conversation as she guided the delicate fabric, Lily decided it was time to put both her indecision and Violet's concerns to one side. For once she was going to be guided by Jill's excellent advice and forget about the old fears of being unlucky in love. There was no point making up problems before they even existed – she was determined to dismiss the 'what ifs' and live in the moment.

Lily had told Flynn that she wanted to go slow and then she changed her mind. But somehow, Flynn hadn't quite got that message. They were going out, hanging out and making out, but every time they got to a certain point, Flynn would pull back.

The other night they had been having a movie marathon at his place. Between the terrifying horror and the action adventure, Lily had kissed him. One kiss led to another, and another, and about at the point that she was ready to forget about the next movie, Flynn jumped up and asked if she wanted a coffee. Bit of a mood changer.

Thinking back over the past couple of weeks, Lily realised that Flynn had reacted similarly on a few occasions, though never blatantly. Well, it was time that she took things in hand

and found out what exactly was going on. She knew that he wanted her just as much as she wanted him – his breath was just as ragged as hers whenever he pulled away.

Flynn Hartley had an effect on her that she couldn't remember ever feeling before, and that was the truth. His touch made her tingle and his kisses made her burn. Just laying eyes on him was all she needed for her heart to skip a beat and her stomach to do that weird contracting thing. So it was time to 'woman' up and take matters into her own hands. Perhaps she'd been guilty of giving Flynn mixed signals but that wouldn't happen again. She needed him to know just how much she wanted him.

Chapter 15

With new resolve, Lily rang Flynn the next morning and asked if he was free for the evening. Violet and Holly were spending the next couple of days at Mac's place, redecorating one of the rooms for Holly. So with the place to herself, she thought she may as well take the opportunity to have a little alone time with Flynn.

They went out to dinner, Flynn organising a dimly lit table in the back corner of the Millstone. He made her laugh with his ridiculous stories as they lingered over their meal. It was comfortable, that's the only way Lily could describe it. He made her feel both at ease and important at the same time.

She did her best to ignore the curious stares they were getting from the other diners. No doubt there would be some juicy stories circulating around the town in the morning. But to her surprise, Lily didn't care. To hell with what people said – who she chose to see was no one's business but hers.

The lightheartedness of the evening shifted towards the end of the meal when Flynn's hand brushed against hers across the table. Lily looked up and saw the same need that had been building in her all day reflected in his eyes. She knew then for certain that she wanted Flynn in her bed – to deny that fact would be lying to herself.

He had looked away and said something silly to make her laugh but Lily wasn't fooled. Flynn might be trying to suppress it but she knew it was burning in both of them.

Flynn drove her home, walking her to the front door and hesitating for a second before he dropped a chaste kiss on her forehead. Lily almost laughed out loud. God, she was doing to her damnedest to get him into bed and he was doing his best to avoid it.

'Listen, thanks for tonight but I'd better get going,' Flynn said.

Like she was going to let that happen. Instead she pushed open the door. 'Why don't you come in for a second?'

'I'm not sure if that's a good idea.'

'Sure it is,' Lily said as she stared back at him as if in a challenge.

'Well, maybe just for a minute or two,' he answered as he walked through the door with Lily close behind him.

There was a tension in the room as Flynn sat on the couch, watching every move she made. She was conscious of his gaze as she walked out of the lounge room and headed for the kitchen. Lily expected Flynn to stay put but he followed her down the hallway.

She took out a couple of glasses and put them on the counter before pulling a jug of iced tea from the fridge. Lily handed Flynn the glass and he almost finished it in one gulp.

'Well, I suppose I should get going. I don't want to disturb Violet or Holly,' he said as put the glass back on the counter. He flashed a smile. 'Thanks again for a great night.'

'They're over at Mac's,' Lily said, catching one of his hands. 'So you see, you don't have to go yet, do you?'

'I've got an early start . . .'

'You always have an early start – you're a farmer.'

He was silent for a second as his hand tightened around hers. Did he actually look nervous?

'Um, I'm trying to do this different,' he said as he let go of her hand. 'I'm trying to do this right.'

'Don't overthink it. Can't we just enjoy the rest of the evening and see where it takes us?'

He bit his lip for a second. 'I just don't want to fuck this up, Lily. I need you to know that I care about you and I don't—'

'Stay,' she interrupted as she closed the distance between them. She was standing near enough to feel the heat from his body without touching.

'Lily,' he said with an exasperated sigh. 'I'm trying to prove to you that you mean something. I want you more than I can say, but I don't want you thinking that's all I'm after. I need you to understand that it's deeper than that.'

Lily wrapped her arms around his waist and looked up at him. 'Flynn, you don't have to prove anything to me. Stay – that is, if you want to.'

'Want to? Jeez, Lily! Of course I want to – it's so hard to walk away from you,' he said incredulously before his mouth came down and claimed hers. His hands spiked through her hair and then gently held her head in place as he ravished her mouth.

It was a scorching kiss, and the longing she'd suppressed all night broke free. She kissed him back, mirroring his longing and urgency. Flynn's fingers moved over her back before he clasped her bottom in his hands and pulled her up against him. She felt the firm planes of his body and his hard erection pressed against her. It felt good to be held this way but it wasn't enough. Lily unbuttoned his shirt and ran her hands over his warm skin. With each touch, each kiss, the fire built inside her and she needed to feel him against her, flesh to flesh.

Flynn pulled back for a moment, his eyes dark and intense.

'Lily, are you sure?' His voice was deep and husky and it rolled over her like warm honey.

She took one of his hands and brought it to her lips. 'Yes, believe me – I'm more than sure,' she said, leading him back down the hallway and towards her bedroom. 'I want this – I want you – more than I can say.'

She didn't get far because Flynn lifted her from behind and carried her all the way to the bed, kissing the side of her neck as they went. He put her down and in one fluid movement pulled off her top. His hands skimmed over her skin, leaving a tingling trail in their wake. Lily spun around in his arms and pushed his shirt off before she started working on unbuckling his belt.

'I want you, Flynn – so much,' she said.

'Not as much as I want you,' he murmured, tugging her skirt over her hips and letting it fall like a slinky pool around her feet.

He took a step back and stared at her. The heat rose in her cheeks and it was all she could do not to cross her arms or dive under the covers. Instead she stood there in her pale green silk underwear and met his gaze.

Flynn gave her a sexy smile as he pulled her back into his arms. Lily rested her head on his shoulder as her hands splayed across his broad, smooth back. The spicy scent of his aftershave rose subtly from his warm body, tantalising her senses.

'You're so beautiful,' he whispered as his deft fingers unhooked her bra and tossed it onto the ever-growing pile of clothes on the floor. She closed her eyes and revelled in the feeling of Flynn's hands slowly sweeping along her shoulder, back and over the flare of her hips.

'You really are, Lily. You're all creamy and soft and silky, and all I want to do is touch you . . . taste you.'

He dropped a series of kisses along her neck, over her collarbone and down, until his tongue circled one of her now taut nipples.

'Flynn,' Lily said as the delicious sensation of his mouth made her draw in her breath. Her head fell back as a shot of heat fired through her body. Her breath quickened and his touch made her quiver. His lips in painstaking slowness made their way back to her mouth. She needed to touch him, to immerse herself in him. Her hand snaked down his chest and abs until it rested on the large mound in his jeans. His cock hardened even more and strained against the denim as her fingers closed around it. There was a growl coming from the back of his throat and he held onto her tight.

'Baby, you're killing me.'

Lily unbuttoned his jeans and pushed the material from his hips. His rock-hard cock sprung from its confines and she encircled it with her fingers, moving, rubbing, teasing. He sucked in his breath with a whoosh.

'Make love to me, Flynn. I need to feel you inside me.'

'Whatever you want, baby,' he breathed against her. 'Whatever you want.'

Flynn lowered her onto the bed and slipped her silk panties off. He took a foil packet from his pocket before dragging his jeans and jocks the rest of the way off, his eyes devouring her hungrily all the while. The mattress dipped with his weight as he joined Lily on the bed. He pulled her close and for a moment he held her tight, as if he was frightened that she'd get away.

Her fingers speared through his dark hair as she tilted her face up and kissed him. The sense of urgency notched up as her tongue rubbed against his.

His touch meandered over her body, lower and lower until he cupped her. His fingers dipped, taunted and tormented her until she arched against his hand and thought she'd go mad with frustration.

'Flynn, now – love me now,' she said breathlessly as her hands fisted in the sheets.

'You make me burn, Lily, honest to God, you do.' He nudged her legs open and settled between her thighs. 'I've been wanting to be with you like this ever since you came back home.'

Lily smiled as she reached up and touched the side of his face. For a moment she thought that she saw something in his eyes – a different sort of yearning, perhaps – but almost as quickly as it appeared it was gone.

He entered her inch by inch until he filled her entirely. Lily wrapped her legs around his slim hips and for an instant allowed herself to bask in the glorious sensation. She opened her eyes in time to see him give her one of his best crooked smiles and her heart seemed to melt a little bit more. Slowly he began to move and Lily felt herself being taken away. The heat and the need spread through her body like a flash fire. With each luscious stroke, Lily was taken closer to the edge.

'Flynn . . .'

'Lily, you're perfect – this is perfect,' he said as he increased the pace and sent them spiralling into the abyss.

Lily clung onto Flynn as the orgasm rippled through her. It was as if he was the only thing keeping her tethered to the ground.

* * *

Flynn's eyes fluttered open and for a minute he forgot where he was – all he knew for certain was that this definitely wasn't his bed. As he lay there, memories of the night before crashed through his mind.

Lily.

A smile tugged at his lips as she moved beside him. She was warm and soft and her hair was fanned across his arm and the pillow. Flynn stared at her for a moment, taking in her beauty. His heart swelled as he swore he'd never seen anyone as lovely as Lily Beckett.

162

He was a lucky man and that was the truth.

Through the lace curtain the sky was beginning to lighten. A cool breeze blew in from outside and set the tinkling wind-chime in motion. Another day in Violet Falls was about to start but all Flynn wanted to do was stay here, cocooned in Lily's bed. He ran his hand over her shoulder and down her arm. She was perfect; everything was perfect.

Flynn relaxed back on the pillow and looked up at the ceiling. He was happy, really truly happy, something he could never actually remember being before. For the first time he thought about a life he could have, the life he pretended he didn't want but deep down yearned for: love, happiness and a family to call his own. He knew thinking like this was moving fast and the last thing he wanted to do was spook her, but maybe one day they could have a life together. It wasn't like he wanted to haul her off to the nearest church or anything – all he wanted was the promise of a possible future.

But she won't love you, not really. One day she'll leave and you'll be left all alone, just as you should be. You don't deserve to be loved.

Flynn shut his eyes as his grandmother's mocking words ran through his mind. This was different – Lily was different – and he wouldn't let the past ruin his future.

A bolt of clammy fear shot through his body. No, his grandmother was just a spiteful old bitch. He couldn't let her win. She was dead and gone and he deserved happiness just like everyone else, didn't he? Just don't take things too fast.

Flynn shook his head as he gently extracted his arm from Lily and sat up. He was thinking crazy thoughts – this is exactly what he wanted, so why was there a sinking feeling in his stomach? He was preparing to run again, the old fear of abandonment and rejection filtering through him. He'd been at this point before but had never reached it so quickly. There was a sense of rising panic that he did his best to push back down but he was fighting a losing battle.

Lily stirred beside him.

'Hey.'

'Hey, sweetheart. I didn't mean to wake you,' Flynn said as he glanced over to her.

'What time is it?'

'About five thirty, I guess.'

'Oh, that's just wrong. Let's go back to sleep.'

'Sorry, I've got to go,' Flynn said as he threw back the covers and swung out of bed. He turned around and caught a glimpse of Lily's luscious curved body before he pulled the covers over her. All he wanted to do was dive back into bed with Lily but the cold hard stone in the pit of his stomach made him step away. It was almost as if he was watching himself from outside his body, like a fricking robot, every step taking him away from her. He knew he was doing it but he couldn't stop.

Lily was beautiful and amazing and she made him burn inside. But she was too much, it was all too much, and in that instant he knew he had to get away and put some distance between them.

'Stay with me.' Her voice was full of sleepy seduction and he faltered for a second. 'Come back to bed, Flynn. Stay.'

He took a step back and started to reach for her but just in the nick of time managed to pull himself together.

He had to leave, to protect himself . . . to try to find his centre. He picked up his discarded jeans and pulled them on. The air and the dark of the bedroom started to close in on him.

'I can't. Last night was amazing but I have to go,' he said as he grabbed his shirt from the floor and shrugged it on. 'I'll call you later.'

Lily sat up and pulled the covers over her delicious breasts. She frowned as her eyes met his. 'For God's sake, Flynn – what are you doing?'

'Nothing. I don't know what you mean.'

Lily waved her hand in the air. 'Really? Because what I'm seeing is a guy desperate to leave. You promised me that this was different. You said you wanted me.'

Flynn took another step towards the open door. 'Baby, you're talking shit. Of course I want you. Just chill, everything's fine – I said that I'd call you later. I just need . . .'

'Yeah, what do you need?'

'There's nothing wrong, I just got to go.'

'Then why has the temperature in here dropped to fifty below? I thought this thing between us was nothing but fun, but you're acting as if I've just asked you to marry me.'

'Lily . . .'

Lily held up her hand. 'God, if you're that scared, just leave.'

'I'm not scared, it's just—'

'You don't have to explain. Just leave. I always knew this would happen.'

Flynn froze in the doorway. His heart hammered and for a couple of seconds he forgot how to breathe. What the hell was he doing? He wanted Lily more than anything, so why was he purposely fucking it up?

You're just your mother's dirty mistake. No one will ever want you.

His stomach clenched as his grandmother's words filled his head. She was wrong – he knew she was wrong! He needed to walk back to Lily, to hold her and tell her that this time he wouldn't go anywhere, but he just couldn't.

'I promise I'll call you later,' he croaked out before he walked out of the room without a backward glance.

'Whatever.'

He could hear the disappointment in her voice but was unable to give her what she needed – reassurance.

Flynn headed down the hallway, his workboots echoing on the polished boards. If he had any sense he would swing around and beg her forgiveness. But the terror of having his heart ripped out kept him heading for the door.

He was already halfway in love with her – if he stayed any longer he'd be a goner, and then how would he ever survive when she left? And she *would* leave him, it was inevitable. Flynn yanked open the front door before he stepped over the threshold and closed it firmly behind him.

He stood on the front verandah with his hand still on the doorknob. He'd hurt her, he'd seen it in her eyes. He sucked in a breath and tried to find the courage to walk back inside and make everything right. He turned the knob but just didn't have the strength to push the door open.

'Jesus,' he muttered as he spun on well-worn heels and headed down the stairs towards his ute. 'Why am I such a fuck-up?'

Chapter 16

Lily sank back against the pillows and stared at the empty doorway.

What the hell just happened?

Flynn had gone from ardent lover to running away as fast as he could. Last night everything had been perfect, but this morning the whole bloody thing exploded in her face.

She'd been dismissed by Flynn Hartley and now had a pretty good idea what each and every one of his women had felt when they found themselves in this position – it sucked.

Lily sat up and pummelled the pillow before landing back on it. She should be angry – no, she should be bloody furious with him for what he just pulled. They'd shared a connection last night, and she wasn't just talking about the hot sex. There had been something deeper, and yet this morning he hightailed it out of here like she was a pariah.

She'd caught a look in his eyes that made her think there was more to it than the obvious – we had great sex and now I'm outta here. There had been a flash of pain when he'd turned away from her.

So the question was, if distancing himself from Lily caused him pain, why was he doing it?

Normally such a spectacular rejection would make Lily roll up in a ball and let every single one of her old fears feed on her soul, internal taunts of not being good enough or pretty enough immobilising her. But not today. A tiny voice inside said that Flynn needed her, and she was determined to get to the bottom of it. That is, once she managed to rein in her seething anger . . .

Lily pushed back the covers and got out of bed. Grabbing her Chinese silk dressing-gown from the end of the bed and slipping it on, she twisted the tie into a bow before heading to the kitchen in search of coffee.

Flynn might have just walked out of her room but she'd be damned if she was going to let him walk out of her life. He was hiding something from her and she had every intention of finding out what it was.

Instead of going on her morning run, Lily treated herself to a leisurely breakfast of toast, marmalade and a couple of cups of steaming coffee before taking a luxuriously long shower. She allowed her mind to wander over the previous night with Flynn and relive how his touch made her feel. Furious or not, she wasn't about to let him cast her aside because he was scared of something. No, she was going to confront him and find out what the hell was going on.

Lily wrapped the thick lilac towel around her as she made her way to her wardrobe and opened the door. The only way to face a situation like this was with a fabulous frock and some bright red lipstick.

***

Flynn unloaded the chainsaw from the back of the ute. He'd been checking the firebreaks on the northern boundary, refilling the water troughs and mentally kicking himself all morning. Not even halfway back from Lily's house this morning it dawned on him that he'd just made the biggest mistake of his life. He'd let his fear overpower him and it could just have cost him everything because, let's face it, he'd acted like a complete dickhead.

Flynn leant against the side of the ute and let out a sigh. In a stupid moment he'd allowed all the shit from the past to come and steal away his future. Damn it, he wouldn't blame Lily if she never spoke to him again. In her eyes, he'd be lower than a snake – maybe even lower than that guy she used to be with. Ever since Lily had returned to Violet Falls he'd wanted her to be with him. And then when she finally was, he made love to her and then ran as fast as he could to get away. When did he turn into such an arsehole?

He ran his hands through his hair. He had to fix this, but how?

Flynn picked up the chainsaw and headed to the shed. Just as he was opening the door he heard the crunch of tyres on the gravel drive. Spinning around he saw Lily's little red car driving up to the house.

His whole body tensed. She was here. That had to be a good sign . . . didn't it?

Lily stopped the car and got out. Her white dress sprinkled with red roses was cinched in at the waist, the skirt skimming her knees. But it was how she carried herself that caught his attention.

Flynn's mouth went dry. God, she was amazing.

She slammed the car door shut and marched towards him.

'You and I are going to talk.' There was a fire in her step and a look of determination on her face.

'Lily, sweetheart, I'm sorry about this morning. I was a jerk.' He held up his hands in surrender.

'Yes, you really were,' she said as she stopped in front of him. Her hands rested on her hips and she glared at him from over her sunglasses.

Flynn moved towards her but she took a step back. He frowned; this could be more difficult than he thought. All he wanted to do was hold her but he'd screwed it all up and didn't know what to do. He'd be lucky if she ever let him near her again.

'Just hold it right there, mister. I heard the apology, but I think we need to talk about this. Just answer my question truthfully: do you want us to stop seeing each other?'

Flynn shook his head. 'No, I don't – not at all. What happened this morning was . . . can we just forget about it and pretend it never happened?'

'Maybe . . . but I still think we need to clear the air,' she said. 'What you did this morning was just plain cold, Flynn. I didn't think you had that in you.'

Flynn noticed she'd lost some of her stiffness. 'I know and I'm sorry. I never meant to hurt you and I promise it'll never happen again.'

'And why should I believe that?'

'Because I want it to be true – it *is* true, and I need a second chance so I can prove it. Please, Lily, come inside and we can talk about anything you want. Let's get out of the heat.'

'I'm fine where I am.'

'Please . . .' He reached out and took her hand; at least she didn't pull away.

Lily was silent for a moment as she stared up at him. She was conflicted, he could see it in her face.

'Oh, all right – but I expect some answers.'

Lily walked beside him, her hand still firmly in his. He led her into the house and across the cool slate floors to the living room; the temperature inside was easily ten degrees lower than outside. He let go of her hand and she wandered over to the large windows that overlooked the gully and Landoc Creek. For a couple of minutes she didn't say a damn thing, and Flynn felt the tension in the room rise.

'So how do I know you're not going to treat me like you have every other girl you've gone out with?' she finally asked. 'Is what happened this morning indicative of how you end all of your relationships?'

'No, you're wrong. I swear that you're wrong. Shit, Lily, I'm really sorry. I won't treat you like the other girls because you're nothing like them and I've never felt this way about anyone else. This is different.'

'How?'

'I don't know, but it is.'

Lily turned around and faced him. 'From what I've been told, you don't do relationships. Once there is a chance of having something, you skip out as fast as you can.'

'You're right, that's what's happened in the past,' Flynn said as he slowly made his way over to her. 'It's about now

172

that I start to feel all panicky and hemmed in, but I don't feel that way with you.'

Lily raised a questioning eyebrow but remained silent.

'Oh okay, maybe for a second this morning I panicked, but I was already kicking myself for being a bloody idiot before I even got home, and that's never happened before.'

'Why do you think that is?'

'I can't explain it. All I know is that I want to be with you. And when we're not together, you're constantly in my head.' He closed the gap between them and placed his hands on her hips, pulling her slightly towards him. 'I suppose that in the past, I've always wanted to end a relationship before it really takes hold.'

Lily put her hand on his chest and looked up through her lashes at him. Flynn swallowed hard – all he wanted to do was kiss her and hold her to his heart.

'But why, Flynn? Why would you sabotage yourself?'

'I guess . . . I guess it all comes down to protecting myself. God, I don't know, Lily – I'm not very good at this sort of shit.'

'I think you're doing fine. But how does running away from a commitment protect you?'

Flynn let out a world-weary sigh and shrugged his broad shoulders. 'Because I end it before it becomes serious and I fall in love with them.'

'That's a pretty lonely way to live, never allowing yourself to be emotionally available,' she said as she reached up and draped her arms over his shoulders.

'Jeez, Lily, where the hell do you come up with crap like that?'

'It's not crap, and don't change the subject. Why do you think you run?'

'Did you just turn into my shrink?'

'Nope, I'm just trying to understand.'

'I reckon there's a long line for that – maybe you had better take a number.' He grinned, but the bitterness in his voice was evident. He tried to cover it up by bending down and dropping a kiss on her lips.

'You can tell me, Flynn. You *need* to tell me, so I can understand.'

'It's all rolled up with a whole lot of old hurts that are better off forgotten.'

'That might be true, but the problem is you haven't forgotten them, have you? Maybe it's time to put them to rest.'

He was silent for a second as the past pushed through his carefully constructed barriers and threatened to swamp him. He stared beyond Lily into the distance as the old injuries started to prick and bleed all over again.

'My mother deserted me,' he finally began, haltingly. 'I don't know why, maybe she just couldn't handle being that young and having a baby. Maybe she just didn't want me. She left me with my grandmother, and maybe she thought she was doing the best thing for me. Guess I'll never know because she never came back. In my grandmother's eyes I was nothing more than a mistake and an embarrassment. I was something that had to be tolerated . . . barely. My

174

grandmother never let me forget that I was a bastard, a dirty mistake that should never have happened. My mother couldn't love me and my grandmother never wanted to. I guess I started thinking that if that was the case, why would anyone else ever want to?'

'Oh, Flynn,' Lily said as she pulled him closer and held him tight.

'So I leave before anyone else has the chance to. If I keep things light and fun then no one will get hurt.'

'Flynn, that's no way to live. You're cheating yourself out of love and happiness and a future. You deserve to have those things – everyone does.'

'I didn't think so; my grandmother had drummed that into me ever since I was old enough to understand. I never really believed that anyone would want me or love me. But I guess that changed a bit when the McKellans pulled me kicking and screaming into their family. They showed me what a real family could be like, and for the first time I felt that I belonged somewhere.'

'But you didn't try to do the same in your love life?'

'Baby, before I met you I didn't have a love life, not really. For the first time, I don't want to push away and run. I want to stay and take a chance on something that I've never had before. I think I could fall in love with you, Lily Beckett, and I reckon I should hang around and find out. You say that you're worried that I'll treat you like the others but the truth is that I'm also terrified that you'll leave me.'

Lily pushed up on her tiptoes and whispered against his mouth. 'I swear, I'm not going anywhere.'

He held onto her and the minutes slipped by. 'Good, because I'm pretty sure that I can't give you up,' he said before he kissed her. The tension inside him released and for a few precious moments he allowed himself to be engulfed by Lily's presence. Her lips moved beneath his. The kiss was warm and drew him in. Careful not to break contact, he lifted her feet off the ground and her arms locked behind his neck.

Lily pulled back as Flynn headed out of the lounge room. 'Where are we going?'

'Upstairs. Is that a problem?'

Lily wound her legs around Flynn's hips and grinned. 'No problem at all.'

* * *

Lily knew that something was up as soon as she walked into the kitchen. A week had passed since she made up with Flynn, and all she wanted right now was some juice and maybe a couple of slices of toast, but it looked as if breakfast was going to come with a lecture on the side. Her stomach grumbled as she took a breath and waited for Violet's displeasure.

'We need to talk,' Violet said as she leant back against the kitchen counter and crossed her arms. 'This business with Flynn. Is it serious?'

Lily stifled a sigh. 'Yes, it is.'

'And you think it's going to be okay?' Violet asked with a frown.

'Well, I hope so, but as I've told you before, none of us get any guarantees. That is, except for you and Mac – you two are going to be happily in love even when you're both a hundred and five.'

Violet smiled. 'And beyond.'

'There you go. But as for Flynn and me, well, I don't know, but there's no point you stressing over it. It is what it is and that's enough for now.' Lily headed to the fridge and yanked open the door.

'Lily, I think we should discuss this.'

'Oh for goodness sake, we did – we are. God, Violet, just stop,' Lily said as she grabbed the juice from the fridge. 'I'm not a little girl – I'm an adult who is perfectly capable of making my own decisions.'

'But Lily—'

'No buts, okay? We've already talked about this. I know that you love me and want to look out for me but who I see isn't up for discussion.'

'I just don't want you to get hurt.'

Lily poured herself a drink. 'I get that, I really do. But this is my life, and because of that I get to make the decisions. I'm not going to stop seeing Flynn because my big sister told me to.'

Violet opened her mouth but after a moment's hesitation she closed it again. She uncrossed her arms and held up her hands. 'Okay, it's your call. I won't say another word about it.'

'Really? Because I'm pretty sure you've said that before,' Lily replied tersely as she reached for her glass.

Violet sighed. 'I know. It's just sometimes I forget that you're an adult. I tend to see you permanently as fifteen.'

'Great – you mean with puppy fat and pimples?'

'No, it's just . . .'

Lily walked over to Violet and put her arm around her. 'I get it – you did an amazing job of bringing me up and protecting me when we ran away all those years ago. You've always been there for me and I love you for it, you know that.'

'Yes, I do.'

'I want you to be proud of me and give me your blessing in most of the big stuff, but you can't help who you fall in love with – you know that better than anyone.'

'You're right, you're right, I'm backing away now. I won't offer any advice on this matter – that is, until you ask me, of course,' Violet added with a grin.

Lily chuckled. 'You just don't give up, do you?'

'Nope, that's what sisters are for. So, what are your plans for the day?'

'We're fitting out the storeroom today. Which means Johnno and Kev are building shelves and clothes racks and I'm supervising. After that, I'm having a quick lunch with Jill and Hailey before spending the rest of the night sewing.'

'Fitting out, huh? I thought Johnno was just doing the kitchen and bathroom for you?'

'That was the original plan, but with the roof leaking, rotten beams and getting rid of graffiti, I thought, hey, this is costing me a fortune already so what's a few more shelves?'

'Are you over budget?'

'Oh, yeah. Let's just say I'll be filling up helium balloons and dragging around floral arrangements at your events for some time,' Lily said with a grin.

'I can always use the help.'

'A good thing for me. So what's on your agenda for today?'

'I'm here all day. I've got to plan out a couple of functions and finally pin down the last details for the Edmonds' party. Oh, and Holly and I will be over at Mac's tonight, so you'll have the place to yourself.'

'Okay. Listen, there may be a few parcels that turn up today. I've been doing a little online therapy.'

'Ooh, anything interesting?'

'Not really, it's just some stuff for the shop. There's a little bit of jewellery and a few decorations, just to give the shop a lift,' Lily said with a shrug. 'I'd better get moving – I'm meant to be meeting Johnno at the shop by eight.'

'See you later then.'

'Yep, have a good day,' Lily said as she hurried past Violet, snagging a piece of her toast as she went.

'Hey! Get your own.'

Lily gave her a grin. 'Sorry, haven't got time.'

179

Chapter 17

Lily frowned as she slipped through the back gate of the shop. It was sitting slightly ajar and she was almost a hundred per cent certain she'd closed it last night. She peered down and took a closer look at the latch; it didn't seem to be broken. With a shake of her head, she straightened up and headed towards the back door. She must have forgotten, that's all.

She'd almost reached the door when her shoes crunched on something.

'What the . . .?'

Glass lay shattered over the back step. It was only then, looking up, that she saw the windows on the bottom level of the shop had been broken. She raised her head further: the first floor window was still intact but it looked like it had a crack in it.

Bloody hell! This vandalism thing had to stop.

Lily dug into her handbag and pulled out her phone.

'Hi, this is Lily Beckett. I think someone's tried to break into my shop.' Lily paused for a minute. 'Um, hang on, I'll check.'

She walked over and pushed against the door but it was still locked. 'Hello? No, the back windows have been broken but the door seems to be okay,' she said as she glanced inside through one of the smashed panes. 'I can't be sure, but it looks like everything is still there – maybe vandalism rather than a break-in . . . Okay, thanks, see you soon.'

Lily blew out an exasperated sigh as the back gate swung open and Johnno came striding in.

'Hey, Lily,' he called out as he came closer.

'Hey. Looks like we've got a bit of a problem.'

'Yeah? What's that?'

'Someone doesn't like my windows.'

Johnno put his hands on his hips and surveyed the damage. 'Shit. Don't worry, the boys and I can fix that up.'

'Thanks, but we're going to have to wait until the police get here and check it out.'

He turned his head and gave her brief smile. 'No worries.'

'Listen, Johnno, do you get a lot of vandalism in town?'

'Nup, I don't think so. Other than a bit of graffiti down along the railway, I can't think of anything. You know, come to think of it, it's a bit odd.'

'What do you mean?'

'First the paint and now broken windows? Have you pissed anyone off recently?'

'Not that I'm aware of.'

'Well, I'm not the police but it seems to me that it's either kids and a bit of senseless vandalism, or you've pissed someone off, or . . .'

'Or what?' Lily said with a deepening frown.

'Or it's a ploy to get me to hang around longer,' he said with a smile.

Lily laughed. 'God, Johnno, like I can afford that!'

'Made you laugh though,' he said, winking. 'Don't worry about it, I'll get these fixed as soon as the police say I can.'

'Thank you, I really appreciate it.'

By the afternoon Lily was standing on the shop floor and mentally planning how she'd decorate the room. The police had come and gone, their official take on the whole incident was that it was vandalism. They were probably right, but Johnno's words had played on her mind. Did someone have a grudge against her? Had she managed to piss someone off to the point that they wanted to destroy her business? She cast her mind back but there hadn't been an altercation or even a harsh word with anyone that she could think of. Pretty much everyone had been nice, helpful – hell, even welcoming. Nope, she couldn't think of anyone who hated her that much.

It had to be kids.

Lily took a breath and tried to clear her head. She should spend her time thinking about what she had to do, not dreaming up some Moriarty-wannabe nemesis who wanted to bring her down. In fact, she hoped that if she did have an arch enemy they would be a little more diabolical and cunning than breaking a couple of windows and chucking about a bit of paint.

Apart from the windows, the shop was looking just as Lily hoped it would. With the last of the painting done, the old store had been given a new lease on life. It felt airy and fresh and brimming with possibilities. Lily walked around the shop floor, imagining how she was going to put everything together.

A spark of excitement flared through her as she saw in her mind's eye where to position the old cheval mirror she'd found at a bargain price in a second-hand shop, where she'd put the old glass counter, and which wall the huge ornately framed mirror would be attached to. Johnno and one of his workers had dragged the old cash register down from the attic; it was a thing of Victorian-era beauty with its big fat keys and floral embossed metalwork. It also kind of worked – with a bit of fiddling she'd managed to get the cash drawer to open and close. But probably it would be included in the shop more for its aesthetic value.

Things were on track and finally coming together nicely, broken windows aside. Now, if she could just get all of her sample dresses finished, everything would be set.

* * *

From the top of the ridge, Flynn looked out over his land. The countryside was parched and sweltered in the late summer heat. He leant against the trunk of a ghost gum and stared off to the south towards McKellan's Run and the town of Violet Falls.

Sweat trickled down the middle of his back. The shade of the tree gave little relief from the forty-five-degree temperature. The sun beat down and fried anything stupid enough to be out in the open – yeah, well, that included him today. One of the worst things about summer was the hot air: somehow it just made the whole business of breathing even harder.

He'd checked the weather report this morning and it was meant to be hot and sunny, with a growing northerly wind. Great, just the type of day that had everyone, especially firefighters, on tenterhooks. Flynn pulled out his phone to check if there had been any fire updates in the area.

Scrolling down the screen he saw that it was clear – so far, so good. He just hoped that it would stay that way.

He pushed himself away from the tree and started to head back down to the house. Yesterday, he, Mac and a couple of hired hands had brought most of the mob down from the top paddock and closer to home. He had them penned in the paddock that was closest to the house. It was smaller than they were used to but it sported a few ancient shade trees and the dam was still half full. Tomorrow he would get the stragglers and the small flock from the northern enclosure. And the day after that they'd be rounding up the sheep from the western paddock. It would take several days but then he would have the majority of his sheep closer to home where he could keep an eye on them.

So far, Violet Falls had been lucky, but the fire season wasn't over yet and everyone was a little jumpy.

Flynn walked back towards the Grange. As it was all downhill from the ridge it would have been pleasurable if it hadn't been for the glaring sun and heat. Just as he reached the paddock by the house, a gust of hot northerly wind blew at his back. He paused for a second, raising his head and sniffing at the air – there was the undeniable taint of smoke in the air. He swung around and scanned the distant hills and countryside. Flynn couldn't see a plume of smoke on the horizon – yet.

Needing a better view, he turned and ran back up to the ridge, sweat now running down the middle of his back. Scrambling up the steep incline to the top, the air was gathering and beginning to whip about him in short, hot bursts, robbing him of his breath and making the climb even more difficult. He stood panting as he studied the landscape and blue sky, looking for any sign of fire. The hot north wind gusted about him as he saw a thin column of smoke rising in the distance. It looked as if it was coming from old Harry Turner's land.

Flynn dug his mobile out of his jeans pocket and punched in triple zero.

'Hi, yeah . . . patch me through to the fire authority. Thanks.' Flynn waited for a second to be redirected. 'Hello, this is Flynn Hartley and I need to report a fire.' He rattled off his location and postcode. 'Yep, that's right. It's burning just north of Violet Falls. I'm at the Grange, right outside of Violet Falls. I'm up on the ridge and can see the smoke in the distance. Yeah, and the wind's picking up from the north. Thanks.'

The wind sent the black smoke spiralling up into the air. Flynn rammed the phone back in his pocket and ran all the way back down the hill.

* * *

Flynn's mind raced as he went over his fire plan. He'd made decent firebreaks all around his property and all he could do was hope that would be enough. There was no dead wood or green waste hanging around waiting for a stray spark to set it alight. Everything was cleared or stowed away.

185

He'd moved some of his sheep down to the bottom paddock nearest the house. The dam there was still fairly full, unlike the others scattered around the Grange. He'd intended to round up the rest of the mob and bring them down as well, but now it was too late.

Flynn turned on the pump in the bottom dam in case he needed to use the water to fight any fire that jumped the firebreaks. Hopefully it wouldn't come to that.

He was almost back to the house when he drew out his phone and pulled up Mac's number.

'Hey, it's me.'

'Hi, Flynn. What's up?'

'Listen, just giving you a heads up: it looks as if there's a fire at Harry Turner's place.'

'Shit! How's it looking?'

'I think it's fairly small at the moment, so hopefully the firies can put it out before it spreads. The problem we've got is that bloody northerly wind. Anyway, I thought you'd want to know.'

'Thanks, mate, and keep me posted. Let me know if you need anything.'

'No worries, thanks.'

'Stay safe.'

'Yeah, you too.'

Flynn hung up and shoved the phone back in his pocket. The hot air blew against his back. The scent of smoke was unmistakable now. In the distance the sound of fire-engine sirens rang out; he could only pray that they'd get there in time. If the fire took hold then the wind would send it

186

straight for the Grange, and then on to McKellan's Run. From Mac's place it was just a hop, skip and a jump to the outskirts of Violet Falls.

He looked behind towards the ridge. Flynn's heart sank; even from here he could see the smoke column rising in the air. The fire seemed to be getting bigger.

Flynn spent a half hour or so closing up the house, turning everything off and making sure things were ready before riding his dirt bike back into the yard. He couldn't herd the mob back by himself so he'd open the gates of the top paddocks. At least there was a slim chance that if the fire came through, the flock might get out of its way.

His phone vibrated. 'Hey, this is Flynn.'

'Hi, Flynn. This is Brigade Captain Lissy Stevens of the CFA.'

Flynn's stomach clenched. He had never heard Lissy sound so formal before. 'What's up, Lissy?'

'The fire at the Turner place has really taken hold. I've got units here at the heel of the fire and we're flanking it on both sides. The problem is that the wind is fanning it and it's shooting out fingers. It's running fast and the head of the fire has just crossed over into your place. I've got a truck heading over to you now.'

'Jeez, thanks for letting me know, Lissy.'

'Flynn, are you going or staying?'

'I'll stay as long as I can. You know what the Grange means to me.'

'All right, hopefully we'll get it out. But if we tell you to evacuate, I expect you to do it.'

'You got it,' Flynn said as he watched a fire-engine trundle up the steep drive.

The fire truck pulled up and half a dozen men in yellow coveralls clambered down.

Flynn walked over and greeted them with a nod. He'd grown up with most of them. 'Hey. How's it looking?'

'It's a bit of a worry,' Jack Sullivan said as he nodded back. 'The wind's up and the fire is trying to get away from us. We've got units on both sides but at the moment it's coming this way.'

'Yeah, Lissy just called to fill me in.'

'There's more units on the way. Let's hope the wind dies down.'

'So what do you want me to do?'

'We'll take care of the head fire. I want you to hang back and protect your house from any spot fires or embers that try to take hold.'

Flynn nodded his head. 'Okay, I'm on it.'

'Basically put the wet stuff on the red stuff,' Jack said with a tight smile.

'Wet stuff and the red stuff – right, got it.'

Jack clamped his hand briefly on Flynn's shoulder. 'We'll do our best to save what we can.'

Flynn nodded but couldn't find the words. He'd worked so hard and poured every cent he had into building the Grange up into a working sheep run that could sustain him and itself. And now the whole thing could be snatched away from him.

'Right, let's get to it,' he said as he turned and headed towards his house.

188

Chapter 18

Lily stepped outside her shop and stared up into the smoke-filled sky. The sun was causing the light to take on a dull orangey tint. Wherever the fire was, it was close. The smoke made her eyes smart and tickled the back of her throat. She turned her head towards the sound of sirens approaching and saw several fire trucks speeding down the main road and out of town to the west.

Lily frowned: they were heading in the direction of Flynn's place. She could only hope that he wasn't in harm's way. She pulled out her phone from the pocket of her jeans and dialled his number. Her frown deepened when the call went straight to voicemail.

Lily was about to try his number again when her phone sounded. Looking at the screen, she saw it was Violet.

'Hey,' she said.

'Hi, Lily. Listen, I just wanted to make sure that you were all right.'

'I'm fine, but it looks like the fire is pretty close.'

'Oh, you don't know? Of course you don't.'

A sliver of fear spiked through her. 'What do you mean? What don't I know?'

'That the fire is at Flynn's.'

Lily sucked in her breath. 'Oh my God, is he okay?'

'As far as I know. He rang Mac a while ago to tell him what was happening.'

Lily's head was spinning and she found it difficult to comprehend Violet's words. 'Why would he ring Mac?'

'Because if the fire goes through Flynn's place, McKellan's Run is just a stone's throw away.

'Of course, sorry, I wasn't thinking straight. Listen, I'd better go.'

'Lily, you can't go out there – you know that, don't you? It's dangerous, and the CFA and police will have the road out of town blocked off. If you want to help, meet me at Holly's school. They're setting up an evacuation centre in the school gym.'

'Evacuation?'

'Yeah, for anyone who lives on that side of town and feels the fire is getting too close.'

'Where's Mac?'

'He's already headed over to Flynn's.'

'I've got to go,' Lily said. 'I'll talk to you later.'

'Lily, I mean it, don't try to—'

'See ya,' Lily said as she hung up. She raced back inside and grabbed her car keys. Maybe she wouldn't be able to get through but all she knew was that she had to try.

Clattering over the old wooden bridge out of town and heading in the direction of Mac's place, she slowed down. The smoke was thicker here and it was harder to see; everything was enveloped in a brown haze. Ahead there were flashing hazard lights and several cars parked on the road. Lily hit the brakes and slowed down to a crawl. A guy in high-vis gear waved her to a stop.

Lily wound down her window; the heat from outside and the smoke wisped into the cabin and made her eyes water.

'Sorry, miss, the road is closed. If you need to get around you'll have to go back through town, over Calsey's Bluff and then over the flats at Moonlight. Once you get to the old Duke of Cornwall mine, follow the old road left and it will get you to the highway.'

'I'm just trying to get to the Grange.'

'That's the last place you want to be. The fire is eating its way through that area at the moment.'

'Listen, my friend is up there.'

'I understand, but I still can't let you through. Best if you go back to town and wait.'

'But . . .' Lily stopped. It was obvious that there was no way he was going to let her through. 'All right, but can you tell me anything about the Grange or Flynn Hartley?'

He shook his head. 'Not really. The fire started accidentally at old Harry Turner's place but the wind is blowing it in the direction of the town. It's jumped the road and crossed into the Grange, but to what extent, I don't know.'

'Okay, thanks.' It was all Lily could say. Turning the car around and driving back to Violet Falls, she let out a frustrated sigh and rubbed the back of her neck with one hand. If she just knew he was safe – he needed to be safe. Lily's stomach churned as a dozen scenarios ran through her brain, none of them good.

Just as she reached the outskirts of the town again she pulled over to the side of the road. Digging her phone out of her pocket, she tried to ring Flynn again.

'Hey, this is Flynn. Sorry, I can't talk right now. Leave a message and I'll get back to you.'

'Damn!' Lily said as she shook her head. All she could do was wait for the beep and leave a message. 'Hi, Flynn – it's Lily. I'm worried about you and the fire. Are you okay? Just give me a ring when you can and be safe.' Lily hung up and then chucked her phone onto the passenger seat.

God, please let him be safe.

* * *

Flynn's heart sank when he looked towards the ridge and saw the first flickers of orange flame. Damn it, that meant the fire had probably burnt through the top paddocks, and the house stood in its direct path. There were several fire-fighters already up on the ridge; he could only hope that they would be able to stop the fire's progress.

The air was thick with smoke, the scent of eucalypts, and flying embers. Flynn attacked another ember with a shovel as it landed near his feet. He caught a movement out of the corner of his eye and turned his head to see Jack Sullivan heading his way.

'Flynn, if the fire makes it over the ridge, I'll need you to get out of here.'

Flynn pulled off the wet scarf he'd tied across his nose and mouth and straightened up, staring Jack in the eyes. 'I have

192

to let the sheep out of the pen – hopefully they'll make it to shelter somewhere, but I'll be staying to the very last minute.'

'Flynn, it would be better if you left. You know we're going to do everything in our power to save your house, but unless the wind shifts we'll be fighting a losing battle. We've managed to get it back at its heel and the eastern side,' Jack said as he pointed to the east. 'But the rate the fire is eating up the ridge, unless there's a miracle or a wind shift, it's going to head straight through here and then onto Mac's place. I'm sorry, mate, but that's how it is.'

'I know you'll do what you can, but I need to stay.'

Jack held his gaze for a second and then shrugged. 'Okay, I can see you're going to be stubborn about this. I understand – I get that you need to try to save your house. But just remember, as painful as it is, you can always replace a house. Not so a life.'

Flynn nodded. He knew Jack was right but he still needed to try.

'We'll keep fighting and monitoring the situation but I can't promise anything,' Jack said before he swung around and jogged back to the fire line.

'Got it,' Flynn said to his retreating back, as another half a dozen embers hit the dry ground. He retied the scarf and started putting the sparks out before they could take hold.

**

Lily looked around the school gym, rubbing her arms. It was filling up with the families from outlying farms. She hoped against hope that if she searched the growing crowd for long enough, she'd find Flynn among their number. Stupid, really, because in her heart she knew that Flynn was still out at the Grange trying to save everything he'd worked for. She glanced at her watch: another hour had dragged by and she still hadn't heard from Flynn. Time seemed to be creeping slowly. Whenever she checked her watch the minute hand had hardly moved.

'Could you hand these out?' Violet asked, coming over with a large tray of sandwiches. 'The Hummingbird Café just arrived with a heap of food.'

Lily jumped at the sound of her sister's voice.

'Sorry, I didn't mean to startle you.'

Lily gave her a slight smile. 'I was miles away,' she said as she took the tray from Violet.

'He'll be fine, Lily. Flynn isn't brainless; he won't put himself in danger.'

'Yeah, you're right. Have you heard any updates?'

Violet dropped her voice and tilted her head towards a young family sitting not far away. 'The Hendersons have lost their house.'

Lily glanced over. The two little girls of about five or six years old sat playing with a little blue heeler puppy. Their parents were locked in each other's arms. John Henderson's jaw was set in grim determination while Lucy had tears shimmering in her eyes.

'Oh no! That's awful.'

Violet glanced across the room and Lily followed her gaze. 'Mrs Bailey said the fire was close to her place but she decided not to wait around. She packed up Mr Tibbs, her cat, and came into town. So far there's talk that several homes have been lost, but the only one confirmed is the Henderson place,' Violet said. 'Why don't you take the sandwiches around that side of the room? Holly and I will do the other.'

'Okay,' Lily said. Looking up she saw Jill and Hailey coming through the door, both carrying bags and boxes. They hurried over to where she was standing and dumped everything on the long table against the wall. 'What's all this?' Lily asked.

Jill gave her a grim smile. 'I've brought some things from the supermarket. It's just bits and pieces, but Mum and I thought that it might be useful.' She opened a bag and peered in. 'This one is tissues, sanitary products, nappies, toothbrushes and toothpaste. That one Hailey is holding has colouring books for the kids. There's juice and snacks, and that bag is fresh fruit. I wasn't sure what you needed so I just kind of grabbed stuff off the shelves.'

'That's brilliant, Jill.'

'And I've been sent by the council,' Hailey said with a shake of her head. 'Don't get me wrong, I'm happy to be here and help out any way I can, but the mayor wants to be *seen* as being involved.'

Lily smiled. 'That's a bit cynical, isn't it?'

'Nah, the election is right around the corner and he's determined to keep his position. Oh, speak of the devil. Give it another ten minutes and the local paper will be down here so he can capture the photo-op.' Hailey rolled her eyes as Grant Somerville and his daughter, Charlotte, appeared in the doorway.

'Is that a bit harsh?' Jill asked.

'Are you kidding? Just wait until a camera turns up. I bet he'll suddenly be handing out cups of tea and pretending that he actually gives a damn about the town and its population.'

Lily looked over her shoulder at the newcomers. Charlotte scanned the room, her gaze landing on Lily for a second. She gave her a brief nod of recognition before turning away.

'Hmmm, that was interesting,' Jill whispered beside her.

'Was it?' Lily said sceptically. 'Hey, I haven't heard from Flynn and I'm really worried about him.'

'The fire isn't near his place, is it?' Hailey asked as she started to get the colouring books and pencils out of the bag.

'Yes, it is. Violet got a message from Mac.'

'Shit,' Jill said.

'I tried to go out there, but the emergency services had closed off the road and they wouldn't let me through. I'm not sure what's happening or just how bad it is.'

'I'm sure he'll be fine,' Hailey said with a smile. 'He's been through fire seasons before. Try not to worry too much.'

Lily gave a nod. 'Anyway, these sandwiches won't give themselves out,' she said as she took a step away from her friends. 'Come on, people need a bit of help and comfort.'

But even though she was keeping busy, Flynn was never far from her mind.

Chapter 19

The fire was edging closer, no matter how hard Flynn and the firies worked to try to stop it. Bathed in sweat from the heat and the layers of clothing protecting his body, he was exhausted but he wouldn't stop fighting – he couldn't. The slow, heavy drone of the helicopter rotor blades made him look up but the smoke haze obscured his line of sight. The copter was water bombing the fire from somewhere above; Flynn could only pray that it would help.

Flynn used the water from the nearby dam to put out the orange flames of the many spot fires which were flaring up around the house. The roar of the fire filled his ears – it had reached the top of the ridge and was now slowly eating its way down the hill towards him.

His mob of sheep were long gone; he could only hope they'd managed to get out of harm's way and headed away from the fire. Flynn watched helplessly as everything he'd spent years building up was burnt to a cinder. He knew that the top paddocks and the sheep pens were gone, along with any of his stock that couldn't outrun the flames. There wasn't much left between it and his house, just a few acres of paddock and the hayshed. If the fire made it to the bottom of the hill that would be pretty much it – all he'd have left was charred land and a few piles of charcoal.

A hand clamped his shoulder.

'Mate, we need to get out of here,' Mac shouted over the sound of the crackling fire.

Flynn pulled down the scarf from his nose. 'You go – I need to stay a bit longer.'

'Flynn.' Mac's eyes said it all. 'We have to go. Leave the rest to the fire brigade.'

Flynn stared at his friend for a second. He could see the inevitable loss reflected in his expression. 'Mac . . . I . . .'

'Come on, it's time – the girls will be worried. The house isn't worth your life, Flynn. You've done all you can.'

He wanted to argue, he wanted to stay until the very last possible second. But he glanced back to the encroaching wall of flames and he knew in his gut that Mac was right.

'You can rebuild it, Flynn, and you know that I'll help you. But it's time to go.'

Flynn took a shaky breath and then slowly nodded. 'Just give me a minute.'

'Do you need a hand packing anything?'

'It's already stowed in the ute. No, I just need a walk through. It could be for the last time.'

'Okay, I'll meet you at the front – don't be too long. I'm sorry, Flynn, I really am.'

'I know, so am I,' Flynn said as he turned and walked back to the house. He stepped into the kitchen and ran his hand over the reclaimed wood island bench. He'd found the slab in the old shed and it'd taken him days to sand and polish the surface. It wasn't that he had a lot of possessions; it was just he'd put so much of himself into renovating the house. And the thought that he was going to lose it left a hard stone in the pit of his stomach. He walked into the lounge room and glanced out the bank of floor-to-ceiling windows that looked out onto the gully below. The smoky haze made it hard to see anything outside now. He swallowed hard as he turned around slowly, committing every detail of the room to his mind. Then, without a backward glance, he strode out to the entrance hall and through the front door, banging it shut behind him.

'You right?' Mac said from where he stood by the utes.

'Yeah.'

'We'll head into town. The girls are at the evacuation centre helping out.'

'Lily too?'

'Yep. According to Violet, when she found out about the fire she tried to come out here, but by then they'd closed off the road.'

'She did?'

'Yes, Flynn, she did.'

The idea that she cared enough to do that warmed him.

'I guess I should've called her, to let her know I was okay. I just didn't think – shit, I'm the worst boyfriend ever.'

'She'll forgive you – you had a lot on your plate,' Mac said with a fleeting smile. 'Come on, let's get out of here.'

'Right, I'll follow you,' Flynn nodded before he started to walk over to his ute. He opened the door and leant against it as he gave the house one last look. A hint of breeze seemed to touch his face as he went to duck into the cab. Flynn stilled and looked across to Mac.

'What's wrong?' Mac called out.

Flynn shrugged. 'I reckon I'm imagining things, or maybe it's just wishful thinking.'

'Flynn?'

'I thought for a second the wind was from the south – as I said, wishful thinking.'

Mac stilled for a second too. 'Nah, I can't feel a thing . . .'

Flynn closed his eyes as a gentle puff of breeze kissed his cheek. 'There!' His eyes flicked open as he swung back to Mac. 'Did you feel that?'

'There's nothing . . . Oh my God – the wind's changed!'

A great wave of relief swept through Flynn. He grinned at Mac before he threw back his head and laughed.

***

It was almost dark before Flynn and Mac walked into the evacuation centre. He'd managed to ring Lily a few hours before to let her know that he was alive. He hadn't meant to worry her but the fire had moved so fast, there hadn't been time until then.

Thanks to the wind change and the diligent endeavours of the fire brigade, the fire was all but out. There were still a few crews mopping up, but his house had been saved. As for everything else, he'd work that out tomorrow.

Flynn rolled his shoulders just as they reached the door. He was tired, hungry and still reeked of smoke, even though he'd showered and changed his clothes. Inside, the school gym was crowded. People sat in clusters on chairs, while some of the gym mats had been laid out on the floor for the kids. There was a subdued murmur in the room, an undercurrent of voices as people wondered and worried about their properties and their future. Once they had confirmation that the wind had changed and the fire was no longer a danger, people would have started returning to their homes. From what he'd heard, six homes had been lost down White Gum Road and another dozen or so had been damaged, but to what extent he wasn't sure.

He counted his blessings and scanned the room looking for Lily. She was standing on the other side of the room talking to old Mrs Bailey. She must have sensed his gaze because she glanced up and stared right into his eyes. Excusing herself with a smile from the old lady, she walked quickly towards him.

There was a look of relief on her pretty face, but there was something else as well. He should've gone forward and met her halfway, but her eyes held him rooted to the spot. No woman had ever stared at him this way. There was a raw tenderness that left a tightness in his throat.

With her last few steps she ran into his arms, and Flynn lifted her up and kissed her deeply. Lily's arms went behind his neck as she clung onto him. She was the best thing to happen to him all day, one bright spot in a hot, smoky and terrifying afternoon.

Flynn could feel the entire room staring at him and he didn't give a damn. Mac cleared his throat loudly, twice, but Flynn didn't care because the one person who meant the world to him was locked in his arms.

How bloody scary was that?

Whereas he'd have been happy to stand in the middle of the gym and kiss Lily Beckett all night, it appeared she had other ideas. Slowly, although he could sense the reluctance, she broke their kiss.

'I was worried sick about you.'

'I'm sorry – I should've rung but everything happened so quickly. One minute I was looking at a smoke plume in the distance and the next I was trying to save the house.'

'I'm so sorry.'

'Nothing for you to be sorry about. Shit happens, and today just happened to be pretty bloody shitty.'

Lily glanced over his shoulder and probably realised that they were making a damn fine spectacle of themselves. 'Um, maybe you'd better put me down.'

'No, I'm right.'

'Flynn, people are staring – some of them are frowning.'

Flynn grinned as he looked over at the smiling Mrs Bailey. 'Well, Mrs Bailey and Mr Tibbs the cat think it's fine, so we're good.'

'Ah, come on, mate, there are children present,' Mac chuckled as he walked past on his way to find Violet.

'Everyone's a critic,' Flynn said as he put Lily down, though still holding her tightly. She placed her head on his shoulder and her body pressed against his. Hell, it felt good.

'So, your house . . .?'

'Is fine, thanks to the fire brigade and emergency services.'

'And the sheep, the paddocks?'

Flynn shook his head. 'I don't know. The sheep were loose, so I can only hope that they got out of the fire's path. As for the rest, well, I guess I'll know more tomorrow.'

'You look as if you could use a coffee.'

'Actually, I'm thinking food, bed and you.'

Lily glanced up at him, a hint of a smile touching the corner of her lips. 'I think we can arrange that. Why don't you ring through an order to Dan's and we can pick it up on our way to my place?'

'I'd love that but what about Violet and Holly?'

'It's not a problem. They're staying with Mac for the next few days, so we'll have the old place to ourselves. I'll just grab my bag and say goodbye to the girls.' Lily stepped out of his embrace and hurried over to the other side of the room.

Flynn grabbed his phone and flicked up the number for the Millstone.

'Hey, Dan, it's Flynn.' He went silent as he was bombarded by questions. 'No, we were able to save the house . . . Uh-huh, yeah . . . I don't know. Reckon the top paddocks are burnt through . . . Yep, that's right. Thanks, mate, I'll let you know if I need any help. Listen, can I order a couple of pizzas and a salad to go? Sure, the usual would be great. Thanks – talk to you then.' As he ended the call, Charlotte materialised in front of him.

'Well, nothing like making an exhibition of yourself,' she said with a small smile.

'Hi, Charlotte – I try my best,' Flynn said with a shrug.

'I hear you saved your house.'

'Well, I did have a lot of help but yeah, it's still standing.'

'I'm glad, it's a great house,' she said.

'Thanks, I think so.' There was an awkward pause. 'Listen, I'd better go, Lily is waiting for me. It's been a hell of a day and I need to eat.'

Charlotte glanced in Lily's direction. 'Well, I won't keep you then. It's just . . .'

'What?'

Charlotte flicked her hair over one shoulder. 'Well, we stopped seeing each other because you weren't ready to take our relationship to the next level. You said that you couldn't commit to something like that and I agreed. And yet, here you are, a number of months on, in a relationship.'

He glanced over at Lily and something inside him warmed. 'Sorry, Charlotte. I understand what you're saying, but truthfully, I don't think this is the right time. I'm tired and can barely think, let alone hold an intelligent conversation. You were right, I wasn't ready, but it seems I am now.'

Charlotte nodded. 'Okay, I'll let you go.' She took his hand and gave it a squeeze. 'I'm glad that you're all right.'

Flynn gave her a smile and gently pulled his hand away. 'Thanks, Charlotte, I appreciate it,' he said, and turned towards Lily.

Chapter 20

The sun was just emerging over the horizon as a glow began to transform the dark sky. Lily was still sleeping when Flynn slid out of bed and crept out of the room. He needed to be alone for a while before he assessed the extent of the damage to the Grange in the cool morning light. It had been five days since the fire and last night he'd received a call from the CFA giving him the all clear to return. Flynn stood by the old ghost gum on the ridge, now just a charred stump. He thought of the countless times he'd sat under its shady branches and sighed: it would be missed.

An ugly burnt-out swathe ran along the ridge and down the hill that encompassed the two top paddocks and beyond. Flynn glanced over his shoulder – the blackened land continued almost to the sheep pen by his house and over through the grazing land to the west. He'd been lucky: unlike some, he'd kept his house, but by the looks of things the only other bit of land that hadn't been touched was the bottom paddock and, hopefully, the shearing shed. Not that he had any sheep left to shear at this point – he hoped they'd scattered but feared he'd find many of their remains in the charred fields.

He had spent the last five years pouring everything into this land to make the Grange a going concern, just like it had been when his grandad had been alive. And now, in one afternoon, he was back where he'd started. Yes, there was insurance, but his land was scorched and the flock was gone, right along with the fences. He'd miss out on the lambing season and he could kiss his next wool cheque goodbye. It would take time to rebuild the Grange to what it was, and things were going to be pretty tight for the next couple of years.

With a sigh he rubbed the back of his neck with his hand. It was kind of heartbreaking, but it could have been even worse. What was that old saying about what doesn't break you? Flynn looked back across the ridge and let out half a laugh in disbelief. His grandmother's white weatherboard house stood unscathed. Part of him was glad that the new owners hadn't lost their home, but another part of him . . . Well, if ever a house deserved to be razed to the ground it was that one.

He drove back to Lily's place. The smell of freshly brewed coffee hit him as he walked into the kitchen. Lily turned and smiled.

'Hey, I didn't wake you, did I?'

She shook her head. 'No. I didn't realise that you'd head out so early. How does it look out there?'

'Pretty dismal. Oh hell, I don't know, I suppose it could be worse.' Flynn grabbed a cup and poured himself a coffee.

'Is there anything I can do?'

'Thanks, but not really. I need to assess the damage and then ring the insurance people.'

'Any sign of the sheep?'

Flynn shrugged. 'Not yet.' A silence settled over the kitchen; he should say something to fill it but this morning he just didn't have the words. Seeing the fire's destruction had left him with a cold hard lump in his stomach. It hurt to see everything he'd worked so hard for go up literally in smoke. He wanted to tell her what he was feeling but it all seemed too raw this morning.

Lily stared at him for a second. 'Um, I suppose I'd better get ready. I think I'll do a short run just up to the gardens today.'

Shit, was he screwing up again?

'Lily, I'm not running and I'm sure as hell not pushing you away. It's just today will be . . . no, *is* a bitch. As days go, I get the feeling this one isn't going to be up there in my favourites.'

Lily stood up and walked over to him. She laced her arms around his waist and gave him a hug. 'I get it, don't worry. But just remember I'm here if you want me.'

Flynn pulled her close. 'I want you – don't ever think I don't. We're good?'

'Yeah, we're good.'

'Okay,' he said before dropping a kiss on her mouth. 'I'll call you tonight.'

* * *

He'd found another group of them. This would make the third lot he'd discovered as he wandered through the burnt-out paddocks. Flynn took off his Akubra and rubbed a hand over his eyes. He told himself it was the ash and dust in the hot air that was making his eyes sting and tear-up. These fifty or so sheep carcasses in the far western paddock, just before the mouth of the gully, looked as if they'd been heading for the creek, but the fire had overtaken them before they could get to safety. So far his grim discoveries had netted somewhere over five hundred of his flock.

For a second he felt overwhelmed. Turning away, he scrambled down the blackened side of the gully to the water's edge. Just deal with it. He'd have to call Johnno's brother, Pete, and get him to bulldoze a pit so he could get rid of the carcasses. But for now, Flynn needed a second away from the depressing sight of his dead sheep, the charred land, the ash and the burnt scent that lingered in his nostrils.

He followed the water downstream; if he kept walking the creek would eventually arch by his house. After a few minutes the burnt earth gave way to the grey green of the eucalypts and wattles that had escaped the fire. The water splashed along its course, running over river stones and glinting in the early afternoon sun.

Flynn squatted down by the side of the creek and dipped his hand into the cool water. He splashed it on his face before sitting back on his haunches and taking in a breath. Down here the air smelt sweet and untarnished by fire. If he closed his eyes for a minute maybe he could just pretend yesterday hadn't happened.

Jeez, stop feeling bloody sorry for yourself and get on with it.

Flynn stood up – no point dwelling on something that

can't be changed, better to keep moving and deal with the things that were in your control. He started to head along the water's edge when he caught a movement out of the corner of his eye. Flynn stuck his hat back on as he went to investigate. Behind a large rock and a bit of a scraggly blackberry bush, Flynn saw a flash of white.

'Hey, what are you doing there?' Flynn exclaimed as he neared.

Baaaaa.

'Well, aren't you a sight for sore eyes.' His eyes looked over the animal; as far as he could see, it was unhurt.

The sheep bleated again as it eyed Flynn moving closer.

Flynn slid off his belt and, after a moment or two of awkward wrangling, managed to loop it around the sheep's neck. 'Come on, mate, we're going home – and there's no way I'm going to carry you the whole way.'

Baaaaa.

'Nope, not going to happen,' Flynn said as he led the sheep downstream and towards the house. One out of two and a half thousand sheep – well, that was a better result than he'd had ten minutes ago.

* * *

Later that day, Flynn was checking the fence around the stock pen near the house when he saw Mac's ute coming up the drive. He walked towards the vehicle as it pulled up.

'Hey, how's it going?' Flynn asked as his friend emerged.

'Pretty good. You?'

Flynn shrugged. 'All right, I suppose.'

'Really?'

'No, it's been a pretty shitty day. The fences have gone along with the sheep. The upside is that the fire didn't touch this,' Flynn thumbed over his shoulder towards the stock pen. 'I've still got the house and the shed, which is a blessing, and the bottom paddock with the shearing shed.'

'Well, your day is just going to get a whole lot better – look,' Mac said as he gestured down the drive.

Flynn frowned at a truck making its way up the steep hill towards the house. He turned to Mac. 'What's this?'

'Everyone in town knew that you had to release your mob of sheep. Anyway, some of us managed to track a few of them down. Mrs Hatton found a dozen of them in her rose garden.'

'No . . .'

Mac nodded. 'Yeah, you can imagine how happy she was about them stomping around her prize roses. You know how touchy she is about them, especially this year after Mum pipped her at the post at the show. Well, I reckon any other day she'd give you an earful, but under the circumstances she was happy to send them back along with her best wishes and a gingerbread cake.'

Flynn swallowed the hard lump in his throat as the truck came to a stop and he saw it was filled with his sheep.

'Added to that we found a few in the old timberyard, and handfuls scattered around pretty much all the way into town.'

Old Harry Turner clambered out of the truck and walked

over to Flynn. He rubbed his hand across his weatherworn face before coming to a halt.

'I don't know what to say, lad. You almost lost everything and it was my fault. There was a spark from my tractor and the damn fire flared up so quick I just couldn't stop it. I'm sorry, I really am.'

Flynn reached over and clasped his hand on the older man's shoulder. 'It's all right, Harry. It was an accident and I don't blame you for it. It's summer and fires happen.'

Harry let out a sigh of relief. 'Thanks, Flynn, I appreciate that. It's not much, after everything you went through the other day, but at least Mac and I are able to return this lot to you,' he said, tapping the side of the truck.

'Thanks mate, I appreciate it. How many did you find?'

'One hundred and eighty-seven. Well, a hundred and eighty-eight, to be honest, but that last one is proving difficult to catch. Last seen, it was hightailing it into the bush towards the winery,' Mac said. 'So how many have you found?'

'Alive, there's a couple of hundred or so down in the bottom paddock. They were all huddled together behind the shearing shed. Other than that, all I've got so far is Lucky.' Flynn pointed over to a lone sheep tethered outside his house.

'Lucky?'

'Yeah, I found her down by the creek. I figure she's my new lawnmower.'

'Mate, it's summer – there's no lawn.'

'Yeah, but there will be one day, and I reckon she deserves it. As to the rest of them, I opened up all the gates, so I can only hope they managed to get away.'

'We'll keep an eye out for them. I'm sure they'll turn up.'

'Everyone in town is talking about you, Flynn,' Harry said.

'Well, I suppose a fire will do that,' Flynn said with a slight smile.

The old man chuckled. 'Oh, it's not the fire or your missing sheep that have got the tongues wagging. It's the fact that you kissed Lily Beckett in the middle of the evacuation centre.' Harry gave Mac a nudge in the side. 'Picked her up and everything, apparently.'

'Yeah, I was there, Harry,' Mac said.

'Really? Well, I missed it.' Harry winked at Flynn as he added, 'Guess I'll just have to wait for my invite to the wedding.'

'I'll keep that in mind, Harry. Come on, are we going to unload this mob or what?' Flynn walked towards the back of the truck, ignoring the laughter behind him.

* * *

Lily paused by the gate as she placed her earphones in and chose some music. Today she was going to go down by the old wooden bridge and run on the opposite side of the creek. Instead of heading into town, it took her farther out until she was almost at the borders of McKellan country. It also put another twenty minutes onto her run but the scenery was worth it. She'd rediscovered the route last week and been running it nearly every morning since.

Breathing in the crisp morning air, Lily set her pace to the pumping beat. She ran along the nature strip and under the spreading branches of the gums. Passing the last house, the nature strip finished and she was forced onto the road. Just to be on the safe side, Lily made sure she ran on the edge. The verge began to dip as the road curved towards the creek.

About fifty metres ahead, the road narrowed just before the old bridge until it was only wide enough for one car to go over at a time in either direction. In fact it was so narrow that if there was a car on the bridge, Lily would have to wait to cross over. On either side of the bridge there was a steep drop as the ground fell away to the rocky creek below.

Nearing the crossing, Lily pulled out her earphones as a precaution so she could listen for any approaching cars. Which was just as well, because she immediately heard a car slow down behind her. Lily moved over right to the edge of the road and, without looking around, waved the car on. She kept running but was almost to the bridge – if the damn car didn't pass her soon, she would have to stop and wait while it crossed.

God, why were they taking so long?

The car moved forward and Lily could feel it almost next to her, as if it was keeping pace. She gave it a quick sideways glance, just long enough for her to register that it was big and dark. The driver was obviously being overcautious as there was still plenty of room to pass her.

Lily gestured again for the car to drive on. She was mid step when the car swerved and clipped her. Catching her on the hip and thigh, there was enough force in it to send her flying through the air.

Pain radiated through her leg as she saw the rough, dry ground rushing up to meet her. Lily raised her hands in an attempt to protect her face. She landed heavily and rolled down the embankment. Sticks, undergrowth and rocks scraped and stabbed at her as she tumbled towards the water. Her head hit something hard as she came to rest on the bank of the creek. Before losing consciousness, she thought she heard a door open and then close before a car drove off.

Chapter 21

Lily sucked in a breath and pushed herself up into a sitting position, then regretted the sudden movement as the world spun around her for a second. She grasped at the ground, her fingers scraping into the dry dirt until the spinning stopped.

A shiver ran through her even though the air was warm. Lily glanced up at the sun; it was higher than she remembered it being.

Shit, how long have I been here?

She looked back down at her legs, with nicks and cuts all over them. Tentatively, she moved one leg – the damn thing hurt like hell but nothing seemed broken. Lily's head pounded and as she ran her fingers through her hair she winced. Her head was tender and when she brought her hand back down she saw that her fingertips were smeared with blood.

Where the hell was the person who did this?

She glanced up at the bridge, the movement making her head throb even more. From what she could see the road was deserted.

Who does that? Who runs someone off the road and keeps going?

Lily stilled for a minute as she tried to think through the throbbing headache. She couldn't stay where she was. But even if she could make it back up to the road, she doubted she could walk back to town. She suppressed the tears that wanted to come as she pulled her phone from her armband. Her hand trembled as she prayed that it wasn't broken.

Relief flooded through her: the phone appeared to be intact. Without any hesitation she called the person she needed most.

'Hello, Flynn?'

'Hey, sweetheart, how's everything? I was—'

'Flynn, I need your help.'

'What's up?' His easy manner had disappeared and there was an edge to his voice.

'I've been in an accident. I'm down by the old wooden bridge – you know, Crickly's Bridge, just out of town. Actually, I'm down the embankment near the creek. A car pushed me off the road.'

'Jesus! Are you alright?'

Lily's voice broke for a second but she tried to pull it back together. 'Yes, no . . . I mean, I'm hurt and shaken up but I don't think it's serious.'

'Okay, sweetheart – just sit tight and I'll be there in a few minutes. Do I need to call a tow truck?'

'No, I was running.'

She heard him gasp as he breathed in.

'I'm on my way.'

***

Flynn felt a cold lump land straight in his guts as he ran for the ute. What seemed like a hundred questions surged through his brain at once. He tried to push them all to one side as he tapped in a number on his phone.

'Come on, come on,' he muttered under his breath, sliding into the driver's seat.

'Senior Sergeant Barker,' a voice finally answered.

Flynn clipped his seatbelt into place and turned on the ignition. 'Steve, it's Flynn Hartley. Can you meet me at the old bridge outside of town?'

'Well, that sounds mysterious, Flynn – you're not winding me up, are you? Because I'm kind of busy at the moment.'

Flynn pushed down a biting reply. 'It's not a joke. I just had a call from Lily Beckett. Someone has run her off the road while she was on a run.'

'Is she all right?'

'I won't know until I get there. She was lucid on the phone but she said she was hurt.'

'I'll call an ambulance and meet you there.'

'Thanks,' Flynn said before he flicked off his phone and chucked it on the empty seat next to him. As quickly as he could he drove down his steep drive and towards Violet Falls.

After a few minutes, Flynn saw the old bridge ahead. His heart was in his throat as he swerved onto the edge of the road and pulled on the handbrake. He scrambled out of the car and for a split second he didn't know where to start looking.

'Lily!' He swore that his heart was going to beat out of his chest.

'Flynn, I'm down here,' a small voice came back to him from the embankment on his left.

He ran blindly down the rough bank of dry dirt and scraggly weeds. Halfway down he saw her sitting near the edge of the creek. She was alive and in one piece, and Flynn let out the breath he hadn't realised he'd been holding.

'Sweetheart, what can I do?' He knelt down beside her.

'Just hug me, Flynn, and don't let go.'

Gently he drew her into his arms and kissed the top of her head.

'Everything will be all right, I promise.'

Lily half hiccupped and half sobbed as she pressed her face against the crook of his neck. 'What are you going to do, slay all the dragons?'

'Whatever it takes, baby – whatever it takes.'

In the distance the sound of a siren rang out in the morning air. At least help was on the way.

'Can you tell me where you're hurting?'

'My leg, but I don't think anything is broken. I must have whacked my head on something because I've got a killer headache.'

'Lily, what happened?'

She sniffed and sounded as if she holding back the tears. 'I was just running. Before the bridge a car slowed down; I thought it was just being overly cautious and waved it to overtake me. It kept pace with me for a second before it veered left and knocked me down the slope and took off.'

'Did you recognise the car?'

'No, all I can tell you was that it was big and dark – sorry. But I'm certain that it stopped and made sure it hit me before it drove away. I guess they must have panicked.'

'There's nothing to be sorry about, sweetheart.' Flynn glanced up in time to see the ambulance pull up next to his ute. He pushed the anger down deep and slammed the door shut. He needed to focus on Lily. What sort of bastard hits a woman and then drives off? One that purposely wanted to hurt her. 'Hey, here come the reinforcements.' As the ambulance crew made their way down the bank, he instantly recognised Cheryl Reece taking the lead, a serious look on her face to go with her standard no-nonsense attitude. Lily couldn't be in better hands.

Flynn gently released Lily and stepped back to give the ambulance crew room.

'Lily, this is Cheryl – she's one of the finest ambos in the district.'

'Well, thanks for the glowing introduction, Flynn,' Cheryl said as she knelt down and gave Lily a smile. 'This is my partner, Nate. Can you tell me where it hurts?'

'My left leg mainly, but I can still move it. I cracked my head when I fell down the bank too.'

'We're going to get you to the hospital straightaway, okay?'

'Thanks.'

Within a few minutes Lily was ensconced in the ambulance and Flynn leant against the door. His heart seemed to contract when he saw her there, lying pale and fragile on the gurney. He looked over his shoulder as Steve Barker's police car pulled up.

Turning back he gave Lily a smile. 'You're in good hands. I'll meet you at the hospital, sweetheart. I've just got to talk to the police for a minute.'

'Flynn, don't tell Violet and Mac.'

'But I think—'

'Please, Flynn – the wedding is next week and I don't want Violet to worry.'

'Lily, I really think she'd want to know about this.'

'Flynn, I'm okay, just a bit bruised.'

He frowned and was far from convinced, but he wasn't about to upset her now.

'Alright, if that's what you want. But how are you going to explain being hurt?'

'Um, I'll just say that I fell over when I was running. It's not exactly a lie.'

'Okay, if you think that's best,' Flynn said as his frown got deeper. 'I'll follow you to the hospital and we'll take it from there.'

'Thank you. I'll see you soon,' Lily said with a smile.

'You sure will.'

Flynn gave Cheryl a nod before walking over to Steve's car.

'Is she okay?' Steve said as he walked over towards them.

'She's going to be fine, but this wasn't an accident. The car slowed down and kept level with her before it ran her off the road.'

'A warning?'

Flynn shrugged his shoulders. 'Maybe.'

'Well, warning or not, I think it sheds some light on the other stuff that's been going on.'

'What do you mean?'

'The graffiti and the vandalism that happened at Lily's shop. We put the first down to kids and the broken windows as a drunken night that got out of hand, but now I'm thinking it could be something more.'

'They're connected,' Flynn said with a nod.

'Yes, I think they are.'

* * *

It had been four days since Lily was released from hospital. The diagnosis had been a slight concussion, a bruised leg and a few nasty scrapes and bumps. The doctor had insisted she stay in overnight just to be on the safe side, but by the next morning he'd been happy enough to let her hobble home. On paper her injuries didn't seem much at all; pity they still hurt like hell.

Sergeant Barker had been in touch. The police were looking into the case but Lily didn't hold out much hope. Let's face it: her vague description of a big, dark car didn't narrow down the body of suspects much. This was Violet Falls, and nearly everyone drove SUVs in various dark colours.

Lily let out a satisfied sigh as she stood in the doorway and looked at the bare bones of her shop, with its newly painted white walls, modern kitchenette and small bathroom. It was a beautifully prepared blank canvas – now all she had to do was plan where everything was to go and dress it. Lily had asked Johnno to divide the storeroom, so now instead of a voluminous space she also had two decent-sized fitting

221

rooms. The shop was perfect – at least, the ground floor was, and the rest of it wasn't too far behind.

She winced as she walked up the stairs. Her leg still hurt, not that she would ever admit that to Flynn. He was hovering over her and treating her like some sort of china doll. She'd tried talking to him and telling him that she was okay but her words didn't seem to get through. Lily just hoped that the impressively technicoloured bruise that ran over her hip and thigh would hurry up and fade away. Because if he caught sight of that . . . well, heaven knows how he'd react.

Making her way into the front room of the first floor, she paused for a second. Light and airy with great proportions, it was going to make a fantastic office. She could picture her desk over by the far wall and the French doors to the balcony open wide. The smaller room behind it had been fitted out as another storeroom. Sticking to her design, Johnno had added hanging space along one wall and a series of shelves and cupboards on the other. All she needed now were a couple of dress racks on wheels and everything would be ready for her designs.

Lily smiled despite the lingering twinges of pain after hauling herself up the stairs. She felt as if she was standing at the beginning of something exciting, a new business and a new love – it was a heady mix of optimism and exhilaration. Coming back to Violet Falls was the best decision she'd made in a long time.

* * *

222

'Seriously, why would you even think about moving out of here?' Violet asked as she stood in her bedroom while Lily fussed with her wedding dress.

'I don't know – I just thought that with you both moving to McKellan's Run you'd want to rent this out, that's all,' Lily said, attempting to tie a bow for a second time without success. 'Will you stop fidgeting? I'm trying to fix your dress.'

Violet looked over her shoulder. 'Don't be ridiculous. This is your home as much it is mine.'

'Well, in that case, we'd better work out how much you want in rent.'

'If you don't shut up about this, I may be forced to slap you.'

'Violet, it's your house, you should be getting something out of it.'

'I am – you. So can you stop being a goose and just drop the whole subject?'

'But Violet, I—'

'Are we really going to argue on my wedding day?'

Lily shook her head. 'No, we're not – and thank you.'

'There's nothing to thank me for. Now, are you finished?'

'There, you're done,' Lily said as she adjusted the sash that was now tied into a small but perfect bow. She took a step back and studied her sister for a moment. 'You look beautiful, Violet, you really do.'

'I feel beautiful, and that's all due to you. Lily, this is the most stunning dress I've ever seen.' Violet gently ran her hand over the deep cream lace skirt. It was a simple design, but the effect of Lily's vision and hard work, including a copious amount of beading, had transformed it into something sublime.

'You asked for a spaghetti-strap dress that wasn't over the top or puffy. It's still the same design, but I just went down the vintage romantic path instead.'

'I love it, I really do. I'm glad you talked me into changing the straps for these beaded appliqués.' Violet turned around and looked at her back in the mirror.

The dull silver appliqués formed a gentle V at the back of the dress, and from them Lily had sewn hundreds of bugle beads in long, free-flowing loops so they cascaded off Violet's shoulders and down her back. There was a wide band of the same beading around her waist. The dress had an ethereal feel to it as well as being reminiscent of another era. There was a sense that Lily may have found it in one of the old trunks in the shop's attic.

Violet pulled Lily into a careful hug. 'You're so clever.'

'Well, thank you,' Lily said as she gave Violet a squeeze. 'I'm so happy that you like it.'

'What's not to like? It's beautiful and it makes me feel pretty and special.'

'You look like a princess, Mummy,' Holly said as she twirled on the spot in her pale pink flower girl's dress. 'Look, at me! I'm a ballerina, or a fairy, but I'm not wearing my wings.'

Lily and Violet stood arm in arm as they watched Holly do another spin.

'Ooh, that was good,' Violet said. 'Maybe you're a fairy ballerina?'

'You're almost done, sweetie, but we still have to put this on,' Lily said as she picked up the small circlet of tiny flowers. Holly stopped twirling long enough for her aunt to fix it to her head. 'Just a sec, Holly. Violet, pass me another bobby pin please.'

'Sure,' Violet said as she grabbed a couple more pins off the dressing table. 'Just stay still for Aunty Lily a tiny bit longer.'

'There . . . and we're done,' Lily said with a grin as she stepped back and studied her niece. 'Beautiful.'

'So are you,' Holly said.

'Well, thank you.' Lily checked out her reflection in the floor-length mirror. She was in a soft dull green that Lily liked to think of as a sea-foam dress. It had the same vintage feel to it as Violet's gown. 'Not too bad at all.'

Violet chuckled. 'Not too bad – you know damn well that you look gorgeous.'

'Oh, I almost forgot your something blue,' Lily said as she grabbed her bag and dug around in it. 'Okay, so this is more of a bluey purple, but it could also cover the something old criteria.'

'What is it?'

Lily held up the old brooch. 'It's a little violet brooch. I found it when I was cleaning up the attic. I can't prove it but I have the feeling that it could have belonged to the first Violet Beckett.'

'It's beautiful.'

'It is, and it's my present to you. The original Violet would have wanted her namesake to have it,' Lily said as she pinned the flowers to the dress strap. 'There, you look perfect.'

'Thank you,' Violet said as pulled her sister into a tighter hug.

Lily pulled back and sniffed. 'Come on, before we start crying.' Lily picked up the small bouquet of dark cream roses and handed it to Violet. 'Are you ready?'

Violet nodded and her eyes teared up. 'Absolutely.'

'Then let's go and get you married before you ruin your makeup,' Lily said as she gave her sister another hug.

Chapter 22

Life is full of beginnings, endings and continuations, and this was a hell of a good beginning, Lily thought as she, Violet and Holly entered the tiny bluestone church. Lily had to bite back the tears as she prepared to walk slowly down the aisle ahead of Violet in the church that both the Becketts and the McKellans had been part of for generations. The pews were full – it seemed that most of Violet Falls had come out to witness the marriage. The early afternoon sun flooded through the old stained-glass windows and filled the church with a myriad of colours. From the entrance, Lily saw Flynn, Mac's best man, nudge him in the ribs. When Mac looked at him, Flynn gestured with a nod and a grin in the direction of the aisle. The look on Mac's face when he turned and watched Violet walk towards him was something Lily would never forget. She knew that he loved her sister but it wasn't until that moment she really saw just how much.

Sarah McKellan sat in the front row, sandwiched between her two other sons, Jason and Dan. Lily noted as she passed that Sarah was already dabbing her eyes.

Lily tried not to tear up as Violet and Mac exchanged their vows but it proved an impossible task. She glanced over to Flynn who grinned back at her before giving her a wink.

The ceremony ended with Mac taking Violet in his arms and kissing her. Applause and a collective 'Ah' seemed to roll through the church as he picked up Holly and set her on his hip before taking Violet by the hand and escorting her back down the aisle.

Flynn offered Lily his arm as they followed Mac and Violet out.

'You look beautiful,' he whispered in her ear. 'I'm loving the way that pretty dress skims over your body.'

Lily turned her head and smiled up at him. 'Thank you. And you look devilishly handsome yourself. I never thought you'd scrub up so well. Who knew what was under all the denim and sheep shit?'

'Liar. I know that you think I'm hot.'

'Hmmm, hot and maybe a little bit vain,' Lily said with a grin.

'Just telling it how it is,' Flynn said as they walked down the church steps and into a cloud of confetti. 'So are you ready to get out of here?'

'We can't – there's still photos and a reception to go.'

'Wouldn't you rather skip the whole thing? I was thinking we could go somewhere a bit less crowded and you could show me just how hot you think I am.' He let go of her hand and draped his arm around her shoulders.

'As tempting as that is, have you forgotten that you're meant to be giving a speech at the reception?' Lily said with a laugh.

'Okay, you win. I guess I'll just have to try a little self-restraint and not throw you over my shoulder like a Neanderthal.'

'Flynn!'

'Can't help it, Lily. You drive me crazy,' he said as he dipped his head and gave her a quick kiss on the lips. 'I want you now – hell, I want you all the time.'

The only way Lily made it through the photo session at the botanical gardens was by ensuring she didn't stand too close to Flynn. The afternoon sun was warm but Lily knew the heat she was feeling had very little to do with the weather and a whole lot more to do with Flynn Hartley's near proximity. She made herself busy by helping Violet with her veil and making sure that Holly didn't end up twirling into the rosebushes.

After about half an hour the wedding party made it to the reception. Mac had thrown McKellan's Run open to pretty much anyone who wanted to celebrate his wedding. The house was filled with a variety of flowers in pale shades. Lily could smell the scent of roses as soon as she stepped inside. Tables and chairs were scattered throughout the great room and Dan and his staff from the Millstone had set up a lavish smorgasbord alongside the far wall. The French doors leading to the courtyard were opened wide and as Lily walked past she saw a local band, 'Amp', setting up. The whole feel of the place was one of welcoming, laidback country elegance, which seemed to reflect both Violet and Mac.

There was laughter, music and good food as everyone came together to celebrate Mac and Violet's wedding and wish them well. The afternoon passed in a warm and fuzzy bubble of happiness that Lily swore she'd never forget.

It was late afternoon when Flynn caught her by the hand and pulled her into the courtyard. The band was playing an old slow love song as he took her in his arms and started to sway to the music. The sun was low in the sky but still held its heat, rays warming the stones of the old courtyard and the lavender bushes that ran around its edges. The air was filled by their fragrance.

'Are you having a nice time?' Flynn held her a little closer.

Lily looked up into his dark eyes and smiled. It felt good to have him hold her like this. She laid her head against his shoulder. Flynn had been trying hard to prove himself to her and Lily was beginning to think that he was solid, maybe even dependable. She prayed that she was right because all her talk to her friends about just being with him for fun was a big fat lie.

Lily wanted him in her life – not just for a few carefree months but for always. She was in love with him and that was the truth. She hoped that he cared enough about her to try to make something out of what they had and not run like he'd done with every other girl in his past.

'Yes, I am, thank you. I swear I've never seen Violet so happy.'

'Yeah, and Mac's been walking around all day looking smug. You know he's been in love with her ever since they were in school?'

'I kind of figured that was the case. It must have been hard for Mac to watch her go out with Jason.'

Flynn shook his head. 'Almost killed him.'

'I thought there might be some tension between them but it doesn't look like it.'

Flynn looked over to where Mac and Jason were talking by the bar. 'Things are always going to be a bit tricky, I reckon, seeing Jason is Holly's father. But I think Jason is genuinely happy for them.'

'Hmmm, well he's never been my favourite person, not after the way he treated my sister all those years ago. But, I suppose I'm willing to give him the benefit of the doubt. Although if he ever hurts Violet or Holly – or hell, even Mac – he's going to have me to answer to.'

'Feisty!'

Lily grinned back. 'You'd better believe it. No one messes with the people I care about.'

'Am I included in that?'

'Maybe you are.'

'I like that.' He dipped his head and gave her a quick kiss. 'So, are you ready to sneak away yet?'

'Aren't you meant to give a speech? Besides, we can't leave until the bride and groom do.'

Flynn let out a sigh. 'You're no fun, Lily Beckett, and that's a fact.'

'That's right, I'm a regular party pooper.'

'Tell you what: I'll stop asking if you promise that you'll come swimming with me the moment Violet and Mac leave.'

'Swimming tonight? Are you serious?'

'Yep, it's going to be a warm night. Let's head up to the falls.'

'Really?'

'Well, a man has to cool off somehow. Besides, I want you all naked and slippery against me,' he said with a widening grin.

Lily looked around at the other couples on the dance floor. 'Shhh, they'll hear.'

'Like I keep telling you, I don't care. So, will you come?'

Lily gave him a slow smile. 'Yes, I will.'

'Great. Now I get to spend the rest of the day imagining what it's going to be like to slip those straps from your shoulders and watch that dress slide off your amazing body. God, I'm getting all hot and bothered just picturing it,' he said as his fingers moved over her bare skin and trailed down the spaghetti straps.

Lily felt an ember of want begin to glow within her but she took a breath and tried her damnedest to ignore it.

'So stop picturing it.'

Flynn leant forward and whispered in her ear. 'Hell, babe, that's like asking me to hold back the tide – bloody impossible.'

* * *

'Okay, can everyone settle down for a minute!' It was an order rather than a request; Flynn stood up and tapped an empty glass with a knife. His voice cut through the noisy room and the crowd turned to look at him.

Flynn loosened his tie before he continued. 'We all know that Mac and Violet wanted today to be a relaxed

232

get-together. They wanted you all to feel welcome and able to sit back and enjoy good company, great music and fantastic food. However, it was decided that we needed at least one short speech, so this is the only formal bit of the evening.'

Lily looked up at Flynn from her seat. She gave him a smile of encouragement. Not that he really needed it – Flynn was used to being the centre of attention. His hand tightened around hers for a second before letting go.

'I'm sure Mac would probably prefer someone else to give the speech . . .' He glanced over in time to see Mac nod his head in agreement. 'See, now that just hurts!'

Mac let out a laugh. 'Oh, just get on with it,' he called out as he draped his arm around Violet's shoulders and pulled her close.

Flynn squared his shoulders. 'I've known Mac all my life and—'

'Hey, I thought you said this was going to be short,' Dan called out.

Flynn sent him a dirty look. 'Anyway, before I was so rudely interrupted, I just wanted to wish you and Violet the very best for the future. Everyone here knows that you both deserve your happily ever after, especially after it took you so many years to get her to agree to marry you. On that note, I also have to say a special thank you to Violet,' he said, turning to look at her. 'Thanks for accepting his proposal: at least now I won't have to put up with him moping about, talking about you and, whenever possible, stalking you.'

'Ah, shut up!' Mac shouted out with a grin.

'Flynn, maybe you'd better tell me a bit more about the stalking?' Violet said with a mischievous gleam in her eye.

'Hey, I thought you were meant to be on my side!' Mac said as he hugged Violet.

'Always.'

Mac dipped his head and kissed her deeply.

'Guys, focus for a second,' Flynn said as he rolled his eyes. 'Come on, you two, there are children present.'

Violet pulled back and gave an apologetic smile. 'Sorry.'

'Nothing to be sorry about, sweetheart,' Mac said before he leant in and kissed her again.

Flynn cleared his throat loudly as a ripple of laughter flowed through the room.

'As I was trying to say, we all wish you a lifetime of happiness, love and good fortune.' He looked down and smiled at Lily beside him. 'We can only hope to find the love of our lives, but you two have done it!' Flynn's gaze reluctantly left Lily's as he continued. 'Anyway, let's all raise a glass: to Mac, Violet and Holly, and to the wonderful family they have just become.'

It took Lily a few seconds to remember how to breathe; that look of Flynn's seemed to say so much, and to her it felt like a declaration to the whole room. Heat flushed her cheeks as she glanced across the room. Jill was giving her a huge grin and a thumbs up and Lily bit back a grin. She turned her head and fell straight into the eyes of Charlotte Somerville. Charlotte stared back at her; she wore a thin smile but Lily caught a look of sadness in her eyes. It was obvious that Charlotte still cared for Flynn, even though, from what Lily had heard, she'd been the one to end their arrangement in the first place.

Lily looked away and tried to put it out of her mind. Today was all about Violet, Mac and Holly, not remorseful ex-partners. With Flynn's toast finished, the revellers went back to, well, revelling. It wasn't until an hour or so later when Lily was heading to the kitchen that Charlotte appeared by her side.

'Can we talk?'

'Sure,' Lily said cautiously.

Charlotte's hand reached out and touched her arm. 'I just wanted to say that I'm glad Flynn has found happiness. He once said that he didn't do commitment and yet he has with you.'

Lily looked down at Charlotte's hand before raising her eyes to the other woman.

'Thank you, Charlotte.'

Charlotte shook her head. 'I care about him. I waited for him but he wasn't ready . . . but obviously he is now.'

'I'm sorry,' Lily said.

'It's not your fault – just bad timing along with a hundred other things. I wish you well,' Charlotte said as she gave a little shrug.

'Thanks, that's kind of you.'

'Not a word most people would use about me,' Charlotte said with a tight smile as she dropped her gaze. 'But I hope it works out for you both.'

Lily wasn't sure but she thought Charlotte's eyes filled with tears as she turned away and disappeared back into the party.

Chapter 23

Later that evening when the moon hung in the warm summer air, Lily stood with the rest of the wellwishers waiting to wave Violet and Mac goodbye.

'Now, be a good girl, won't you?' Violet said as she hugged Holly tightly. 'I miss you already.'

'Come on, Violet. Holly is always good,' Lily said with a grin. 'Except when she isn't.'

'Aunty Lily, I'm good,' Holly said with a pout as she looked up.

'Just teasing, sweetie,' Lily winked at her niece before glancing at her sister. 'Go and have a great time. Don't worry, Holly will be fine.'

'I know she will, it's just I've never been away from her before.'

Lily gave Violet a quick hug. 'Stop worrying and we'll see you in a week. Come on, Mac, get her out of here.'

Mac sauntered over and draped his arm around his bride. 'So, Flynn, if there's any problems just—'

Flynn rolled his eyes. 'Jeez, Mac, you're only going for a week. I'm sure the Run and the rest of us will be just fine. Seriously, we've got this covered, so go and sit on a tropical beach and enjoy yourselves.'

'Right,' Mac grinned. 'Thanks. Let's go, sweetheart.'

Violet bent down and wrapped Holly in another hug before dropping a kiss on her forehead. 'We'll call you tomorrow.'

Mac scooped Holly up and planted a kiss on her cheek. 'Okay, fairy, you're in charge until we get back.'

Holly giggled. 'I can't be in charge of McKellan's Run – I'm only seven.'

'Course you can,' he said with a smile as he handed her to Flynn. 'And don't you let this one boss you around.'

'As if I could,' Flynn said as he balanced Holly on his hip, pulling Lily into a hug with his free hand.

After another couple of minutes of happy, weepy goodbyes, mainly from Violet and Sarah, Mac finally managed to get her in the car and drive off. Lily smiled up at Flynn as his fingers drew slow circles against the bare skin of her shoulder. His touch sparked the dormant lust inside her. She'd wanted him all day and now finally she'd be able to act upon it – maybe there was something in this whole delayed gratification thing after all.

Lily left Holly in Sarah's capable care. Both grandmother and granddaughter were looking forward to spending the next week in each other's company. It was a win-win situation, with Holly getting spoiled and Sarah being able to do the spoiling.

Most of the guests had drifted off by the time Flynn took Lily's hand and led her to his ute. She leant against him as they drove away from McKellan's Run and towards the other side of town.

238

The falls had been an integral part of the community ever since the town was founded. Landoc Creek snaked its way through the bush and just outside of town it ran over a high rocky face and formed a steady flowing waterfall, which poured into a natural pool before continuing its journey as a fast-moving stream.

But the blessing of the falls was that no matter how hot the summer was or even if the town was caught in a drought, the water still flowed.

Flynn brought the ute to a stop in the small car park from which the falls were a couple of minutes' walk away. The town had been careful to try to protect the area so, other than a couple of lights around the pool edge itself, the rest of the place was pretty much unchanged. The only concessions that had been made by the council were the car park, a toilet block and a gas barbeque, all tucked away from the natural beauty of the site.

Lily got out of the front cab and stood for a moment, listening to the sound of the falls in the warm darkness. There was something special about this place and she'd always felt a connection to it. Flynn walked around the bonnet and took her hand, a chorus of cicadas sounding as they began to walk.

'Looks like we're the only ones here.'

'Oh yes, the picnickers are all long gone,' Flynn said. 'Still feel up to a swim or are you going to chicken out?'

'Well, that will depend on just how cold the water is,' Lily answered.

Together they walked down the narrow path, the sound of the rushing water becoming louder with each step. When

239

they reached the falls, one light shone on the cascading waters while the other lit up part of the pool. Along the banks of the falls were scattered rock formations and several clumps of willows and gums. As they reached the water's edge, the cooler air and water mist blew across Lily's body.

Lily knelt down and dipped her fingers into the water.

'Too cold?' Flynn asked as he leant against one of the willows.

Lily shook her head as she stood up. 'You don't think anyone else will turn up?'

'It's pretty unlikely at this time of night, but if you want to go, we can.'

Lily reached over and touched his cheek, her fingers trailing down the side of his face.

'No, I don't want to go. I want to stay here with you.'

He pulled her into his arms. The kiss was long and slow and made her glow inside. Her tongue sought his and within a heartbeat desire kindled and fired within her. Lily wound her arms around him and pulled him closer. The thought of swimming slipped from her mind. She wanted Flynn – no, she needed him.

'You burn me up, Lily,' he murmured against her lips.

She didn't answer, instead grabbing the hem of his shirt with both hands and pulling it up and over his head. A couple of buttons seemed to pop but she needed to touch his warm skin, craving the smooth muscled planes of his shoulders and defined chest. The necessity to feel his heart beat against hers was overwhelming.

As Flynn's shirt floated to the ground, he slipped the

240

straps from her shoulders and tugged the bodice of her dress down. Lily's head fell back as Flynn's mouth closed over her breast – hot, wet and searing. Her breath caught for a moment as her insides contracted.

'Flynn.'

'I'm here, babe, and I swear I'm not going anywhere.'

Her dress slithered down her body and the beaded pale green chiffon pooled at her feet.

'You're so beautiful, Lily. I swear I just can't get enough of you.'

'I want you, Flynn. I want to feel you against me, wrapped around me . . . inside me.' Her fingers ran slowly over his warm skin as the heat inside her began to build.

Flynn sucked in a breath. 'You've got a hell of a way with words, Lily. I thought I'd try to do something romantic – you know, an almost full moon, a hot summer's night and the falls. But now I can't think straight. All I know is I want you so much. Hell, I can't even put it into words.'

Lily's hand meandered over his chest, the hard muscles of his abdomen, until she cupped his rock-hard erection. Leaning forward, she whispered in his ear. 'I appreciate the thought. It was a sweet romantic gesture and I promise I'll give it my full attention . . . later. But right now, let's just get naked.'

'Babe, you don't have to ask me twice,' Flynn said, a wolfish grin spreading over his face.

In about two seconds flat Lily found herself standing bare in front of an equally naked Flynn. Lord, he was so hot standing there in moonlight that he almost made her breath stop. His eyes travelled up and down her body and Lily stared back.

The old Lily, the Lily before she fell in love with Flynn, would have tried to hide from his gaze. The moment would have been ruined because of all her self-doubt and never quite feeling comfortable with her own body. But not anymore. She saw the way he looked at her and how it made her feel: wanted, coveted and, for the very first time in her life, beautiful.

She heard the faint crinkle of the foil as Flynn opened a condom packet.

'Would you like me to . . .?'

'That's something we can explore in greater depth later. Right now, I'm just doing what you asked me to do,' he breathed raggedly.

'And what's that exactly?' asked Lily, equally breathless.

'Holding you against me.'

Her breasts brushed against the hard planes of his chest. She felt his hot skin searing hers, his cock straining against her. He bent down and dropped a series of burning kisses along the side of her neck. Lily leant into him and tilted her head to the side to allow him access. Warmth pooled in her belly at the sensation of his lips on her skin.

'Wrapping myself around you,' Flynn whispered as his arms encircled her and held her close.

She loved this feeling of being cocooned by his heat, his strength, his essence. Lily wound her arms around his shoulders and kissed him. His hands slid down her body before lifting her up, and instinctively she locked her legs around him.

'Being inside you,' he said as he slowly entered her.

Lily closed her eyes as the delicious sensation filled her again and again.

'Ah, Lily, you turn me upside down.'

She held on tight as they found their natural rhythm, her breath quickening as the fire grew inside her. Lily opened her mouth to reply but the words never materialised, swept away by the reaction that Flynn stirred within her. All she was left with was the fire in his touch, and it consumed her.

* * *

The Monday morning after the wedding, Lily went through some of the photos she'd taken before the ceremony. She smiled as the image of Violet in her wedding dress flashed up on the screen, turning back to face the camera. The light coming in from the windows gave her an ethereal quality; she was beautiful and the dress looked sublime. The shot was perfect for the website she was developing for the Gilded Lily. She'd been trying to find the perfect name for her business pretty much from when she had the idea of opening, but nothing had seemed right until now. She knew that she'd left the whole naming thing a bit late, but she'd finally commissioned the sign-writer and ordered her business cards.

The repairs and remodelling of the shop were finally finished, so now all she had to do was dress the space and complete the last handful of designs. Lily hoped that she could pull everything together for the opening in just over two weeks.

Flicking through the images on the screen, it occurred to Lily that she could use them not only on the website but in the shop as well. This sweet photo of Holly in her flower girl's dress skipping through the old rose garden at Mac's place, for instance. The photos were imbued with a sense of romance, which was just what Lily wanted for her business. She'd have them blown up and mounted in ornate gilt frames. Running with the decision, Lily was downloading some favourite images onto a thumb drive when her phone rang.

'Hi, Lily – it's Mandy from the *Violet Falls Gazette*.'

'Hi, how are you?'

'Good. I was just wondering if it would be okay to do another little article on your shop. I know you're not open yet but, as I said before, I think we could generate a great buzz.'

'That'd be fantastic,' Lily said as she perched on the arm of the couch. 'I'm planning to open in a couple of weeks, so the timing could be great. When did you want to do something?'

'I know it's short notice but how about today?'

'I think I can do that. So, what do you want to do exactly?'

'Some shots of the inside of the shop would be fantastic as well as a couple of your dresses.'

'Sure thing.'

'Great! How about I meet you at the shop in a couple of hours? Is that too soon?'

Lily glanced at her watch. 'That's fine – I'll see you then.'

When Lily parked her car in front of the shop just before eleven o'clock Mandy was already there, waiting in a white van with *Violet Falls Gazette* in a cursive font along the side.

'Hi,' Mandy said as she got out and walked over towards Lily. 'Thanks for coming at such short notice.'

Lily gave a smile before she turned and unlocked the front door. 'Not a problem.'

Mandy looked back at the van and motioned forward a young guy with cropped blond hair and a slim-fitting black jacket. 'This is John, our photographer.'

'Hi, John.'

'Hey,' he said with a curt nod.

Lily pushed open the door and turned on a light. 'So this is it. Go in, I've just got to grab the dresses from the car.'

'I'll give you a hand,' Mandy said as she followed Lily back to the kerb.

'Thanks.' Lily opened the passenger door and reached in to grab the pile of garment bags. The large A4-sized prints she'd just picked up of Violet and Holly were sitting on top, so she moved them onto the back seat.

'Wow, can I have a look?' Mandy asked.

Lily straightened up and handed the photos over. 'I took them at the wedding and I've decided to use them in the shop.'

'They're beautiful – I mean it. And Violet's dress is just stunning. I'm really bummed that I couldn't make the wedding, but I saw the dress that night when we all went to the movies before you had finished it. At the time I thought it was gorgeous but now . . . wow,' she said again.

Lily felt a little warmth in her cheeks. 'Thanks, Mandy, that means a lot.'

'Could I use that picture of Violet in the article? I mean, do you . . . would she mind?'

'That's fine. Violet already knows that I'll be using some of the photos I took for promotion. She says she's fine with it as long as she's not pulling some weird face or has her mouth stuffed full of food.'

'Yeah, and I bet if that was the case, she'd still end up looking amazing.' Mandy handed the photos back and Lily placed them carefully on the back seat.

Lily handed a couple of the garment bags to Mandy before she draped the remaining ones over her arm. 'Exactly! I don't think I've ever seen a bad photo of her.'

Just as they walked back into the shop together, John the photographer looked up from his camera.

'It's a lovely space – it has good light and a nice feel about it.'

'Thanks, I think so too,' Lily said as she unzipped the bag and took out the first dress, an elegant sheath in white silk.

'Ooh, that's gorgeous. I love white,' Mandy said as she came closer. 'Unfortunately, it doesn't love me. I always – and I mean always – manage to drop or spill something indelible on it.'

Lily chuckled. 'Me too. I always gravitate to black – at least that way no one can see the coffee stains. So, where do you want me to put these? I have an antique dressmaker's dummy – should I put one of the dresses on that?'

'That'd be good,' John said. 'And I think we'll hang the dresses up there and then have you sit on the old counter. Yeah, that'll work.'

'I meant to ask – when will this go into the *Gazette*?'

'Wednesday, if all goes to plan. Plus, the article will be online as well. I know we're only a small paper, but with the website a few of our articles get interest from Bendigo, and even in some cases, Melbourne. So I'm hoping that it will give you some exposure,' Mandy said with a smile.

'That's great – thanks, Mandy, I appreciate it.'

For the next half an hour while John snapped photos, Lily chatted to Mandy about everything from her aesthetic, to her design process, to why she was opening a business back in Violet Falls.

On Wednesday morning there was a knock on Lily's door. Lily frowned as she glanced at her watch; it was only 8.17. She hurried down the hallway and opened the door.

Flynn stood there with a grin on his face, holding a newspaper. 'So, my girl is a celebrity,' he said before bending down and giving her a quick kiss.

Lily would've liked the kiss to continue but curiosity got the better of her. 'What do you mean?'

'I mean you've got a full page in the *Violet Falls Gazette*.' Flynn handed her the opened paper as he walked into the house.

'A full page! I thought I was just getting a teeny article, and maybe a picture or two if I was lucky,' she said as she followed him down to the kitchen, scanning the article as she went. The headline read "Sew in love – the Gilded Lily – the essential dress stop location". Along with the article, which highlighted the bespoke aspect of the business, there was a picture of her sitting on the counter surrounded by

247

her dresses, the photo of Violet in her wedding gown, and another of her blue damask silk on the antique dummy. 'This is amazing!'

'Sure is. I reckon you'll be chained to your sewing machine with all the orders that will stream in,' Flynn said as he headed over to the kettle and flicked it on.

'Do you really think so?'

'Definitely – apparently your dresses are "sublime" according to the article, and besides that, you're brilliant.'

Lily walked over and slipped her hands around his waist. 'Brilliant, hey?'

'Absolutely,' he said before he scooped her up and kissed her.

Chapter 24

As much as she would have loved to spend her Friday night wrapped up in Flynn's arms, Lily had reluctantly turned down his idea of dinner at the Millstone so she could spend the time sewing. With the opening looming closer, Lily needed to get everything finished so she could concentrate on decorating the shop.

It was getting late but Lily was pleased with what she'd accomplished. She'd managed to create a small but cohesive collection that displayed her style and sensibilities. Half of the collection was young and a little flirty, a mixture of skirts, tops and dresses. Added to that there were two other dresses with more structured designs and boned corsets. Beautiful and fashioned in dark cream silk, either one would make the perfect wedding gown. But of course, her centre-piece for the display was Violet's wedding dress, which she was borrowing for the opening. There was also a sea-green silk that flowed like water and could have been seen on the red carpet in the 1930s. Everything was done, finished and rechecked, all except the last dress. A barely pink silk, it was almost complete, with just a dusting of crystals to be hand sewn onto the bodice and the skirt needing to be hemmed.

Over the hum of her sewing machine, Lily heard her phone ring. Taking her foot off the pedal, she reached over and snatched up the phone. Lily glanced at the incoming number but didn't recognise the caller.

'Hello?'

'Lily? It's Edwina Partell here.'

'Edwina! What a surprise.'

'I hope I haven't caught you at a bad time. I was wondering if we could have a little chat?'

'Of course. How can I help you?'

'Well, firstly, I guess I should congratulate you on the newspaper article.'

'You saw that?'

'A friend of mine lives near Bendigo and she sent me a link. From the photos, your designs look stunning.'

'Thank you, that means a lot.'

'I have to say that I was sorry to hear that you resigned from our team. I was hoping that you were going to stay with us longer than you did.'

'But you know why I left, right?'

There was a pause on the other end of the line. 'I was told that you were returning back to your home town to be closer to family.'

'Edwina, I returned home because I basically had no other option than to quit.'

'What do you mean?

'Sam Worth took the credit for one of my designs. I felt that I couldn't stay at the company after that. Even if I backed down and didn't say anything, there were no guarantees that she wouldn't do the same thing again in the future.'

'I'm sorry, Lily – I wish I'd known. I guess at the time I was busy in London then opening up the new shop in Sydney.'

'I know. I tried to get in touch with you several times but I don't know if you received my messages.'

'No, I didn't, and I can't say I'm surprised. All I can say is that some people have been let go.'

'Is Sam one of them?'

'Yes. Sometime after you left I was approached by others on the design team – it seems you weren't the only one that had happened to. Several designers, interns and junior designers came forward to complain about Sam passing off other people's garments and designs as her own. It appears that this had been going on for quite some time. Your name was mentioned a couple of times, and I did wonder if she'd done the same thing to you.'

Lily let out a sigh. 'Yeah, she did.'

'The burnished copper dress was yours, wasn't it?'

'Yes, yes, it was.'

'And Sam passed it off as her original design. I remember that you were still with us and then, after that meeting I had with Sam, you weren't. I should have put two and two together. It's a great dress, Lily. I can see that you not only have the ability to be a successful designer but you also have an individual aesthetic.'

'Thank you.'

Edwina made a brief dismissive noise. 'Now, getting down to the crux of the conversation: I want you to come back, Lily, and be part of our team again. You'll be welcomed back as a fully fledged designer, not a junior.

I know you've made plans in Violet Falls but if you come back, I'll make it worth your while.'

The lump in Lily's stomach got heavier. God, wasn't this what she'd wanted, designing for an established house? There was a pull, an instinct to burst into a dance of joy and say 'yes'. But she bit her lip and was silent. What about her new dreams – her business here and, above all of that, what about Flynn?

'Lily, are you still there?'

'Yes, I'm still here. I'm sorry, Edwina. It's just an awful lot to take in, that's all.'

'I see . . . Well, you don't have to give me an answer right now, take some time and think about it. If you would like to come back to us you'd be more than welcome. Working here, working with me, could push your career to greater heights. It just depends on what you really want. I'm not saying that you wouldn't be successful if you stayed where you are; clearly you've got the talent. It's just that if you want a shot at reaching an international audience and clientele, I think you may have a better chance with me. As a design house we're beginning to take off. We'll be attending Melbourne Fashion Week next March and have some features coming up in several international fashion magazines. I can't say more at the moment because we're still working out the details, but this could be very big for our label. And I just hope that you will consider returning to us.'

'I understand, Edwina, and I'd like to thank you for the opportunity. I'll give it some thought and be in touch soon.'

'Good. I look forward to it. Bye then,' Edwina said before she hung up.

Lily sat there for a minute and ran over the conversation in her mind. She felt torn and confused. Yes, she did want her own business, to have the freedom to design what she wanted and see her vision realised. But to design for Edwina Partell was a chance to make it in the higher echelons of the fashion world. The label was garnering more and more interest and, after years of hard work, Edwina Partell was beginning to take off. What Edwina was offering Lily was potentially a chance at something big, but the question was, did she still want it enough to give up everything she'd just found?

The phone rang again in her hand and made her jump.

'Hi, Flynn.'

'Hey, just thought I'd see how you were going. Missing me, I hope?'

'Always,' Lily said as a smile touched her lips.

'Good. So whatcha doing?'

'Um, I'm just sewing . . . um . . . that's all.'

'Lily, what's wrong? You sound distracted or something. Did I catch you at a bad time?'

'Oh no, it's nothing. It's just I got a strange phone call and it's turned me about.'

'Strange as in heavy breathing and asking what you're wearing? Sprung, that was me.'

Lily chuckled. 'No, funnily enough there wasn't any heavy breathing involved.'

'Shame. Personally, I could do with a bit of heavy breathing about now.'

Lily laughed. 'No, it was strange as in my former boss just offered me a job. I mean, it was really out of the blue and the last thing I was expecting.'

The line was silent for a moment. 'I see. So what did you tell her?'

'Nothing, she asked me to think about it.'

'Right. Okay then.'

Lily frowned; his tone was short and clipped. 'It would have been rude of me to reject her offer after she asked me to think about it. It's a huge opportunity and not the sort of thing you dismiss on the spur of the moment.'

'So you're actually considering it?'

'No, well . . . it was just such a surprise.'

'But what about all these months of hard work trying to get the shop ready? What about your dream of having your own business? What about . . .' He paused for a second before he went on. 'Look, it doesn't matter. Just tell me when you get around to making your decision.'

Again with the silence.

'Flynn, I—'

'Listen, I have to go. I'll catch you later.'

And before Lily could reply the line went dead. Damn.

* * *

Flynn tossed his phone on the table as a wave of coldness washed through his body. She was going to leave him, just when he'd started to believe that his life had changed. He placed his hands on the table, lowered his head onto them and closed his eyes for a moment.

No one will ever want you. You don't deserve to be loved.

His grandmother's spiteful words circled in his head like a murder of crows as he retreated into himself. Why had he thought that this would be any different? They all left him in the end because he was unlovable.

Flynn took a breath and it seemed to keep at bay the darkness that threatened to envelop him. He was jumping to conclusions and allowing that twisted old bitch to screw with his mind again. Well, this time he wouldn't let her. Lily cared about him, and deep down inside he knew that. There was something between them, something solid and tangible like a foundation, and with work maybe they could build on it.

He took in another breath and slowly straightened.

No matter what her decision was he'd support it. There would be some way for them to be together even if she moved back to Melbourne; he'd just have to be creative.

A frown formed on his brow as he rewound the conversation with Lily. Yeah, he kind of mucked things up again. It was just the thought of Lily leaving that sent him into a tailspin. He should call back and apologise. He snatched up his phone and she answered on the first ring.

'Hi.'

'Lily, listen, I'm sorry if I was weird before. It's just come as a surprise that you would consider moving back to Melbourne.'

'Flynn, I haven't agreed to anything.'

'I know. I just wanted to tell you to do what's best for you. We'll find our way around it even if it means I have to move to the city to be with you.'

'Flynn, you can't give up the Grange – it's in your blood.'

'Maybe, but the question is, what do I want more? Anyway, all I'm saying is do what you need to do because whatever your decision is, I've got your back. I told you that I was here for the long haul and one way or another I'm going to prove that to you.'

'Flynn, you don't have to prove anything. I believe you.'

'Good, great. It's all I need to know. Night, babe, talk to you tomorrow.'

'Night, and Flynn . . .'

'Yes?'

'Thank you,' Lily said before the phone went dead.

* * *

It was an accident, he never meant to do it – why would he? He tried to tell his grandmother but she just wouldn't listen to him.

As he reached over the table to get the butter his arm had caught the highball glass and knocked it over. All he could do was watch it, the whole scene playing out as if it was a slow-motion clip from a movie. The half-filled glass toppled, spilling orange juice over the snowy white table-cloth. He tried to snatch it up but before he could it rolled with what seemed like agonising slowness across the damask cloth and over the edge of the table. Flynn winced as he heard the sharp tinkle of the glass shattering into a thousand pieces on the black and white linoleum floor.

'Look what you've done, you stupid, stupid boy!'

'I'm sorry, Granny, I didn't mean to,' Flynn said as he jumped up from his seat and hurried towards the sink. 'I'll clean it up.'

But he never made it across the room. His grandmother caught him before he could take three steps. Her thin bony fingers were like needles as they bit into his shoulder. Flynn cried out in pain as well as surprise.

'Idiot, clumsy boy – no wonder your mother never wanted you. I took you in when no one else would have you. I know it was my Christian duty but I swear to God it was the worst mistake I ever made. Then your grandfather goes and dies on me and all I'm left with is you, a bad bargain if ever there was one.'

Her fingers dug deeper into his shoulder as she bent down and whispered in his ear. 'You're more trouble than you're worth.' She propelled him through the kitchen and out towards the tiny closet sandwiched between the utility room and the back verandah.

A thin flare of panic flickered through Flynn the closer he got to the door.

'No, please, Granny. I'm sorry, I'm sorry.' He tried to twist out of her grip but she held on so tightly that he wondered if she would push her finger right through his skin. He dug in his heels but the soles of his shoes skidded across the slippery linoleum.

'Well it's too late for that. You should've been more careful,' Edith Hartley said as she pushed him through the little door.

Flynn stumbled forward and banged his arm against

the bank of shelves that lined the three sides of the narrow cupboard. He never knew what was meant to be housed in here but he was sure it wasn't a boy. The cupboard was so skinny there was only just enough room for him to stand upright. Swinging around, he caught a glimpse of his grandmother's smug face before she slammed the door shut and left him in total darkness. His stomach lurched with fear and the hairs on the back of his neck quivered. It was so dark that he couldn't make out anything.

'You can stay there until I come and get you,' she said as she turned the key in the lock. The sound was hollow and deafening at the same time.

It was so dark in the cupboard, he couldn't see what was in there with him.

Don't think that! His mind shouted as Flynn squeezed his eyes shut. 'Don't think that,' he whispered. 'I'm alone in here and there's nothing to be afraid of. Nothing, nothing to be afraid of.' He repeated the words over and over again in the hope that he would eventually believe it.

The inky blackness pressed down on him like a great stone and Flynn tried to remember how to breathe. He leant against the door and held on to the handle; it gave him an anchor to concentrate on. Taking in an even breath, Flynn tried with all his might not to imagine the horrific monsters that could lurk behind him in the velvety shadows.

The silence enveloped him and he strained his ears to try to hear something from the sunlit world outside. But there was nothing. It was as if he was floating in a great black void that nothing could ever penetrate.

258

'There's nothing there, there's nothing there.'

Flynn clutched the door handle so tightly that the metal bit deeply into his flesh. He didn't know if the moisture he could feel in his palms was sweat or blood.

'There's nothing there.'

But a shiver skipped up his spine as he heard a faint scratching coming from somewhere behind him.

'It's only a mouse, it's only a mouse,' Flynn whispered over and over again as the scratching became stronger. In his mind the phantom mouse grew into a monstrous shadowy creature with talon-like claws sharp enough to slice him in two. His legs trembled as he sank to his knees and tried to tuck his feet underneath him. He made himself as small as he could, his hand still gripping onto the door handle. His heart was beating so hard he thought it may jump right out of his chest. Flynn pinched his eyes shut.

'There's nothing there. There's nothing there,' he chanted as the huge cupboard monster edged closer. The hairs on the back of Flynn's neck stood on end as hot tears ran unchecked down his cheeks. Any moment now he'd feel its fetid breath on the side of his face – any moment now it would lash out and tear him limb from limb.

* * *

Flynn sucked in a breath as he sat bolt upright in bed.

'Fuck!'

A shudder ran through his body as he rubbed his hands over his face and then through his hair. Fucking nightmare!

259

God, it had been years since he'd suffered through one of them but they were always the same. They would start with the memory of him breaking that stupid bloody glass and end up in some sort of hellish nightmare where he'd be pulled apart by a mutant rat-like creature.

Throwing back the covers, Flynn got out of bed. He walked over to the large bank of windows and stared out unseeing into the night, his mind still half trapped in his eight-year-old self and that bloody cupboard.

His grandmother had a hell of a lot to answer for. He knew that deep down, for his own sake, he shouldn't hold grudges, but God it was hard. She'd always called him the 'devil's spawn', and threatened him with the fires of hell.

Well, wherever she was, Flynn hoped that she was nice and toasty warm next to her own private hellfire.

He rolled his shoulders and glanced over to the clock on the dresser: 11.37 pm. Great, he'd been asleep less than half an hour and he had to get up in four and a half hours. It was useless even thinking about going back to bed now; he needed to blow away the last vestiges of the nightmare first.

Flynn couldn't count the times his grandmother had locked him in the cupboard, but it stopped by the time he reached twelve. A slight smile touched the corner of his lips as he remembered the day he was finally able to shake off the old bitch's hold. There had been a sense of relief and, he supposed, a touch of power when he spun around and faced her and saw the glimmer of fear in her pale eyes. In that moment the rules had changed and so did his world in some ways. The punishments and beatings stopped but the harsh words, criticism and undermining continued to the day she died. No matter how old he was, somehow Edith Hartley had the ability to get inside his head and screw with it.

Eventually Flynn had turned to humour to deflect each of her savage barbs. Sometimes he managed to brush them off but every now and then one would stick. He used humour both as a weapon and, on more than one occasion, to defuse a situation. Better he say something outrageous or do something stupid than let it turn into an ugly scene. Besides, when he acted like a fool it annoyed the crap out of his grandmother, which in Flynn's opinion was always a win.

He opened the window and let the warm night air blow over him. It was soft and comforting, and it eased the jittery feeling that still tied his stomach up in knots. No point dwelling on the past, it was dead and gone. His time would be better spent looking to the future he could have with Lily.

His grandmother was gone and she didn't have the power to hurt him anymore. No matter how much poison she'd tried to pour into his brain, Flynn now knew that he deserved to find happiness and love.

No point going back to bed yet; his head was still spinning and his mouth was dry. Might as well head to the kitchen for a drink. But as he started to turn away from the window, he swore he caught a hint of smoke in the air. He opened the window wider and scanned the bush outside; all seemed as it should. Flynn strained his ears but all he could hear was the soft trickle of water at the bottom of the gully.

He sniffed the air again; the smoky taint was still there. Flynn strode out of the bedroom and over to the narrow

Victorian windows on the landing. Peering into the darkness, he glimpsed a soft orangey glow from the hayshed.

'Shit!'

He whirled back to the bedroom, dragging on jeans and a t-shirt as quick as he could before ramming his feet into his workboots. Grabbing his phone from the dresser, Flynn was dialling triple zero as he ran down the stairs.

Chapter 25

Lily took her foot off the pedal of the sewing machine, the whirl of the engine instantly dying. With a sigh, she raised her arms and stretched against the chair. A series of little cracks ran down her spine – that can't be good. She'd spent too many hours hunched over this sea of pale pink tulle and lace.

Lily rolled her shoulders and moved her neck from side to side. What she needed was a break. Pushing back the chair she stood up and glanced at the wall. To her surprise the clock had just clicked past midnight.

'How did that happen?' she mumbled beneath her breath. Last time she'd looked it had only been coming up to 9 pm. It was obvious that she didn't just need a break – she needed her bed. The dress would have to wait until tomorrow.

The house was so quiet. She supposed she'd become used to sharing the space with Violet and Holly. The only sound were her footsteps as she walked across the wooden floors. The silence was beginning to give her the chills, and she hadn't even watched one of those horror movies that Flynn loved so much. Lily picked up the remote and turned on the radio, the soft music instantly flowing through the quiet void – better. She stood for a second and listened to the familiar song before tossing the remote on the couch and heading to the kitchen. Halfway down the hall she heard a siren off in the distance. Lily frowned and prayed that it wasn't another fire.

Just as she was about to enter the kitchen there was a loud knock on the front door. It made Lily jump and suck in a breath.

'What the hell . . ?' Sighing heavily, she tried to shake off the creepy feeling and walked quickly back up the hall. Lily flicked on the outside light and attempted to ignore the prickling sensation at the back of her neck.

She'd just reached the door when the knock sounded again, louder this time and more demanding. For the second time Lily almost jumped out of her skin.

'Shit!'

She peered through the peephole and saw the verandah was illuminated in a comforting pool of light, and that a familiar figure stood waiting. With a sigh of relief she unlocked the door and pulled it open.

'Jeez, Hailey, you scared the crap out of me!' Lily said with a nervous laugh. 'What are you doing here at this time of night?'

Hailey gave her a bright smile. 'Sorry, I hope I didn't wake you? I was coming back from Bendigo and my bloody car broke down. It didn't even make it all the way to your place,' she said as she pointed up the road. 'You don't mind if I crash here for a minute, do you?'

Lily was about to step back and let Hailey into the house when the sound of the siren blared closer – it was a fire-engine – and it was speeding out of town.

'I wonder where that's going.'

'Don't know,' Hailey said as she turned in the direction of the siren. 'I didn't see any smoke when I was driving back. Surely it can't be another bushfire already. So Violet's still on her honeymoon, I guess? How is it being on your own again?'

Lily smiled. 'I like it, but I have to admit I miss Violet and Holly.'

'So, you're definitely staying here now that Violet and Holly will be moving out to McKellan's Run?'

'Yep, that's the plan,' Lily nodded.

Hailey linked arms with Lily. 'Hey, don't suppose I can mooch a coffee off you before I head across town?

'Of course, but I can drive you back to your place if you want?'

'Thanks but it's not that far. I was just going to head straight there but I saw your lights on and I thought I could grab a drink and whinge about my stupid car breaking down.'

Lily went to shut the door but lingered for a minute as she tried to work out where the fire might be. 'I'll put the kettle on. You're officially my very first guest since Violet's been away. I think I'm a hermit.'

Hailey gave her a smile. 'Great. But what about Flynn? Hasn't he been here?'

'Sure, but my boyfriend doesn't count as a guest as I figure he'll be spending almost as much of his time here as I will be at his place.'

'Right, so I'm the first?'

'Like I said,' Lily smiled as she stepped inside. 'Can you smell that?'

'What?'

'I don't know – it kind of smells like petrol with a touch of smoke.'

'Ah, the fire must be closer than we think.'

'Maybe.' Lily glanced up at the tree in the front yard. Its leaves oscillated and swayed in the night air. 'I suppose the wind has picked up a bit. Come through to the kitchen and I'll make you a coffee.'

'Thanks, Lily, I appreciate it,' Hailey said as she trailed behind Lily. 'So, how's the shop going? Has Johnno finished everything?'

'Yep, he sure has, and it looks amazing. He did a great job – you'll have to come by and check it out.'

'I will. What have you been up to tonight?' Hailey asked. She pushed a strand of brown hair behind her ear as she sat down at the skinny marble-topped counter.

'Oh, not much. I've been sewing all night,' Lily answered as she went to fill up the kettle. 'Everything's pretty much set for the opening but I wanted to try to finish the pink silk dress.'

'Is that the one I saw the design for a couple of weeks ago?'

'Yep, that's it.'

'I love it, it's so beautiful.'

'Thanks. I just need to finish the beading and that's about it,' Lily said with a smile. 'Now, would you like coffee or tea?'

'Actually, I think I'll have a tea, thanks. So anything exciting happening other than sewing?'

'Not really, and I'd hardly call sewing exciting. Although I did have an interesting phone call earlier on.'

'Oh?'

'Yeah, my old boss called to offer me a position at Edwina Partell's.'

'Ooh, wow – that's great.'

'It was certainly a surprise.' Lily grabbed the kettle and started to fill it under the tap. 'She saw the article that Mandy wrote about me.'

'That's a huge opportunity for you, isn't it? I mean, it could make your dresses famous, couldn't it?'

'Well, it would certainly boost my career and put me on the right path in the fashion world. Edwina's fashion house is gaining some interest overseas, so yes, I guess it's a big deal.'

'So when do you leave?' Hailey said with a widening grin. 'Come on, you're going to do it, aren't you?'

'I admit I thought about it for a few minutes. It's really tempting, but I know I'm where I'm meant to be. I thought I was, but I wasn't a hundred per cent sure until another option suddenly arrived. I suppose I still harboured the tiniest doubt about Flynn's willingness to commit, which was wrong. But now . . . well, let's just say that everything became crystal clear a few hours ago, and now I couldn't imagine living anywhere else,' Lily said as she glanced up and saw the frown on Hailey's face. 'Oh, don't mind me – I'm rambling, sorry.'

'Seriously, you're not going to take the job?'

Lily shook her head. 'No, I'm not. I've found too many things to keep me here.'

'You're so very lucky, aren't you?'

Lily had just reached up to grab the tea canister out of the cupboard. She glanced over her shoulder at Hailey.

'I don't know what you mean.'

'Of course you do. You're talented and have your own business. Everyone wants you, everyone loves you,' Hailey said with a smirk.

Lily started making the tea. She shook her head and let out a soft chuckle. 'Yeah, well, Grandad might have left me the shop but in a little over a week I'll have risked all I have on a business, one which is only going to survive on a wing and a prayer. I've got everything riding on this and if it nose-dives into a disaster, I will have pretty much lost it all.'

'Maybe, but you still managed to pull everything together.'

'It wasn't easy, and I did have help,' Lily said as she placed the cup in front of Hailey. 'I couldn't have got this far with the shop without Violet, Mac, the tradies and, of course, Flynn.'

Hailey took a sip of the tea. 'Of course they helped you, they love you.'

'Even Johnno and his crew?' Lily laughed. 'Well, maybe he loved the big fat cheque I handed him the other day.'

'You know what I mean. Besides, as I said, you're lucky, people care about you and you're beautiful and—'

'Will you stop already? You know that I've never seen myself like that. Ever since school I've been struggling with my self-image. You know that I don't have some perfect, charmed life – none of us do. You work with what you're given and get on with it.'

'Maybe, but you're pretty, you know. Otherwise, what would Flynn see in you?'

If Jill or Violet had said it, Lily would have just laughed

the comment off, but there was a look in Hailey's eyes that sent a chill through her.

Lily stared at Hailey for a second. Something felt off and for a moment Lily was uncomfortable. Normally Jill was always with them, but without her here to cushion Hailey's comments, Lily noticed for the first time just how intense she could be. Lily picked up her mug and leant against the far bench, the kitchen island forming a buffer between them.

'That's a really weird thing to say.' She tried to sound upbeat and pretend that Hailey's behaviour wasn't sending up more than a few red flags.

'Oh, I didn't mean it to be. Sometimes I'm not as articulate as you and Jill. Say, you wouldn't have a biscuit would you?'

Lily nodded and grabbed the biscuit barrel, placing it in front of Hailey. 'Help yourself.'

'Thanks,' Hailey said as she peered into the jar. 'Hmm, chocky-chip, my favourite. So, don't you think it would be better for you, for your career, to take the offer and go back to Melbourne?'

'I've put a load of time and money into getting the shop ready. I need to see it through. Besides, I've discovered that I do fit into this town. When I was younger I never seemed to, but it's different now.'

'Why? Because of Flynn?' Hailey looked up and caught her gaze.

'Yes, partly. And also because my family is here and so are my friends.'

'I guess, although now the shop is renovated you could always sell it or rent it out.'

'Yeah, call me sentimental but I can't sell it. After all, it's been in the family for so long, I'd feel like I was letting everyone down,' Lily said before she took a sip of her coffee.

'Rent it out then.'

'Hell, Hailey, I'm beginning to think that you want to get rid of me.'

* * *

'At least let me give you a ride home,' Lily said as she opened the front door.

'No, I'll be fine,' Hailey said as she stepped up to Lily and gave her an awkward hug. 'Everything will be fine. See you.'

'Bye.'

Lily stood by the front door and watched as Hailey hurried down the steps and along the drive. She turned just as she reached the footpath and waved. Lily raised her hand and then went back inside, locking the door behind her. She sighed as she walked down the hallway and back into the kitchen.

Grabbing her coffee mug, she sat down on the nearest stool and wondered if Hailey was all right. She'd said some weird things and Lily had to admit the whole visit had creeped her out. Hailey's behaviour had been odd and part of Lily was kind of glad that she'd left.

But another part of her was now wondering how she could have just let her childhood friend walk out of here in the middle of the night. Jeez, what had she been thinking? Admittedly, there wasn't a lot of crime in Violet Falls, but there was still a loony vandal, or maybe even a gang about. What would happen if Hailey accidently ran into him or them?

The more Lily thought about it, the more agitated she became.

'I can't let her walk by herself,' she muttered as she got off the stool, grabbed her keys and stuck her phone into her jeans pocket. 'She can't have got far.'

Lily hurried out of the house and jumped into her car. Pulling out of the driveway, she headed in the direction Hailey had walked off in. To get home, she'd follow this road right along to the main street and then turn right just before the supermarket. It wasn't that far, but it would take her a good ten minutes.

Lily drove along slowly, scanning both sides of the road, but there was no sign of her. She kept going until she hit the streetlights of the town centre and still Hailey was nowhere to be found. With a sigh she pulled up outside her shop. Hailey must have run up Fletcher's Lane, it was the only other option. It shaved off about half a block but it wasn't as well lit. Lily sat there for a second and wondered if she should keep driving around. Maybe Hailey had decided to drop into Jill's place as well. It was odd that she couldn't find her, as if she'd just vanished into thin air.

But as she was here, she may as well grab the vintage crystal brooch she was going to use as a final touch to the dress she was working on. At least then it wouldn't have been a wasted trip.

Lily got out of the car and listened for a moment. Everything was quiet except for the wind whipping the leaves in the nearby trees. A car was driving somewhere in the distance but Lily couldn't pinpoint it. There were no footsteps or voices; the town appeared to be dead. Lily hurried across the footpath and slipped in the front door of the shop. She didn't bother turning on the shop light as the light at the top of the stairs was always left on.

Lily walked up both flights of stairs to the attic, the glow from the streetlights below shining through the uncurtained window. She walked over to the desk and flicked on her work lamp. The attic was a work in progress. It had been scrubbed, painted white and a couple of ready-made shelving units had been installed, but that was pretty much it. Lily hadn't brought all her supplies over yet; they were still boxed up and vying for room among the bolts of fabric and completed dresses in her small workroom at home. Although, just to give herself enough space to actually sew, Lily had dragged over a few boxes of trimming and several armloads of material a couple of days ago. And of course, somehow the tin of vintage Aurora Borealis crystal jewellery she'd been collecting for years had managed to get mixed up in it.

An old wooden barrel stood by the tiny walk-in cupboard at the other end of the attic. Lily had found it when she'd been cleaning up the attic months ago. It was old, interesting and she'd been loath to part with it. So she had put it to use and it now held bolts of colourful fabrics.

Lily scanned the shelves near her desk looking for the small tin of jewellery but it wasn't there. She picked up a bolt of mauve silk taffeta that was propped against the shelf – heaven only knows how it ended up there, it should have been in the barrel with the rest of the material. She tucked it under her arm as she continued her search.

Damn it, where the hell did she put it? She placed the lid back on a plastic storage tub by her desk chair and scanned the room.

She blew out a breath and closed her eyes for a second to focus. 'Oh, I'm an idiot,' she whispered, remembering that she'd stacked a pile of boxes in the walk-in cupboard. She hurried across the floor and poked the mauve taffeta into the barrel as she went. But just as she stepped into the cupboard there was a crash behind her. Lily whirled around just in time to see the barrel tipping over and the cupboard door slamming shut.

'Oh shit,' she muttered as she pushed against it, but it was stuck. The only light source in the small space was the small window. She braced herself against the old shelves and tried to kick the door open, just like Flynn had done, but she couldn't budge it.

Lily was about to pull her phone out when she heard the bang of the back gate opening. She stood up on tiptoes to see out of the tiny pane, which looked down onto the courtyard. Relief surged through her when she saw Hailey come into view. Maybe she'd seen her car parked out the front.

Lily tapped on the window. 'Hey, I'm up here!'

Hailey didn't look up but scurried towards the back door carrying some sort of container. Lily was about to call out again but stopped when she saw that Hailey had a jerry can. Why on earth would she be carrying around a jerry can?

273

Did she need water for her car? No, that couldn't be right because if that was the case she would have got it at Lily's home. Besides, she said the car had broken down.

Lily rested her head on the nearest shelf as she tried to make sense of what she'd just seen. It couldn't be possible, could it? Was it Hailey who had defaced the shop and broken the windows – and even run her off the road? But why? Why would she do it?

Lily took out her phone and called Flynn.

'Hey, baby. Listen, I can't talk – the hay shed's on fire.'

'What! Are you okay?' Lily asked.

'Yeah, the firies are here now. They're not a hundred percent sure but we think it was done on purpose.'

Lily eyes opened wide as the realisation hit her. 'Flynn, I'm trapped in the walk-in cupboard at the shop. I knocked over the barrel, which closed the door . . . anyway, I can't get out.'

'Okay, I'm coming.'

'Flynn, there's more. I've just seen Hailey downstairs in the courtyard and she's carrying a jerry can.'

'You don't think?'

'I don't know what to think,' Lily said as a noise in the courtyard caught her attention. 'Hang on a tick.' Lily peered through the window again. She was pretty sure that had been the sound of the back gate closing. 'I think she's gone.'

'Okay, so why would you—'

Lily caught sight of a flickering glow downstairs. 'Wait, Flynn – she's lit a fire at the back door! I can't put it out because I can't get out of this bloody cupboard!'

'Hold on, Lily, I'm on my way.'

Chapter 26

Flynn pulled up outside Lily's shop. The only light he could make out was coming from the attic, but as he jumped out of the ute he could smell smoke in the night air. He ran to the front door and was thankful that she'd forgotten to lock it. As Flynn crossed the shop floor, the smoke became thicker and he could hear the hiss of the fire. As he hurried to the staircase, he saw that the flames had already started to devour the back door.

He took the stairs two at a time and called out as he made it into the attic.

'Lily! Lily, don't worry – I'm here and everything is going to be okay.'

'Flynn – oh, thank God!' came her voice from behind the stuck door.

He quickly pushed the barrel out of the way and pulled at the door handle, but it didn't move.

'Lily, it needs more force. On the count of three, I want you to kick the door like I did last time we were stuck in there.'

'Uh-huh, all right.'

'Okay, here we go. One . . . two,' Flynn grasped the handle and strained back with all his strength, '. . . three!'

Lily kicked the door and it swung open. She flew out of the cupboard and into his arms, holding on tight and burying her head in the crook of his neck. 'Thanks for the rescue, again.'

'Anytime.'

She raised her head and looked at him. 'We are so taking that bloody door off its hinges.'

'Oh yeah. Seriously though, you're not hurt, are you?'

Lily shook her head. 'No, I'm fine.'

'Good, because we have to get out of here. The fire is burning through the back of the shop as we speak.'

'Oh no! We have to put it out. I can't lose the shop now – not after everything that I've put into it.'

Flynn took her by the hand and tugged her towards the stairs.

'No, we're getting out. I want you safe. The fire brigade is already on the way as well as the police.'

'But—'

'We'll work it all out once we're safely out of here.'

They were almost to the bottom of the stairs when the sound of a police siren blared as it pulled up at the front of the shop.

The smoke was thick; it made her eyes sting and caught at the back of Lily's throat, making her want to cough. Flynn's arm went around her waist as he pulled her closer and guided her through the shop and out the front door.

'Are you both okay?' Senior Sergeant Barker said as he clambered out of the car. Another police car pulled up alongside the first as well as a divvy van.

Flynn tucked her protectively under his arm as they stepped out into the street. Lily was glad to have his strength bolstering her up because when all was said and done, if ever she needed a bit of bolstering, it was tonight.

'Yeah, we'll live,' Flynn said as he guided Lily towards his friend. 'Thanks for getting here so quickly.'

'Not a problem.' Steve glanced at Lily. 'Are you sure that you're unhurt?'

'I'm all right,' Lily replied. In truth she wasn't, but she wasn't about to tell Flynn or Steve that she kind of felt sick in the stomach and her legs were a wee bit shaky. It was a bit of a shock being betrayed by one of your best friends. I mean, on the level of *our friendship no longer exists*, this was pretty much up there.

'Well, you don't look it,' he said. 'I need you to sit in the car until the area is secure. PC Donaldson will stay with you for a second until everyone else arrives.'

Lily opened her mouth to protest as a fire truck flew around the corner with lights flashing and siren blaring. She'd never been so happy to see a fire-engine in all her life.

PC Donaldson walked up. 'Would you like to come and sit over here, out of all the confusion?'

Lily gave him a nod. 'Sure,' she said, but she turned back to Senior Sergeant Barker. 'Hailey lit the fire. I don't know why but I saw her do it from the attic window. I think she may be responsible for the vandalism and maybe even running me off the road.'

'I understand, Ms Beckett. You look as if you need to sit down – go with PC Donaldson and I'll come and let you know what's happening in a little while.'

She settled into the seat and waited. Police Constable Donaldson stood in front of the open door, obscuring her view of the shop. She asked him to move once so she could see what was going on, but he just gave her a smile and acted like he hadn't heard her. If she leant to one side she could just see Flynn and Senior Sergeant Barker talking near the front steps.

A distant shout went up in the night, and several of the cops took off down the side street. Lily tried to stick her head out of the car to see what was happening but PC Donaldson literally stood in front of her.

'Could you move a little to the left?'

'There's nothing to see, Ms Beckett.'

With an exasperated sigh she slumped back against the seat.

'Hartley.' Donaldson nodded as Flynn hurried towards the car. He stepped aside and allowed Flynn to slide into the car next to Lily.

'What's happening?'

Flynn shook his head as he took her hand. 'I'm not sure but I think they must have found Hailey. I was talking to Steve and then all of a sudden he told me to come over here.'

Lily reached out and touched his cheek. Flynn raised his eyes and gave her a look that made her insides go a little mushy.

'Are you okay?'

'Yes, I'm fine – really,' Lily smiled. 'I'm fine.'

PC Donaldson opened the door. 'The ambulance is here, Ms Beckett.'

'I don't think I need—'

'Yeah, you do,' Flynn said as he stood up. 'Just let them give you a look-over, just to be sure.'

'Flynn, it's not necessary, I'm fine.'

'Please, for me.'

Senior Sergeant Barker hurried over to the car. 'We've got her. She tried to escape via the back laneway.'

'Steve, I think she must need medical help,' Lily said. 'I mean, a normal person doesn't go around doing these sorts of things.'

'Did she say why she did it?' Flynn asked Steve as he stepped out of the car.

'Well, not as such, but she was rabbiting on about how you and she are together and that Lily here is intent on coming between you.'

'But that's crazy! We went out a few times but that was years ago.' Flynn shook his head and looked back at Lily. 'I just don't understand.'

'We'll get to the bottom of it,' Steve said as he glanced down at Lily. 'And you need to get checked out.' He motioned one of the ambulance guys over. 'We'll talk tomorrow, when I have a better idea of what's going on.'

Flynn helped Lily out of the car and guided her towards the ambo. Just as they reached the ambulance there was a disturbance from the side street.

'Flynn! Let go of me! You don't understand, I need to see Flynn. Flynn, tell them to let me go. Lily will go now and we'll be together, just like we should – just like we've always been.' Hailey's voice cut through the air as a couple of policemen tried to bundle her into the divvy van. 'Flynn,

280

look at me! Flynn, why won't you look at me? I love you . . . and I know that you feel the same.'

* * *

As the divvy van door clanged shut, Flynn didn't turn around but just held onto Lily a little tighter. He was so thankful that she was alive and in one piece. It could have turned out very differently but any way he looked at it, Flynn kept coming to the same conclusion: it was all his fault. He'd boasted for years that whoever he dated knew the score, that it was all for fun and there were no feelings attached. But this whole thing with Hailey had slipped by him and he almost lost the one person he'd ever cared about. God, how could he not have seen that Hailey was unhinged and fixated on him?

He helped Lily up into the ambulance. 'I'll be right behind you.'

'Good, I'll be waiting.' She gave him a smile and he swore that there were tears in her eyes.

A hard stone seemed to settle in the middle of his stomach. Shit, how could he ever make this up to her?

'Flynn, let's not tell my sister what happened until after they get back from their honeymoon.'

'If that's what you want.'

'Yeah, it really is.'

'You know that both of them will be as mad as hell at us for not saying anything, don't you?'

'Yeah, but they'll forgive us. And besides, by the time they find out they will have already had their loved-up honeymoon.'

Steve walked up next to Flynn to address Lily. 'Are you ready to go?'

'Sure.'

'Alright then. I'll be over to grab a statement from you first thing in the morning.'

'I can give it to you now if you like,' Lily said. Giving a statement was a better option than going to hospital.

Flynn shook his head.

'It'll keep till tomorrow,' Steve said with a brief smile. 'Go and get some rest.'

The divvy van reversed out of the parking bay and momentarily stopped by the ambulance. Flynn thought he could hear his name being called but it was muffled by the metal sides of the police van. He didn't turn around, he couldn't. Instead he stared straight ahead at Lily, who watched the car as it crept past. He saw the pain in Lily's eyes and it just about killed him.

'Are you ready?' Flynn asked the ambulance officer.

'Yes.'

'Good, then get the hell out of here,' Flynn said before he looked back at Lily. 'I'll see you there.'

Lily gave him a smile. 'Okay.'

Flynn closed the ambulance door and then rapped on it twice before standing back. He stood there for a moment and watched as it drove off into the night, towards the hospital.

'You have to let it go,' said Steve from beside him.

'I don't know what you're talking about.'

'Yeah, you do,' Steve said.

Flynn turned his head and stared at the policeman.

'You're standing there all riddled with guilt.'

'I'm not.'

Steve raised an eyebrow. 'Sure,' he said, but it was obvious that he was far from convinced.

'Oh shit, you're right.' Flynn ran his hands through his hair and let out a sigh. 'It's a total fuck-up, and I'm the one who caused it. Me, I did it, okay? I put Lily in danger.'

'Hailey Waters is to blame, not you. You didn't know that she was crazy. Look, this is hard when we all grew up together. I get that we're friends and acquaintances and we probably all know way too much about each other. We all like Hailey, but no one picked this up – no one. So don't go blaming yourself. At least now she'll get the help she obviously should've had a long time ago.'

'But I should've seen it. Jeez, she could have killed Lily.'

Steve clamped his hand on Flynn's shoulder for a second. 'Don't do this to yourself. It won't help you, and it sure as hell won't help Lily.'

Flynn nodded, but he couldn't get past it. 'I'd better get to the hospital. I'll give you a call as soon as we get the all clear.'

'Right then.'

Flynn walked away and headed to his car.

Chapter 27

Lily's eyes flickered open and for a moment she didn't know where she was. Everything seemed pale and hard-edged, and through the partially open door there was a brightly lit corridor. She must have nodded off; maybe she was a little bit more worn-out than she thought. She turned her head and saw Flynn sleeping in the chair next to her bed.

Ah, she was in the hospital. Yeah, it was all coming back to her now . . . unfortunately.

The doctor who attended her said that she was fine but had been called away for an emergency before he could sign her off. So Lily had laid back against the pillows and waited. She guessed she must have fallen asleep.

She studied Flynn. He had a pillow wedged under one arm and his head tilted to one side. Lily had to wonder how anyone could possibly sleep in such an uncomfortable-looking position. She looked up and straight into Flynn's eyes.

'Hey.'

Flynn rubbed his face as he sat up before reaching across the bed and taking her hand.

'How are you feeling?' he asked with a hint of a smile.

'A bit tired. I wonder how long I'll have to wait to get out of here.'

'Yeah, well, don't push it. You need some rest.'

'Flynn, I'm okay.' Lily squeezed his hand and gave him a smile. 'You didn't have to stay. I doubt that sleeping in a chair is very comfortable.'

Flynn shrugged. 'It was alright. Besides, I didn't want to be anywhere else.'

His words warmed her. 'I'm glad.'

A shadow passed over his face. Lily knew that something was wrong because she saw it in his eyes. 'What's up?'

He was silent for a second. He let go of her hand and sat back in the chair, creating a sudden distance between them.

'I'm so sorry, Lily. I know that you must hate me at the moment and I just don't know how or even if you want us to move forward together. I know this whole thing with Hailey is my fault, but I'm hoping that with time you'll forgive me. I know I don't deserve it and I won't blame you if you want to walk away. It'll kill me, but I won't blame you.'

Lily stared at him, stunned, as the words sank in. 'I don't blame you – none of this is your fault. God, I sometimes wonder what goes on in that mind of yours!'

'You don't . . .?'

'No, I don't blame you. This was all Hailey, not you.'

'But if I hadn't taken her out, if I hadn't been so careless, this might not have happened.'

'You're not responsible for Hailey,' Lily said. 'Really, you're not. Do you know where she is?'

'Yeah, Steve rang a while ago. She's been taken to

a hospital in Bendigo to be evaluated, whatever the hell that means.'

Lily gave him a smile. 'I need to talk to someone to find out that she's okay.'

'Jeez, Lily, she could have killed you.'

'But she didn't.'

'You were in the shop when she lit that fire.'

'Yes, but to be fair, she didn't know that I was there.'

'She ran you off the road when you were jogging! As I said, she could have killed you.'

'We don't know that for sure.'

Flynn locked eyes with her. 'Yeah, we do. Apparently she told Steve that she was trying to force you to leave. That way we'd be together again. So yes, baby, she's responsible for the vandalism and hitting you with the car and the damn fire.'

'But has she done this before? I mean, I'm not the first woman you've gone out with.'

'Yeah, but you're the only one that I've ever been serious about, and I guess Hailey knew that.'

'Which is why she became unhinged,' Lily said with a sigh.

'Yeah, something like that. When I think how close you came to . . . I don't know what I would do without you and I don't want to find out. Lily, you scared the hell out of me and you shouldn't go anywhere near her.'

'She's sick, Flynn.'

'I keep telling myself that, but it's gonna take a while for it to sink in.' He stood up and gave Lily a grin. 'So, you don't blame me and you're not breaking up with me?'

Lily shook her head. 'Don't be an idiot, of course I don't. As it happens, you're stuck with me because I'm not going anywhere.'

'Really? What about the job? No, sorry, I shouldn't have brought that up. You haven't had time to make up your mind.'

'It was lovely of Edwina to offer it but I'm not taking the position.'

'You're not? I mean, are you sure? Isn't it your dream?'

'Maybe it was once but I've traded it for a better one. As I said before, I'm not going anywhere.'

Flynn's grin got bigger. 'Good, 'cause neither am I.' He bent down and tugged off his boots.

Lily eyed him suspiciously. 'Flynn, what are you doing?'

'I need to hold you and I'm sick of sitting in that bloody chair.'

'Is that even allowed? I mean, we're in a hospital.'

Lily scooted over as Flynn stretched out alongside her and pulled her into his arms.

'I'm not sure we should be doing this.' Lily placed her head on his shoulder. It felt good, she had to admit.

'I think it's a great idea.'

'Yes, but I'm sure there's rules about this sort of thing.'

'Like I care,' Flynn said as he dropped a kiss on the top of her head.

* * *

It took a little time to put the events of that night behind her. Longer than Lily thought it would. She'd decided as she lay

287

in Flynn's arms in that narrow hospital bed that she needed to feel his warmth and protection around her. It wasn't as if she'd fallen into the helpless damsel in distress mode, but she was definitely feeling fragile and a little vulnerable. She still couldn't quite wrap her head around what Hailey had done. How could the woman sit there and commiserate with Lily about her shop being wrecked and be responsible for it at the same time? How had she not seen through Hailey and realised that she was troubled and needed help? And that's how it was for Lily, her mind swinging back and forth like a pendulum: she was angry at Hailey and then felt sorry for her.

The biggest problem, although also the easiest to fix, was the damage to the shop. The fire had eaten its way through the back door and half the bathroom, and the small back porch had been destroyed altogether. There was nothing to do but delay the opening of the shop and call in Johnno and his team.

The next problem was trying to allay Violet and Mac's fears and concerns when they got back from their honeymoon. Oh, there had been a whole lot of 'Why didn't you call us?' and 'I can't believe that you and Flynn didn't tell us' conversations, but after a bit of fast-talking and reassurances, both she and Flynn were forgiven.

Violet was so rattled by the idea that Hailey had tried to hurt her baby sister that she wanted Lily to move into McKellan's Run, but Lily had given her another hug and said firmly that wasn't going to happen.

Jill was floored by the news and blamed herself for not seeing that Hailey was ill. Lily had told her that it wasn't Jill's fault, just like it wasn't hers or Flynn's or anyone else's, for that matter. They spent an evening crying, laughing and remembering when they were kids and life hadn't been this complicated.

Of course the story circulated around the town, exaggerated in some cases, but nearly everyone came to the same conclusion: that it was a sorry state of affairs and young Hailey Waters needed some professional help.

In Lily's case, everyone had been supportive – she had forgotten what the town was like when it was showing its best. Even so, she hadn't counted on just how encouraging the residents of Violet Falls could be until the middle of autumn, when she finally opened the doors of the Gilded Lily.

Fifteen minutes before the official opening time, a large crowd of women were standing patiently on the covered footpath, waiting to get in. It was more than Lily could ever have hoped for, and then some. The McKellans en masse had been a pretty awesome crew in the final days. Sarah had helped in the lead-up to the opening wherever it was needed, even if it was just turning up with a sticky bun and coffee. Dan had organised the hors d'oeuvres for the event, which were all amazing bites of deliciousness. Violet had taken on the opening just like any other of her events, double- and then triple-checking everything. From ordering the drinks, to the press release and lining up the local newspaper, Violet managed it all without even breaking into a sweat.

Lily leant against the counter of the Gilded Lily and smiled. After a huge amount of hard work and endless nights hunched over her sewing machine, her shop was officially open for business. For the past week, she and Flynn had worked their butts off getting the shop to look perfect. Lily quickly found out that Flynn was very good at hanging pictures, moving furniture and always had the right answer when asked for the fiftieth time, 'Does that look alright?' Really, she couldn't have pulled this opening together without him.

If someone had told her that within a year she would turn her life around by starting a business and finding love, she would have laughed in their face.

She looked over the crowd of potential customers and saw Flynn across the room. He was standing next to Mac and leaning against the wall. Did he look out of place in this very chic and girly space? Hell yes, but she was grateful he'd come.

The finished shop matched the vision she'd had in her head from the very beginning. A dark wooden floor contrasted perfectly with the white walls. Everything was light and delicate, with the exception of the oversized gilt mirror attached to the wall. Lily had placed several large crystal vases of pastel roses around the floor space, and the room was lit by the two vintage chandeliers she'd found on her travels. Her sample designs were displayed around the shop, including Violet's wedding dress, which she'd borrowed for the opening.

The shop was clean, bright and above all feminine, and Lily loved it. She only hoped that she'd be able to build a business. She glanced back to Flynn and he caught her looking at him. He nodded to Mac before winding his way through a bevy of women until he was standing in front of her.

'Well, it looks as if the Gilded Lily is a success.'

'Fingers crossed. I've already had a couple of bookings for consultations later this week.'

'Hey, that's great,' Flynn smiled.

'Yes, it is.'

'Is there anything you need a hand with?'

'Nope, I think everything is under control,' Lily said, looking deep into his dark eyes.

Flynn opened his mouth but before he could say anything more Jill ran behind the counter and gave Lily a hug.

'This is fantastic! The shop is beautiful. Oh, hi, Flynn – sorry, but I have to drag her away for a second.'

Flynn gave Jill a smile. 'No problem.'

'You really like the shop?' Lily asked her. 'Hey, thanks Jill. I'm glad you do.'

'Are you kidding? I love everything about it. Your designs are just stunning, and as for the accessories – well, I can't wait to get my hands on that necklace over there,' Jill said as she pointed to the jewellery display. 'Please tell me no one's grabbed it.'

Lily shook her head. 'No, it's yours if you want it.'

'Great! Oh and I brought along a couple of girls from work. Annie, come over here and meet Lily!' Jill dropped her voice. 'She's just got engaged, so I figure she'll be wanting a wedding dress in the not-too-distant future.'

'Ah.'

'Ah, indeed. You never know, she may need a frock for an engagement party as well. And then we'll guide her towards Violet's event planning.'

'We'll have to put you on commission at this rate.'

'Hey, you know that's a pretty good idea. Hmmm, we'll have to talk details, probably after I've plied you with a couple of glasses of wine.'

Lily glanced at Flynn and gave him an apologetic smile.

'I'll be over there if you need me,' he said with a wink before he made his way back to Mac.

Lily gave herself a second to watch him walk away. She loved the way he moved.

'Lily? Lily, this is Annie.'

Lily turned her attention back to Jill. 'Right. Hello, Annie, thanks so much for coming,' she said as she shook the woman's hand.

'You have such a beautiful shop, Lily. I just love all your designs.'

'Thank you, Annie. It's lovely of you to say so.'

'So, am I right in thinking that you can make the dress I've always dreamt about?'

'Well, I would certainly try. My dresses are as unique and beautiful as my gorgeous customers.'

Annie smiled back at her. 'I like that. Can I drop in tomorrow and have a chat about my wedding dress?'

'Of course, I'll look forward to it.'

'Great. Oh, I finish work at five – is that too late?'

'Nope, I'll see you then.'

'Thanks so much,' Annie said before disappearing into the crowd.

Lily and Jill waited until her back was turned before they did a little 'I've just booked another consultation' dance.

'Aunty Lily, why are you dancing?'

Whoops. Lily looked over the counter and saw Holly standing there.

'Hi, baby girl. I'm just happy.' She gave Jill a quick grin as she went and picked Holly up and sat her on the counter. 'So, do you like my shop?'

Holly nodded her head. 'Yep, it's so pretty, almost like a fairytale.'

'Nailed it! Speaking of pretty, you look like a princess today.'

'It's my new dress that Grandma Sarah gave me yesterday.'

'Is she spoiling you?'

Again Holly gave an exaggerated nod.

'Excellent.' Lily tapped her finger on the end of Holly's nose. 'Because you deserve a good spoil. Jill, could you please pass me that little tiara on the shelf behind you?'

'This one?' Jill pointed to the smallest of the glittery tiaras.

'Yep.'

'Wow, first I get a commission and now I'm a shop assistant. Pretty soon I'll end up being the manager,' Jill said with a laugh as she handed the tiara over.

Lily shook her head as she placed it on Holly's head. 'There, every princess should have a crown.'

'What are you two up to?' Violet said as she draped an arm around Lily.

'Oh, you know, the usual – playing princess,' Lily said as she gave her sister a one-armed hug. 'You've been gone for a while – and if it was new husband related, I don't want to know.'

Violet chuckled. 'No, I was helping Dan with the food for *your* opening, and then I got roped into taking a couple of trays of champagne around to your thirsty guests.'

'Aw, thank you, but you know that's what big sisters are meant to do.'

'Funny, I don't seem to remember reading that in the job description.' She bent down and gave Holly a cuddle. 'How's it going, sweetie?'

'Good. Aunty Lily gave me a crown.' Holly pointed to the top of her head. 'Isn't it pretty?'

'It sure is.' Violet lifted her off the counter. 'Hey, Jill. Are you enjoying the opening?'

'Of course. The shop looks wonderful.'

'She's trying to get a commission out of me,' Lily said with a grin. 'You'd better be careful, she'll be after you next.'

'You said it, not me. Besides, I was just being a good friend and sending business your way,' Jill quipped.

'Is that true?' Violet asked.

'Yep. Jill brought a bride-to-be with her, Annie. She's dropping in tomorrow to have a chat.' Lily waggled her eyebrows.

'Ooh, that sounds promising,' Violet said.

'It sure does, and I've gently pushed her in your direction as well as Lily's. Now, both of you say after me, "Thank you, Jill, you're the best".'

'Thank you, Jill, you're the best,' Lily and Violet said in unison before dissolving into laughter.

'Mummy, I'm going to show Mac my new crown,' Holly said as she tugged on Violet's hand.

'Sure,' Violet said, glancing around the crowded shop. 'Look, he's just over there talking to Flynn.'

Holly let go of her mum's hand. 'Thanks for the crown, Aunty Lily,' she said before she skipped towards Mac. 'Daddy! Daddy, look at my new crown.'

Lily heard Violet suck in her breath next to her.

'What is it?'

'Did you hear that?' Violet asked as she gave Lily's arm a squeeze. 'It's the first time she's ever called him that.'

Lily followed Violet's gaze. Mac had stepped away from Flynn and had a stunned look on his face as Holly ran up to him. He scooped her up in his arms and sent a stare to Violet that probably caused her ovaries to explode. It was hard to tell from this distance, but Lily was pretty sure he had tears in his eyes. Although she couldn't be certain of that because everything was suddenly blurry as she felt herself well up.

'Go.' Lily gave Violet a gentle push as she wiped away an errant tear with the back of her hand. She watched as Violet hurried over to her family.

Flynn sauntered in that sexy way towards her. 'Did I just miss something?'

Lily wrapped her arms around his waist. 'It was the first time Holly has used the word "daddy".'

'Ah, which would explain why he broke off in mid-sentence and looked like a stunned mullet.'

Lily slapped him on the chest. 'Oh, so much for you having warm and fuzzy feelings.'

'Oh, I have them alright. Just wait until you close the

shop and I promise to show you.' He bent down and kissed her neck.

A series of familiar tingles swept through her body. For her own sake she dropped her arms and stepped away from him. He gave her a cheeky grin and a wink; yeah, he knew the effect he had on her, damn it. Lily glanced at her watch. Funny, all of a sudden the end of the day couldn't get here fast enough.

Chapter 28

Flynn had considerately kept his distance from Lily until the shop was closed. When all her friends and family had finally left, he came up behind her and wrapped her in his arms.

'Are you happy?'

'So happy. Everything went really smoothly and I've even made a handful of appointments, plus a heap of contacts.'

'I'm proud of you, you know that?'

'Yeah?'

'I mean it. You had a dream and you went for it.'

'Thank you, but you'd better stop or you'll have me all teary,' she said as she turned around in his arms and leant her head against his chest.

'Well, we wouldn't want that. Anyway, I just wanted to say that I think you're pretty amazing,' he said before he bent down and kissed her.

It felt so right to be in his arms. A familiar flare of want and heat coursed through her as the kiss deepened. They clung to each other and all other thoughts in Lily's mind fled: she needed to touch him.

He pulled back for a moment. 'I thought that maybe you'd like to get out of here for a while. I was going to take you to dinner . . .' The rest of the thought was left suspended in the air as he nuzzled her neck.

'Why don't we go upstairs instead?'

He looked down at her, his eyes darkened with passion. 'You know, you have the best ideas.'

His gaze held her; moments slipped by and Lily found herself unable to look away. What she felt was deep, intense and sometimes even raw. It was scary but in a good way, and she knew that she never wanted to give that up.

He took her hand and brought it to his lips before turning it over and kissing her wrist. Her stomach contracted and the heat began to kindle and build.

Yeah, never giving him up.

'Let's lock up,' she said with a sense of reluctance as she gently pulled away from him.

'I'll get the back door,' he said as he gave her one of his best smiles, the ones that almost always had her reduced to a wobbly jelly.

A minute later they met at the bottom of the stairs.

'Are we all set?' Flynn asked.

'Yep. Hey, what are you doing?'

'This,' Flynn said as he scooped her up and strode upstairs.

'Put me down,' Lily chuckled as she wrapped her arm behind his neck. 'You'll strain something.'

'Well, babe, we can only hope.' He gave her another lopsided grin and Lily had to physically restrain herself from sighing. Yep, she had it bad, and the only thing she was sure of was that she wouldn't have it any other way.

Lily expected him to put her down once they got inside but he just kept holding her tight. Flynn kicked the office door shut behind him before he carried her to the couch. God, this man made her heart explode.

Several delicious hours later, Lily went to get up but a strong arm snaked around her waist and pulled her back.

'And where exactly are you going?'

Lily turned her head and smiled at Flynn. 'Well, you did promise me dinner.'

'Eating is overrated.'

He ran a series of kisses along her neck and Lily's head tilted to the side to give him better access. But then, spoiling what was shaping up to be a promising moment, her stomach growled – loudly. Flynn moved back and let out a sigh.

'Okay, I get the hint. You're hungry.'

'In my defence, other than muesli for breakfast, I've only had a handful of Dan's asparagus spears with prosciutto at the opening.'

'But what about the sandwiches Sarah brought from the Hummingbird Café at lunchtime?'

'Um, I was so wound up and busy, I kind of forgot to eat.'

Flynn frowned. 'You have to take care of yourself, which means eating regularly. I know everything that's gone on in the last couple of months has been crazy but I don't want you getting sick.'

Lily let out a chuckle and shook her head. 'Yeah, like I couldn't afford to lose a kilo or two.'

'You're perfect just the way you are and I love every inch of you.' He reached up and cupped the side of her face with his hand.

EK.

Lily stilled for a moment and locked her eyes onto his. 'What does that mean?'

'That I love you, Lily, and I want us to be together. I need you in my life because you make it better – you make me better.'

'Flynn . . .'

'I mean it. For the first time in my life I feel whole and you did that,' he said before he kissed her. 'I probably don't deserve you but I've got you, and I'm sure as hell not letting you go.'

'I love you too,' Lily said as a warmth flowed through her.

'Well, I know that,' he answered with a cocky grin. 'So, do you think you'll hang around and see what the future brings? I reckon with a bit of work we could have something special – that is, if you're up for the challenge?'

Lily wound her arms around him and held him tight. Happy tears blurred her vision as she whispered in his ear. 'You bet I am.'